Nina Macwan

MAY YOU DIE IN IRELAND

An inherited property leads American professor William Foley to visit Ireland for the first time. He is unwittingly chosen as a courier by men of wicked designs, and he is pursued through the city of Cork and the County of Kerry. His experience of Ireland proves to be no restful holiday but becomes more violent and intriguing than he could ever have imagined...

MAY YOU DIE IN IRELAND

Michael Kenyon

First published 1965
by
Collins

This edition 2002 by Chivers Press
published by arrangement with
HarperCollins Publishers Ltd

ISBN 0 7540 8608 9

Copyright © 1965 by Michael Kenyon

British Library Cataloguing in Publication Data available

Printed and bound in Great Britain by
Bookcraft, Midsomer Norton, Somerset

Chapter 1

Breathless from overweight and a mild attack of asthma, Foley boarded the Aer Lingus Boeing 707 at Kennedy Airport. His spirits were high. He was on vacation and he knew nothing of the government secret in the black plastic folder beneath his arm.

More accurately, the secret was on the folder. The contents of the folder were glossy holiday nonsense: brochures as bright and shining as a dentist's drill, schedules, hotel reservations. Emblazoned in white letters on the folder's cover was the proclamation, Travel Wide with Thomas Hide; and underneath, Thomas Hide Travel Bureau, New York, Chicago & Los Angeles. In more modest lettering upon a top corner of the folder was the bearer's name, academic rank, destination, and a final flourish of advertising: Dr. William Foley, Ph.D., Travel-Wide Passenger to Ireland. The secret was on a microdot film one sixteenth of an inch square which had been glued beneath the F in Foley at the junction of the vertical stroke and the topmost horizontal. The writing on the film was of an eighteen-page draft report which was to be submitted to the President of the United States by the Senate Committee on Submarine Agronomy.

A preface to the report was directed to Shamrock. On June 12, said the preface, the Committee was expected unanimously to recommend allocation of two million dollars for industrial development of chloriodine, pending the findings of the La Calla Research Unit. The Committee, the preface added, would also advise that Professor Holstein and key staff at the Marine Biology Station, Kerry, be immediately invited to continue research in the United States; Shamrock would act accordingly.

Had this intelligence appeared in the copy of the *New York Times* of June 7 which he had abandoned in the departure lounge when his flight was called, Foley would have raised an eyebrow at the two-million figure, scowled in ignorance at the chloriodine, smiled in recognition at Kerry—Bejasus and was not that a corner of the ould Ireland to which he himself was travelling?—and passed quickly to news that was not, from start to finish, gobbledegook. Foley knew as much of Senate Committees on Submarine Agronomy as he did of the microdot film on his black plastic folder.

" Good afternoon and welcome aboard," purred the feline hostess with the green uniform and the freckles.

Her smile burned like a candle. Foley was aware that the smile was not for himself alone but for vacation purposes he chose to believe that it was. Was he not a fully-paid, docketed, documented, honoured and honourable Travel-Wide Passenger to Ireland, and determined as all heaven and hell to have the holiday of his life?

" Hallo there," he wheezed, and smiled back.

Breathing heavily through his mouth, he entered the aircraft, the recommendation of the Senate Committee snug under his arm.

A letter from Aunt Rhoda in Sioux Falls had brought Foley the first hint of his journey to Ireland.

The envelope, postmarked March 26, bore a printed sticker with his aunt's name and address. The mail that morning was agreeably thin: something unmentionable from the telephone company, a circular from a soap maufacturer, the second circular in a week from a publishing company which Foley had never heard of, Aunt Rhoda's letter, and a communication from the Dean of the Graduate

College. Foley thumbed open the Dean's message. Would he attend for cocktails on Wednesday at six o'clock? Foley supposed he would. The Dean's cocktails were notorious for their numbing foulness. What went into them apart from the whisper of gin which might have been measured from an eye-dropper was a mystery which no faculty member had yet fathomed. Still, no one lightly rejected a summons from the Dean. Foley put the invitation in his pocket-book and dropped the remainder of the mail unopened on the kitchen table. It would wait until evening. He did not feel committed to the belief that no news was good news, but increasingly with the passage of years he had found that news came to no harm by being allowed to mature. At least there was nothing from Joy. Since the bother over the concert tickets, Joy had taken to writing sniffy letters which Foley dreaded to receive. He had fallen hopelessly out of love with Joy, and though some day she would realise this she had not done so yet. Her last letter languished for three days in a drawer before Foley had dared open it. He had hastily scanned the careful handwriting to make sure there was nothing he actually had to do and pushed the letter back into the drawer. The letter had ended: " I remember the nights, darling Willie, what has happened?" This cannot go on, Foley told himself miserably aware that he would never find the nerve to call a halt. He felt too old for emotional crises.

Foley drew little comfort from being still on the underside of forty. He looked older. From birthday to birthday he watched his waistline become paunchier. His hair sprouted only on the extreme rear of his head, and the heavy glasses which he wore to counter galloping myopia gave him a faintly owlish look. His face was round and cheerful, his figure chubby. When he smiled, the gold filling in a lower left molar glinted, and when he laughed it dazzled.

The onset of what would clearly be a flabby middle age was distasteful to Foley but not distressing. He had never been athletic. His appetite was robust and he slept well. Occasional bursts of hay fever in the summer, and asthma at any time, were irritations which he had suffered from childhood; his health was otherwise good. His worries were professional and marital, or rather non-marital, and even with these annoyances he had almost come to terms. When he first realised that his dream of making shining discoveries in mathematics was just that—a dream—he had been despondent. Now he had lived with the knowledge long enough to accept it philosophically. Being a good teacher was almost adequate compensation, and though the Univeristy had been slow to grant him tenure, his worth had eventually been recognised and his position in the department was secure. The non-marital outlook was more dismal, for this was a continuing problem which should have been capable of solution. Foley was a bachelor who would have liked to have been married with six children. Those of his academic friends who were not divorced or separated were married with six children, and this seemed to Foley a condition infinitely preferable to that of a bachelor. He was not yet resigned to being a bachelor. He frequently felt sexy, and he would have liked someone to cook *boeuf bourguignon* for him in the evenings and support him at faculty cocktail parties. He liked children, he was a loyal friend, and looking back he could not understand why his luck with girls had been so poor. In twenty years he had chalked up a respectable total of dates, but of the two brunettes with whom he had progressed so far as to propose marriage one had said she would think about it and had disappeared out of his life, the other had said no with a sharpness which Foley thought unnecessarily defiant. He had contemplated proposals to several others before changing his mind. So help him, he reflected, but he had even thought of marrying Joy. A girl who fell silent for an entire evening because he had left two trifling concert tickets in another suit, and who subsequently took to composing emotional letters when she might more easily have telephoned, was plainly unsuitable. In any event, Joy was a girl no longer, she was thirty-seven. Foley blamed himself for the initial error over age, interpreting his poor judgment as a sign of desperation. Six children? He would as easily have had six children from union with an antelope.

He put on his hat and coat, closed the door of his apartment and hurried out to the parking lot. If he could find an untenanted parking space at the other end he would be able to steal ten minutes in the reading-room before sophomore calculus. Aunt Rhoda's letter did not enter his mind again until evening.

He had enticed Oscar Hensen back from the campus to hear a new Callas recording. He put the letter on the tray with the coffee and carried the tray into the sitting-room where Oscar was lying on his back in the most comfortable chair with his eyes closed. Oscar taught chemistry. He was big and shaggy and had an English wife who doted on him to the point of warming his slippers in the oven. Unlike Foley, who had lived in Duluth until his parents died, Oscar was Chicago born and bred: the birthplace had been a slum, the breeding ground an arena of back alleys where Oscar had led a gang called the Vikings. In one electric week in the winter of 1941 his mother had gone off with a car salesman, his father had fallen drunk down the stone steps from their tenement and broken his neck, and Oscar had been dragged into a basement room at the police station and pummelled into oblivion by three uniformed cops. The next week bombs dropped on Pearl Harbour. Oscar spent a harassed war capturing steamy Pacific islands, being chased off, and wading ashore again to the curses of officers and the whining and banging of shells. He had decided that if he was still functioning after the war he would begin by buying an education in Chicago, then see what turned up. After the war he found he functioned better than before, and education and Oscar agreed so well together that he stayed on at the University after graduating, and on. Like Foley he was now an associate professor. Foley had been exempt from military service, his medical examination having lasted four minutes. The doctor had recorded a jumble of words and figures on some forms and said: "Run along home, son, and get better."

Foley sat in the chair with the patched arm and the inkstained seat and read Aunt Rhoda's letter. Oscar lay supine in his chair. After reading the letter Foley let it rest on his lap while he looked up at the ceiling. For a minute he did not speak, then he said: "I've inherited a castle in Ireland."

Chapter 2

"Dear Willie,

I can just see your surprise at a letter from Aunt Rhoda! I hope you got our Christmas card safely. We certainly enjoyed yours. You really must visit with us soon but I know your students keep you 'on the hook.' Now the reason why I am writing. Your Uncle Jay has had this letter from a lawyer in Ireland, Mr. Casey—he calls himself a 'solicitor'—who asks is he the eldest son of Arthur Renfrew Foley or a grandson of David Foley because if he is he has this Castleferry coming to him in an inheritance deal the Irish have. Well of course as Jay says Arthur Renfrew Foley was his father all right but the eldest son was your poor father Matthew, rest his soul. Jay still puts the poem in the newspaper every year on the day. Now you must be the one Mr. Casey is after because you are Matthew's only son and he says this deal is a 'male tail' which means the castle goes down through all the eldest sons. I wish I had the letter but Jay took it to the depot. He cannot remember his grandfather but he says his father used to mention an ancestor or someone coming out here from Ireland because of famine or the British or something and people starving. I have written Mr. Casey your address and his is Emmett Street, Bandon, Co. Cork, Ireland. He doesn't give a number so it must be a short street or he is very well known. You must write him. The castle is at Ballykilleen. Isn't that quaint! It could be thousands of years old. I say it may be someone's idea of a joke but Jay says no it sounds the real thing but he does not want anything to do with it. He is working hard at the depot and still never misses a ball game. Do you remember Janice and Marty? They had their fourth last month. I must say good-bye now.

Yours affectionately, *Aunt Rhoda.*"

Foley looked at the letter in his lap. He looked at Oscar. He said again: "I've inherited a castle in Ireland."

"Where's Ireland?" Oscar said, opening one eye.

"Have you heard of a male tail?"

"Are you kidding?"

Oscar opened the other eye. He reached forward for Aunt Rhoda's letter and lay back again, horizontally. As he read the letter he started to grin. He struggled up to a sitting position. He read on and unleashed a joyous, "Ha!" The grin grew broader. Before he reached the end of the letter his shoulders were shaking with laughter. When he reached the end he brandished the letter above his head.

"You've got a castle," he cried.

"I keep telling you."

Foley started to smile, then he laughed. Oscar was on his feet waving the letter high like a diplomat bringing home a peace treaty.

"You've got a castle," Oscar hooted.

Convulsed with laughter the two linked arms in the centre of the room and circled round in a tiptoe dance chanting, "Got a little castle, got a little castle."

"Willie's got a castle, castle in Ireland," sang Oscar, solo.

"Castle in Ireland—Ireland, Ireland, Ireland!" they chanted together.

The letter floated to the floor. The associate professors subsided panting in their respective chairs. The room fell silent except for heavy breathing and occasional eruptive chuckles.

Foley said: "I'll ring Jacobs about this male tail. He should know."

Jacobs lectured in law and once a week played bridge with Foley, Oscar and an economics lecturer called Kodac. Foley dialled a number. Jacobs answered.

"Just a minute," Foley said into the telephone. "Let me get this down."

He retrieved Aunt Rhoda's letter from the carpet and scribbled on the back while Jacobs talked. Jacobs talked for several minutes. He enjoyed explaining the law. His voice crackled over the phone.

"And that'll cost you a hundred dollars," Jacobs said finally.

"What's money to us landed gentry?" said Foley.

"I'll come visit you in Bally-wherever. Keep me a room in the keep. Get it? With a view over the moat."

They hung up.

"It's not male tail, it's tail male," Foley told Oscar. "A Freudian slip by Aunt Rhoda."

He studied his note.

"Jacobs says that last century the thing to do if you were a man of property was to try to found a dynasty by tying up your estates in strict settlement in this tail male. He says this probably happened in this case. Some old

Irish Foley settled his land on his eldest son, then on his eldest son's eldest son, and so on into eternity. Except that maybe at some stage there wasn't an eldest son so everything had to go sideways to a second son's eldest son, or to a daughter, and the system went off the rails. Are you with me?"

"No."

"He says there could have been a Foley who was raving or didn't get married or who had nothing but bastards. Apparently bastards don't stand to inherit. So the castle went to the second son who'd escaped to America and got lost, and that second son might have been my grandfather, to wit, David Foley."

"So the castle's yours. Willie Foley, Lord of Castleferry. Now you write to this Casey and tell him about your male tail. Tell him to make with the deeds and everything. Then go over and lay the ghost. You could have fun there—could be a nice girl ghost."

Foley hesitated. "I was going to teach summer school again. I can't go this year."

Oscar frowned impatiently. He shook the last cigarette from a squashed king-size packet.

"Go this year," he insisted. "By next year the I.R.A. will have blown the castle up. Do you know about the I.R.A.?"

"No."

"Well, they blow up castles, particularly castles owned by peace-loving American professors. You'll probably have to fight with knives to keep your castle."

"I'm not fighting for any castle."

"What about the honour of the Foleys?"

"This'll turn out to be the greatest load of bull. Jacobs said he knew nothing of Irish law. He only remembers the male tail thing from his undergraduate reading. He said that was English law and he didn't know if Ireland was the same."

Oscar sighed. " So your castle turns out to be a phoney—what do you lose? Okay, it's a heap of mouldering rock with sheep and cows in residence. So go look at the Mountains of Mourne, see the world—you'll have a ball. If it weren't for Ann and the kids I'd go with you."

" Will this castle make me a duke or squire or something?" Foley asked.

The man in the apron brought a beer and a large vodka and set them down on the table. After this large vodka she'll have another large vodka and then a third, Foley thought. He was sorry for both of them but sorry especially for Joy. He suspected that she knew it was the end and would charge him all the vodka she could put away so that he would know she knew it was the end. Neither would utter a word which might hint it was the end.

" I found this travel bureau on South Wabash Avenue," Foley said.

He traced a finger through the condensation on his beer glass. The lightness in his voice was forced. He prattled on helplessly. " Thomas Hide. Purest accident. I've never heard of them. They're a tiny place. They've done the lot: plane ticket, hotel reservation, everything. I'm picking it all up to-morrow."

He paused. Keeping his eyes on the beer glass, he said: " How about lunch?"

" I can't make it to-morrow," Joy said.

Foley stared through his heavy glasses at the beer. He saw that he had written " beer " in the condensation. Joy was looking at a point somewhere behind his left shoulder.

When this is over I shall tread on air, Foley thought. I shall float. When we part this time I shall find a real bar and have a real beer and sing a song with the barman.

" Yessir, we in Chicago are the parent branch. My younger brother runs the West Coast office. That's Los Angeles.

In New York we have Mr. Dempster. Between you and me, Dr. Foley, we are a small organisation—but with a big service. Yessir, a big service. Personal contact with the client, that's our motto."

Quickly, as though some other motto had unaccountably slipped his mind, Mr. Hide added: "Travel Wide with Thomas Hide."

Mr. Thomas Hide, founder and president of the Thomas Hide Travel Bureau, had emerged from his inner office to beam at Foley and send him off across the world with the set speech on the excellence of the Thomas Hide Travel Bureau. Mr. Hide had a long thin nose and squinty eyes which glistened with self-approval. The two clerks at the counter had instructions to inform him of the presence of any client who might be preparing for a journey of reasonable distance and cost. (He was not to be disturbed in instances of internal travel of only a few hundred miles.) Mr. Hide, who had not long been in business, had reduced to fifteen seconds the time necessary for acquainting himself with a client from the filing system kept by Miss Marrs, his secretary. At the sixteenth second he would erupt from his office in a frenzy of goodwill, his nose piercing the air like a rapier, his hand, hot with bonhomie, extended for personal contact.

"Yessir, Ireland, land of the leprechauns," chuckled Mr. Hide, who had never travelled farther east than Nantucket. "Kiss the Blarney Stone, see the birthplace of Robert Burns."

Foley nodded eagerly. The enthusiasm was infectious. Mr. Hide tapped the black plastic folder which Foley held in his hands like a school prize.

"You'll find it all in our all-in comprehensive Travel-Wide Tourist Kit," Mr. Hide said.

From a cabinet stacked with identical black folders, all overstamped with the Bureau's name and slogan, one of the clerks had picked the top folder. Before Foley's enchanted eyes he had equipped it with air ticket, insurance, travellers' cheques, luggage labels and a wad of highly-coloured brochures which explained Ireland to the American visitor. The brochures included explanations of Irish customs and currency, exhortations to stay at hotels of unrepeatable value, a guide to the best fishing, a painless history of the Irish people, and a publication of Bord Fáilte Éireann titled *Holidays in Ireland.* To all this Foley had added his first passport. Now he was impatient to leave Mr. Hide, his goal the nearest drug store, where he could sit with a coffee and dream slowly through the shiny literature. Foley had travelled even less than Mr. Hide.

The correspondence with Mr. Casey had been airy, vague. Mr. Casey's letters were warm. Foley had forwarded on request a copy of his birth certificate and received it back by return with a letter remarking that so far as Mr. Casey was concerned Castleferry belonged to Dr. Foley and he could move in to-morrow. If Dr. Foley were seriously considering visiting the seat of his forefathers, would he care to call on Mr. Casey for refreshment and the completion of formalities? Further, if Dr. Foley chanced to be interested in fishing, Bandon was as fine a centre as any in Ireland and would he care to stay a few days with Mr. and Mrs. Casey? So long as he did not delay his trip until September, when they were accustomed to taking a holiday at Juan-les-Pins. Dazed by the story-book inheritance, and not being of an adventurous nature, Foley had been inclined to ask Mr. Casey to put Castleferry on the market. He was in two minds whether to forget the whole business. Ireland was far away and he always enjoyed summer school. The persuasive influence was Oscar, who almost lost his temper when Foley argued that he did not greatly care to travel all that distance to gaze on a pile of rubble surrounded by a moat. Oscar reminded him that Mr. Casey had mentioned in one letter that

Castleferry was in good repair. If he did not budge from his rut and shift his fat bottom out of his chair and set out immediately term ended to claim the inheritance of the Foleys, he was a poltroon and a drip. Aunt Rhoda wrote to say much the same. Joy sent a letter four pages long setting out the reasons why it was not for her to offer an opinion one way or another. The next day she sent a photograph of herself signed " Joy."

Once Foley realised that he would make the trip he became almost rigid with excitement. He ran to earth a research assistant in sociology who had studied at Trinity College, Dublin, and volleyed questions at her about Ireland's climate, food, transport, towns and countryside. Would he be welcome? What did they think of Americans? Would they swindle him out of his last travellers' cheque? He dipped deep into a bank account which had grown almost obese from lack of exercise and discovered the Thomas Hide Travel Bureau by chance while walking the quarter mile from his parked car to the City Book Store. With one of the clerks he discussed the merits of air travel over sea travel, travel dates and hotels. Then he continued to the City Book Store and bought nine books on Ireland. At a department store he bought a camera, a tweed suit with a greeny-blue fleck, an expanding suitcase and a hotwater bottle. From Fulbright scholars returned from Europe he recalled grisly histories of unheated bedrooms.

" *Bon voyage,*" Mr. Hide was saying. " And don't forget to send us a happy card from Ireland."

A happy card from clients in foreign parts was a sales notion dreamed up by Mr. Hide and, in spite of unforseen hazards, not yet discarded. Framed on a wall in the Bureau were two such cards from satisfied customers, one from Acapulco, the other from Stratford-on-Avon. The response of other clients to this mild form of advertising had proved disappointing. Of the tiny minority of Travel-Wide tourists who had posted a card, several had written rudely about the country they were touring and one or two had attacked the Bureau. A Mr. Leibnitz had written from Rome: "Thank you for our reservations here at the wonderfully popular New Mazzini Hotel. I don't know how you managed them because the hotel has not yet been built. We spent the night looking for a place to sleep. Hoping you are sick of the palsy, Yours truly, Harold P. Leibnitz."

Foley shook Mr. Hide's hand, thanked him for all he had done, and made off from the drug store.

At 3.18 on the afternoon of June 7 Mr. Hide returned to his office after a long lunch. Miss Marrs said: "Mr. Dempster has been calling you from New York. He said he'd ring again at three-thirty."

At 3.30 the telephone rang. Mr. Hide picked up the receiver. He listened, frowning. "Right," he said. "Right. As soon as possible . . . Yes, immediately . . . How should I know? . . . Yes, absolutely vital . . . Hold on a moment."

He lowered the receiver and said to Miss Marrs: "I wonder if you'd fetch me some aspirin. My migraine, I'm afraid."

"I have aspirin right here," Miss Marrs said. She burrowed in her handbag.

"And a chicken sandwich," Mr. Hide said, taking out his bill-fold. "Buy yourself some candy while you're out. How about some of that nice turkish delight?"

Miss Marrs eyed her boss quizzically. She accepted the dollar bill and went out closing the door behind her.

"Damn her," Mr. Hide muttered. He laid the receiver on the desk and hurried over to the filing cabinet. He flicked through a batch of cards and extracted one headed: "Ireland. Dr. William Foley. June 7."

He glanced at the calendar on the wall and returned to his desk with the filing card in his hand.

"Hallo?"

He listened to the voice at the other end of the telephone, then spoke rapidly.

"Here it is. Dr. William Foley, Flight LT Four-One-Six to Shannon, departing Kennedy Airport nine hundred hours —to-morrow. Play it exactly as before . . . Yes, the new folder . . . Hell, I don't know. Fat, wears glasses . . . I don't care, just do it. Then it's up to them . . . Look, you'll have to make time . . . No, don't phone me. Wait a minute——"

Under Mr. Hide's sword-nose the mouth creased into a smile like a crack in cement.

"If the remuneration is—let's say, commensurate, someone's going to be able to lie back and whistle. I've an eye on two thousand acres outside Phoenix. What have you an eye on?"

He hung up without waiting for an answer.

Chapter 3

The Boeing vaulted high into the sky over the Atlantic. Over the loudspeaker a voice as soft as grass told passengers they could unfasten their safety belts and smoke if they wished. Those who wished to smoke would find an ashtray in the arm of their seat.

Foley took out his pipe, tobacco pouch and a box of matches. This was it. His ears buzzed painfully but the asthma had subsided. This was it. The voice intruded again to announce where the aircraft was going and at how many feet and what the weather was like. The weather was good. Foley felt reassured. He recognised the voice of his hostess, or one of the hostesses. He had seen several, all as bright as pins. They had scooted up and down the aisle with boiled sweets, now they were scooting up and down with newspapers and magazines. Foley chose *Newsweek*. An elderly man in the next seat asked a hostess for a whisky. Foley asked for a beer. He returned his pipe unsmoked to his pocket and settled down with *Newsweek*. Through the window, and falling farther and farther away below, cloud stretched like a great snow-pack. Foley was reminded of pictures of the white wastes over which Scott had trekked to the South Pole. Or was it Amundsen, or was that the North Pole? He ordered a second beer, stuffed *Newsweek* into the sagging pocket on the back of the seat in front of him, and meticulously examined the contents of his folder. Everything was there. He had checked many times but he remained apprehensive about the possibility of losing a vital document and having to cable Mr. Hide for help. Maybe he would cable Oscar, not Mr. Hide. He would not cable Joy, he would spare her that, though he guessed that nothing would please her more than an urgent call imploring assistance in time of trouble. He put his glasses in his pocket and tipped back his seat so that he might dream of hostesses.

The plane crashed into the sea and everyone aboard drowned except himself and the hostesses. No, Foley objected, the loss of life was too upsetting. Everyone was rescued by helicopter except the hostesses and himself who were thrown far out to sea when the plane hit the waves and were washed ashore on a desert island. That was it. The night was warm, stars twinkled. The girls were too fatigued to swim the last hundred yards to the island so he had to help them, each in turn, using a powerful sidestroke as he towed them ashore. One by one he carried them up the beach and gently laid them on the sand. They were breathing, so that was all right. The sea lapped at their ankles, which were delicately bruised but not disfigured. Their green tweed uniforms were in tatters. In fact all uniforms had been lost or cast off in the perilous swim ashore, and the girls were covered only by sodden, ragged slips which clung like skins to their firm bodies. The most magnificent hostess, the freckled one, had lost even her slip. She had also lost her brassière. Beads of salt water glittered on her perfect breasts as she lay unconscious on the sand. Exhausted as he was, he staggered over and covered her with his jacket. He could not take advantage of this helpless creature. Tenderly he kissed her forehead. Later, on some such night as this, she would thank him with the simple passion of her woman's nature. So would all the others. They would live together on the desert island, naked and free as children. He would show them how to build houses out of palm leaves. They would make love, eat paw-paw, and he would teach them to spear the succulent flying fish. The biggest and most succulent fish they would single out for him. Sometimes they would quarrel among themselves for his favours but he would resolve disputes with a quiet word, dispensing justice equitably and treating all with a fairness which won their undying devotion. An exception would be made for the freckled one. She would sit at his right hand at supper, and because of her sweetness and sense of fun the other girls would love her as much as she loved him.

"Excuse me, sir, dinner is about to be served."

A hostess was adjusting the folding table above his legs. She was not freckled but she had wide green eyes and Foley marked her down as a satisfactory runner-up. She could sit at his left. He smiled at her. She smiled back and tripped away down the aisle, adjusting tables. Foley ordered another beer, and with his steak he had a half bottle of red wine. After the tinned pears, cheese and coffee, he lit his pipe and tried to peel his name off the front of his Travel-Wide folder.

The letters had been stuck on with a rubber solution which had not effectively hardened. They peeled away like tiny scabs. Foley dropped the letters in his folder. He had been surprised when Mr. Dempster had approached him at the airport and introduced himself. Such a send-off confirmed Foley's impression that he had chanced upon a travel agency with an exceptionally personal service. Other travel agencies might offer a similar service but he doubted it. Less pleasing was the "new improved tourist kit" which Mr. Dempster had pressed on him in exchange for the folder handed out in Chicago. The folders were identical except for the addition of his name in the top corner of the improved version. Foley considered this no improvement. The name and the Ph.D., bared to the world, seemed an unnecessary refinement, but to have refused the new folder on these grounds would have been churlish, and Mr. Dempster had assisted in transferring into it the contents of the old. Before the aircraft taxied off, Foley thought he saw through the window the distant figure of Mr. Dempster, standing on a viewing platform, keeping himself a little apart from the main body of spectators. He appeared to be looking in the direction of the Boeing. He was not waving.

Foley peeled the letters of his name from the folder, dropped some into the folder, rescued them, shuffled them round on his knee. The m of William was missing and he located it clinging to the inside of the folder. He picked out the letters which spelt "Travel-Wide Passenger to Ireland" and dropped them on the floor, then found the Ph. and the D. and dropped these on the floor. From his pocket-book he took the photograph which Joy had sent him. At what stage should an old photograph be shed? he wondered. Immediately, as a gesture of independence? After a month, or year? Never? He surveyed the full mouth, the tall slightly formidable forehead. She was not unattractive. He found the capital W and pressed it on to the tip of Joy's nose. It stuck. He pressed the capital F upside-down on the centre of the forehead. The other letters he arranged higgledy-piggledy until much of the face was obscured. He left one eye unadorned and it peeked at him, silently accusing. Foley giggled. He returned the defaced photograph to his pocket-book. Poor Joy, he thought.

The Boeing lowered its belly through the clouds. Foley looked down through the window at Ireland.

He did not see much. The aircraft was closer to the ground than he had expected but he saw the landscape only dimly through a cloak of rain. Flat fields, cows in one of the fields, a car creeping along a road. A church with a conical tower and a spire loomed into view through the drizzle and was gone. The scene was uninspired, but Foley was not disappointed.

Conditioned by the coloured brochures, even in the grey rain he saw Ireland as imperishably green. The ballads, stories and pictures in his haul from the City Book Store had prepared him for rich hills and meadows, a country peopled by charmers. A " love-affair with an emerald land " he had been promised, and the love-affair he intended to have. In his head, heart and folder were gaudy notions. Foley arrived in Ireland ready to be romanced off his feet, and if there turned out to exist a tougher Ireland at odds with the romance, so much the worse.

" If you ever go across the sea to Ireland . . ." he hummed to himself.

A man in a dark uniform gave the new passport a peremptory glance. Another man in uniform chalked a squiggle on the expanding suitcase. He had made it, he was abroad, a foreigner. Foley's feelings hovered between delight and anxiety. His hat and the shoulders of his coat were wet from the race across the tarmac. He stood in the crowded hall and looked at the signs on walls and doors. " Medieval Tour." " Taxis." " Departure to Dublin." Some signs were in Gaelic. A discreet chart was divided in two under the respective headings " Catholic Services " and " Religious Services." Around him boiled a commotion of embracing relatives. He spotted a pair of unarmed guards and awarded himself top marks for recognition. Irish police were, in Irish, gardai. One garda, two gardai. He recalled the knowledge from the brochures. He felt a hand on his arm. A tall bald man in a white raincoat, and a younger man with a briefcase, big shoulders and a navy-blue duffle coat, had appeared from behind.

Foley turned. His porter put down the suitcase. The bald man said: " Excuse me—Dr. Foley?"

" That's right."

" My name's Parker," said the bald man. " This is Mr. McCarthy. We represent the Thomas Hide Travel Bureau in Ireland."

Foley was not greatly surprised: and after this fresh example of personal service he would not have been surprised if the Thomas Hide Travel Bureau had tucked him into bed at night and brought him orange juice in the morning.

" Good evening," he said. " Mr. Hide never mentioned there'd be someone to meet me."

" We act for several leading travel agencies in America and Europe. We meet clients when we can."

Mr. Parker's accent did not sound Irish. Foley could not decide what it was. Australian, maybe, or cockney.

" If you have a few moments," Mr. Parker continued, " may I propose some small refreshment? A sort of Irish welcome?"

" That's good of you."

" Excellent."

Mr. Parker exchanged a word with Mr. McCarthy who in turn spoke to the porter and handed over a coin. The porter trudged off with the suitcase.

"You will be comfortable at the Erin Hotel," Mr. Parker said. "The Erin is the newest hotel in Ireland."

"Mr. Hide said it was the oldest," Foley replied. "He said Queen Elizabeth slept there."

Mr. Parker's smile slipped. He recovered quickly and said: "Mr. Hide is a humourist. He enjoys pretending that Queen Elizabeth slept everywhere. Of course in Ireland it is not good taste to mention Queen Elizabeth, or Cromwell."

They sat in deep chairs round a table in the lounge.

"Have you tried our Irish coffee, Dr. Foley? You must have a glass. We shall all have a glass."

He crooked a finger at a waiter. His fingers were bony and white, the third finger wore a signet ring inscribed with his initials, or somebody's initials. The truth was, he explained, that new buildings were going up so rapidly in Ireland that from day to day it was difficult to say which was the newest. Hotels, factories, houses, offices—Ireland was beyond doubt the country of the future—well, one of the countries of the future. Ireland was small of course, with a small population, but it was booming. Booming, and most beautiful at this time of the year. The arrival of such distinguished tourists as Dr. Foley showed that Ireland had much to offer.

Foley decided that he did not care for Mr. Parker.

The trio drank Irish coffee and Mr. Parker called for a second round. Foley began to wonder how long the welcome would continue. To be sociable he talked about Castleferry and his plans, after meeting Mr. Casey and inspecting his castle, for touring Ireland. Yes, he supposed he would sell the castle but he could not be sure until he had seen it. Mr. Parker nodded understandingly.

The burly young man in the duffle coat did not move except to raise his glass to his lips. He might have been a religious boxer who had taken a vow of silence. If he possessed small talk he was keeping it to himself. He had not uttered a word except to the porter. As one half of a reception committee he was plainly a waste of time. Foley looked at the young man and started to offer a smile. McCarthy was watching him without expression. Foley abandoned the smile and looked away, feeling uncomfortable. Not merely a waste of time but a jumbo-sized handicap, Foley thought. He sipped his Irish coffee. It slid down his throat without difficulty. He wondered how it would taste made with bourbon.

"Sláinte," announced Parker, raising his glass.

"Here's looking at you," Foley said.

He dabbed away a blob of cream from his lip. McCarthy drank with his eyes on Foley. Foley looked at him and looked quickly away, increasingly uneasy. He's new to the job and never seen an American before, Foley decided. He took out his pipe.

Parker said: "Ah, a pipe smoker. Let me introduce you to a good Irish tobacco."

Foley allowed himself to be led to the bar. Though he did not need new tobacco his nature was to comply rather than to protest, and especially so on vacation. Parker pointed out the flakes and mixtures on a shelf behind the bar and recommended a two-ounce tin for which he paid from his own pocket. Foley protested meekly. If free tobacco were part of the service, fine. When they returned to their table McCarthy was on his feet with his briefcase in his hand.

"There's a flight due which I'm afraid we must meet," Parker said. "Will you excuse us? Perhaps we can find you a taxi. The Erin is only five minutes away. They're expecting you there."

Foley gathered up his hat, camera and folder and walked with his reception committee to the main entrance. The Irish coffee had warmed him. Outside, the evening was growing dark. Rain was still falling. He shook the bony hand of Parker and the big limp hand of McCarthy.

"Thank you," he said. "You give a nice service."

"That's our job," Parker said. "Any difficulties at all, any questions, just get in touch with us."

"Where do I find you?"

"We're in the telephone book: the Parker Tourist Service. I hope the castle is a success."

"Thanks for everything."

Foley and Parker said good-bye. McCarthy inclined his head. He's so overwhelmed with my personality he's tongue-tied, Foley told himself as the pair retreated within the airport building. He climbed into the taxi. He would try another Irish coffee at the hotel. Two were hardly enough for such a very important Travel-Wide tourist.

The taxi drove through the Shannon industrial estate. Foley gazed out of the window but could see little through the rain and the late evening gloom. The factory buildings were low flat shapes in the half-darkness. There were rows of brightly-painted new houses. The prospect was of bleak modernity.

Foley regarded the back of the taxi-driver's head and admitted to himself that there was nothing strikingly Irish about it. The back of taxi-drivers' heads in Chicago looked much the same. He touched the camera to make sure that it was still in his possession and struck a match to check the documents in the folder. Two miles from the airport the taxi turned off the road on to a gravel drive and halted outside the Erin Hotel. Foley handed the driver one of the Irish banknotes with which the Thomas Hide Travel Bureau had equipped him. He received a handful of coins in exchange and fed most of these back into the driver's palm. From the profusion of thanks he guessed that his tip was grossly extravagant, but on his first night abroad he was not going to worry about foreign coinage and rates of tipping. He was puzzled enough over his reception committee at the airport. What in hell had they been up to? Why should they have swapped his folder without telling him? The letters on the top corner of the folder which he carried when he met Parker and McCarthy were on the photograph of Joy in his pocket-book. The folder he now held spelled out his name in small white letters, and after the name the Ph.D. and Travel-Wide Passenger to Ireland.

"And see the sun go down on Galway Bay . . ." he sung to himself, less merrily than before.

He resolved to soak in a bath as hot as he could bear it, change every stitch of clothing, and sample some more Irish coffee.

Chapter 4

The Shamrock bar at the Erin Hotel smelt of varnish, floor polish, air freshener and whisky. By day, for all the chrome, the room was a dim and melancholy place. At night the soft lighting and the patrons combined to offer a semblance of cosiness. Foley sat on a high stool at the counter and studied the signed photographs pinned on a board at the back of the bar. Though he could recognise none of the faces he presumed they were celebrities, Irish celebrities, who had graced the Shamrock Bar and happened to have handy a picture of themselves. His bath had turned him pink. He wore a green knitted tie, white shirt and his new tweed suit with the greeny-blue fleck. The suit was ill-fitting. It had been bought off the peg and was tight under the arms. Though the idiosyncrasies of his figure called for advanced feats of tailoring, Foley bought his suits from the ready-made ranges of department stores. The prospect of measurings, fittings, chalkings, queries over cloth and decisions about whether the lapels should be high, low or attached to the collar with silver rivets thrilled him as much as one of his asthma attacks. Or a letter from Joy. He unbuttoned the coat so that it hung free. Sooner or later all suits wore themselves down to fit the figure: more or less. He rested his elbows on the bar. He tried to feel happy. He felt very far from Chicago.

The Irish coffee was a long time arriving. Fifteen minutes previously the barman in the scarlet jacket had said it would take " less than a second." The bar was busy, and while the coffee bubbled in the percolator the barman lunged from customer to customer, receiving orders and pouring drinks. Several customers were Americans. A middle-aged couple with slow Southern voices drank egg nog. A younger couple from a remote world of their own drank whisky. The girl had lemon-coloured hair and wore a black wool dress and a string of pearls, the man was in a cashmere jacket and an orange shirt buttoned at the neck. Both were suntanned. California, Foley guessed. Film people, or maybe ski instructors, stopping off for local colour on the way back from St. Moritz. The barman arrived with the Irish coffee.

"Now, sir," he said briskly, and was off to another customer without waiting for a reply.

Foley peered through his glasses at the black brew topped with cream. A voice at his side said: "That stuff'll take you to the moon. Why mess around with spaceships?"

He was Foley's age, perhaps a year or two younger. The accent was of a kind which English people identify as American but which some Americans mistake as English. To Foley he was undiluted four-star Ivy League. He wore close-clipped hair and a dark tailored suit with a striped tie. Even on the high bar stool he seemed to recline, as though mere sitting would require needless effort. He was drinking a Martini.

" I've seen you before—and you've seen me," he said.

" This afternoon on the plane," Foley said.

" Right. I'm Phil Minton."

Foley waited for him to add that he was a travel agent. When the man said nothing, Foley introduced himself and waited for Ivy League to make the next move. Normally Foley took people at their face value. He was sociable, and unless a stranger was unintelligible or obviously malodorous he was prepared to like them, but he reminded himself that he was the stranger, in a stranger country, knowing no one, and after the mystifying encounter with Parker and McCarthy he considered it advisable to set up some sort of guard. He was at a loss to know what lay behind his reception at the airport. McCarthy was probably Irish, and somewhere among his reading—not the brochures —Foley had noted that a shortcoming of the Irish was a deviousness which amounted to deceit. Was it in *The Great Hunger*? Right or wrong, the theory had a scholarly ring which was totally lacking in the brochures. For historical reasons, according to the theory, the Irish had been forced to lie and cheat in order that they might practise their religion and even survive, and down through the generations something of the tendency had survived. The theory was uncharitable but so were people who treated you to a drink then swapped your travel folder when your back was turned. Anyone who wanted to change folders had only to ask, as Mr. Dempster had asked. Foley considered asking Minton point blank if he had a folder he intended to swap, because if so he should speak up. The thought was unworthy and he rejected it. Foley was no judge of character but he liked what he saw of Minton. The face was open, friendly. Foley judged that he was married with six children.

" I don't know how well you know this country," Minton said. " Maybe I'm speaking out of turn. But this is my second trip this year—business. I go to Cork to-morrow, then London, Paris, Brussels and Cologne. Then home. You know something? If someone dropped dead and left me a million I'd retire—right here."

"The Erin Hotel?"

"Not quite the Erin. But somewhere in Ireland. Cork maybe . . . the south-west."

"Rent my castle."

Foley had discovered that as a conversational gambit the castle was a winner. Electrical shock treatment probably had much the same effect. If he had suffered from an inferiority complex he might have dreamed up just such a castle simply to impress.

"Your castle?" Minton's eyebrows went up. He even forgot to recline. He sat upright, alert, and the Martini which was in passage to his mouth paused in mid air.

Foley told him about the castle, starting with the letter from Aunt Rhoda. Minton was an appreciative listener. The "tail male" defeated him as it had defeated Foley and Aunt Rhoda and Oscar. He had never heard of Ballykilleen but he knew Bandon and spoke of it as the kind of market-town haven he had in mind for his retirement when the million-dollar windfall wafted his way. He called for an Irish coffee for Foley and a Martini for himself. Ireland, he told Foley, was the last outpost of the western world where a man could live at the speed of a long-playing record and not grow tired of doing nothing. Every time you put your head out of the window a different bird was singing a different song. All news was rumour, all rumour news. In spite of new industries, noises in the Dáil, the setting up of costly embassies round the world and the dispatch of Irish soldiers to trouble-spots, Ireland remained a country parish, a green suburb of the world. A man in Ireland could snap his fingers at the thermonuclear ash. True, Minton said, he could not so easily snap his fingers at bishops and priests, but if he had a fishing-rod and a handful of pennies for a drink he could live like Rockefeller without the worries.

"Why wait for the windfall?" Foley asked.

Minton grinned. "I go for the birdsong and greenery but I was raised a Yankee. The money angle has stuck. If I were left a million I'd buy into Pittsburgh Pharmaceuticals Incorporated. I'd send all the kids to Harvard and one of them would become President of the United States."

He handed Foley a card. It read: "Phil T. Minton, European Sales Director, Pittsburgh Pharmaceuticals Inc., Pittsburgh, Pa." Minton took the card back and wrote on it the name of a hotel in Cork and a telephone number.

"Look me up," he said. "I'll be there till the fourteenth. Maybe by then we'll be ready to ache together with nostalgia for central heating and the Ed Sullivan Show."

Foley bought the next drinks: a lager for himself, another Martini for Minton. He felt cheerful again. He wondered if he should mention Parker and McCarthy and the mystery of the swapped travel folder but decided against it. Minton would make no more sense of it than he could himself. *The Case of the Swapped Travel Folder,* Foley mused, by Erle Stanley Gardner. The alcohol made him sleepy and happy. He described to Minton a day in the life of an associate professor of mathematics and Minton said it seemed a good life. Minton told Foley about the drug industry. Foley said drugs seemed a good life but all things considered he would keep on as an academic. They discussed lysergic acid and Aldous Huxley. Then they moved on to civil rights and the World Series. Foley looked at his watch and was surprised at the lateness of the hour. Though he had eaten no supper he was no longer hungry. The ski-instructors had left, taking their suntan with them. Their place at the bar was occupied by a blond man in a dinner jacket. Except for the clothes he had an air of the primeval forest. The yellow hair grew like a mane down his neck. He was tall with handsome rather brutal features, the nose was straight as a stick, the mouth fleshy, the overall effect mildly dramatic. He held a Coca-Cola while he surveyed the customers. His eyes toured the bar, hesitated as they met Foley's, then continued their incurious journey.

"That's the manager," Minton said. "He's a German. If you want to sell your castle don't sell it to me, sell it to a German. They're the ones in Ireland with the money."

Foley was not listening. He was thinking of Joy and hoping this might be the last time he would think of her, at least until his vacation was over. The affair had been a mistake from the start, but if there was any blame it was as much hers as his. He hoped she did not blame herself too much. She needed confidence more than he did. He was annoyed to think that she probably did not blame herself at all.

"Good night," Minton was saying. He had stood up. "Glad to have met you. Don't forget you've my Cork number."

Abruptly he was gone. The manager with the blond mane had gone. Only four or five customers remained in the bar and Foley was on his own at the counter. He opened his pocket-book and drew out the photograph of Joy. He looked at the high forehead with the capital F upside-down in the centre. Other letters obscured the mouth he used to kiss. He peeled off the F and stuck it on the back of the photograph. The letter left no mark on the cerebral forehead. By peeling off the other letters and sticking them on the back of the photograph he restored the face. Some letters which no longer would stick fell on to the bar. He dabbed them up with his finger and dropped them into the ashtray. He beckoned the barman.

"What do they call you?" Foley asked.

"Sean, sir," the barman said. He was a cautious man

who had learned most of what he knew about life and love from the tales poured out to him by solitary, half-soused drinkers. Attentiveness had sometimes been worth a banknote.

"Mine's Willie Foley." Foley stretched his hand across the bar. The barman held it for a second and gave an uncertain smile.

"Do you know who this is, Sean?" Foley held the picture of Joy before Sean's eyes.

The barman scrutinised the face.

"Is it a film star?" he asked.

"It's Audrey Hepburn," Foley said. "Will you pin it up there with the others?"

Sean hesitated. "That's not Audrey Hepburn. I've seen Audrey Hepburn, she's gorgeous. She was in a film with Cary Grant."

"I know nothing about Cary Grant," Foley said, "but this is Audrey Hepburn all right. It's an old picture—before she became famous. You'll not see many pictures of her like this."

"She looks old there. She was much younger with Cary Grant."

"That's make-up, Sean. You'd be surprised what they do with make-up in Hollywood. She's much older than she looks. Nearly forty."

"I don't believe you," Sean said.

He did believe, though, and the new light on Audrey Hepburn was like a knife in his heart. Foley watched Sean readjusting his feelings towards the aged Audrey Hepburn. He held out a dollar bill. The barman took the photograph and the dollar bill.

"It's signed Joy," he said indignantly.

"You're sharp," Foley replied. "Joy's her pet name. Her friends call her Joy."

He took back the photograph and with his pen across Joy's neckline he wrote: "To Sean, with all my love,

Audrey." He handed the photograph back to the barman. Sean grinned.

"It's a cod," he said in triumph. "I knew it was never Audrey Hepburn."

"You're not easy to fool," said Foley.

"I'll put her up anyway. The boss'll never know. He wouldn't know Audrey Hepburn from Old King Cole."

Sean pinned Joy to a blank space on the board. He winked at Foley.

"The boss wouldn't know Audrey Hepburn from the President of the Republic," he said.

That'll be the President of the Irish Republic, Foley thought as he navigated carefully out of the bar. He had drunk liberally, but not so much that he would fail to find his room.

He woke up wondering what the time could be.

Whoever else was in the room had awakened him by bumping against the bed, a chair, something. Foley opened his eyes. The room was totally dark. He lay on his side holding his breath and told himself not to panic. He felt the thumping in unison of his head and heart, the one from a surfeit of Irish coffee and lager, the other from fright. He lay still, waiting. If I knew who it was, he thought, what it was, everything might be all right. His chest ached. As he started slowly and silently to release his breath a voice whispered. "Now!"

The whisper came from by the door. Foley remembered that some kind of lamp stood on the bedside table. Which side? He knew he should fling himself out of bed and snatch up the lamp but he was not built for flinging. He tried to roll out of bed but his feet tangled in the bedclothes. Other feet scuffled on the carpet. His own were trapped in the blankets. It was a moment of horrible farce. He struggled to push the blankets away with his hands. Should he shout? If he shouted he would awaken the hotel and there would be scenes and explanations. Something touched his hip. A hand gripped his arm, released itself, then clutched his ear. The nails of the hand cut his skin. Foley flailed out with both arms in the darkness, touching nothing. There came a rush of air close to his head, leaving him an instant in which to wonder whether this would be like the court cases in which the witness says: " I blacked out, your honour."

Foley was thinking along these lines when half the Erin Hotel moved into him at a speed of fifty knots.

Chapter 5

Sergeant Burke followed the blond manager into Foley's bedroom. The Sergeant was the favourite uncle of fourteen nephews and nieces; large and gentle, near retiring age. Behind the Sergeant trotted a detective from the junior end of the salary scale. Guard Croft had no family responsibilities and was ambitious only for himself. He put into a deposit account a substantial part of his small income, and when he had a free evening he would study biographies and memoirs of retired policemen in search of clues to advancement. He set out on a tour of the room, examining the walls, floor and furnishings. The room suggested the aftermath of a bulldozer rally. Mattress and bedclothes lay on the floor, drawers had been pulled out, and in places the carpet was ripped up.

" Dr. Foley?" the Sergeant asked.

" I guess so," Foley said. " Don't ask me to prove it."

He winced from the effort of speaking. " They've taken the lot," he added. " Passport, everything."

"Can you describe them?"

"It was dark. I didn't see a thing."

Foley sat obediently still while the doctor wound a bandage round his head. The doctor worked briskly without speaking. He was in a bad humour. He had been called out in the night and had not long returned to sleep when the telephone summoned him to the Erin Hotel. Foley's head hammered, his eyes watered from shock and misery. Round his waist he wore a bath towel embroidered with the words "Erin Hotels Ltd., Dublin & Shannon." His feet were bare.

Sergeant Burke wore uniform. He lowered himself on to the bed. "Pyjamas too?" he asked.

"Pyjamas too," said Foley. "They forgot my glasses, or maybe they left them so I could see what they'd done. They were on the floor."

"How much money?"

"About twenty pounds in Irish notes and a thousand dollars in travellers' cheques."

"I see."

"I'd hoped to take most of it home with me."

"What else?"

"A camera, watch, all my papers—return air ticket, passport, pocket-book. The paper stuff was in a black folder. All my clothes. I'd not unpacked my suitcase. That's gone, everything."

"You should have phoned immediately and not waited till morning," the Sergeant scolded.

"I didn't see what anyone could do."

The manager interrupted to apologise on behalf of the Erin Hotel. His name was Kurt, his accent German. He had shaved hurriedly and nicked his skin, the blond hair was damped down with water. He was sorry he could not attend personally to Dr. Foley in his misfortune, he said, but he was due in Dublin for a meeting of the board of Erin Hotels. In fact he must leave immediately.

He would ask Mr. Cotter, his assistant, to see that Dr. Foley was loaned sufficient funds to be able to continue his holiday. If speaking had not heightened the hammering in his temples, Foley would have replied that he no longer had any intention of continuing his holiday beyond a quick look at his castle. Mr. Kurt bowed and left the room. The doctor told Foley he would live and retired into the bathroom. Guard Croft came out of the bathroom holding the remnants of a bar of soap.

" Someone's slashed the soap to shreds, Sergeant. It was all over the washbasin."

" That's where you should have left it."

" It should go for analysis."

The Sergeant ignored him and looked at Foley. " Any ideas about the soap?"

" Soap's for washing."

" This wasn't a casual break-in," Guard Croft said.

" You're bright to-day," Sergeant Burke said.

The doctor emerged from the bathroom and picked up his bag and coat. " Stay in bed," he told Foley. " You've had a nasty knock."

" What with?" Sergeant Burke asked.

" A blunt instrument," the doctor said, striding out of the room.

" Smart pants," Croft muttered. " I'll not forget that one."

You will when you've met as many as I have, the Sergeant thought. He sat on the bed with his hands on his knees. An American, a wrecked room, slashed soap . . . he suspected he would not be long on this case. If he was, it would be to carry the pencil of someone from Dublin, or even Washington. He could be wrong but he did not think he was. It was not simply the butt-ends of clues, such as they were. Clues were for Croft and the crime manuals. Here there was an overall smell that was undefinable but more pungent than that of workaday larceny or breaking-and-entering or assault. Of course he could be wrong. He would make out his report and there would be no mention of smells, atmospheres. Rheumatism needled his leg. He was getting old.

Mr. Cotter arrived, attended by the hall porter. The assistant manager had never before had to cope with a bludgeoned guest and was suffering from a sense of inadequacy. He fussed over Foley like an aunt, eliciting information about preferences of colour and styling for an emergency suit. The hall porter worked phlegmatically with a tape measure. Foley asked for non-committal grey.

"Non-committal grey, Sanders," Mr. Cotter repeated to the hall porter. "Have you got that now? Non-committal grey."

Sanders took no notice. He stretched the tape measure across Foley's shoulders and jotted down a figure on the back of a cigarette packet. Mr. Cotter tucked back his cuff and glanced at his watch.

"I suggest a loan of a hundred pounds if that's agreeable to you, Dr. Foley. You should see the American Consul as soon as you feel well enough."

"Where do I find him?"

"In Dublin. I'll get you the address."

"I don't want you to go to any trouble."

"No trouble at all."

Mr. Cotter looked again at his watch. He was terrified that the hotel would be invaded by newspaper reporters. American tourists were not beaten over the head every day.

"We shall of course find you another room," he said.

"I think I'll check out as soon as I've some clothes. I was leaving to-day anyway. My travel-agent organised a hire-car for me. The name was in my folder. Shanklin or something. I was to phone them."

"Shanklin, exactly. Shanklin Motors." Mr. Cotter was vehement in his support of Shanklin Motors. "Sanders, will you ring Shanklin's and see about Dr. Foley's car? I must see to the loan."

Mr. Cotter scuttled out. Sanders followed, trailing the tape measure. Sergeant Burke said to Foley: "You said 'they' took everything."

"Somebody said, 'Now.' He wasn't talking to himself. Maybe he was. Anyway, somebody said something."

"That doesn't prove anything," Guard Croft said.

The Sergeant ignored him. He said to Foley: "You'd better tell me about it."

"I don't know any more. I woke up and somebody hit me. The room was black."

"Can you describe the voice?"

"No. It was a whisper."

"Irish?"

"I'm sorry, I couldn't say."

"How long were you out?"

"Long enough for them to get on with this." Foley gazed round the overturned room. "I was on the floor when I woke up again. It was getting light outside but it wasn't morning so I sat where I was until it got lighter and I heard people moving about. Then I phoned downstairs."

"You asked for Mr. Kurt?"

"I didn't ask for anyone. I just said someone had smashed up their room and knocked me out. I guessed they'd want to do something about it. What's the time now?"

"Quarter to eight."

Was that all? Foley wished it were evening and bedtime. He shivered in the bathtowel. Sergeant Burke rose from the bed and picked up a blanket from the floor. He dropped it on Foley's lap. Foley wrapped it round his shoulders.

"It's ludicrous," Foley said. "Why—why? Did they get the wrong room?"

"Possibly."

"What do you mean—possibly?"

"You tell me. Can you think of anything you have that someone might want? Apart from cash, that sort of thing?"

"No."

"You're sure?"

Foley was fairly sure. He was no longer a hundred per cent sure. He told the Sergeant about the travel folder and his meeting with Parker and McCarthy at the airport. The Sergeant listened impassively. At one point in the story Croft started to interrupt and was silenced by an angry bark from the Sergeant which took both the young guard and Foley by surprise.

"Somebody must have heard something," Foley argued. "Will you have to question the whole hotel?"

"Some. Croft's going to get on to that right away, aren't you, Croft?"

Croft left the bedroom. The Sergeant rose slowly. The rheumatism continued to nag.

"I'd like you to stay here, sir, until I've had a word on the phone."

For the time being Foley had no intention of going anywhere. He held the blanket tightly under his chin, trying to console himself with the thought that he was meeting the Irish.

The suit was more non-committal in colour than in cut. A uniformed guard led Foley along the corridor. They halted at an anonymous door and the guard knocked.

"Come in."

Inspector Sheridan sat behind a cluttered desk in the borrowed office. The floor was brown linoleum. "Sit down," the Inspector said. The guard left, closing the door and leaving Foley alone with the middle-aged man behind the desk.

"Beggars can't be choosers, eh?" the Inspector said, looking at the trousers which hung like sails on Foley's legs.

Foley considered the remark in poor taste but in the past twelve hours his ambition had become the avoidance of further trouble. He put on a small smile, not ingratiating, but not sarcastic; just a small smile designed to let the man know that he was ready to be amiable.

With a hundred pounds in his pocket and the hammering gradually abating, Foley felt a little better. In the street outside the Limerick guard station stood the car hired from Shanklin's, a blue, freshly-scrubbed Morris 1100 which seemed to function in all gears and promised to convey him safely on the two hundred miles to Bandon, Ballykilleen, and back to Shannon; so long as he remembered to keep to the left side of the road. He had looked for Minton before checking out of the Erin but his Ivy League drinking partner had already left. Foley was not sorry. He did not yet feel sturdy enough to cope with the sympathy of compatriots. Sergeant Burke, having sat with him while he ate a slice of toast and drank three cups of coffee, had accompanied him in the Morris to the guard station. All the Sergeant would say was: "Inspector Sheridan is coming down from Dublin. He's with the Special Branch."

The short drive brought Foley his first sight of the Irish countryside and a glimpse of Bunratty Castle. The castle stood massive and stark at the side of the road a few miles north of Limerick. Foley decided to leave his future plans open. To return to Chicago after seeing no more of Ireland than Bandon and Ballykilleen, if ever he got as far as Bandon and Ballykilleen, would be feeble. Certainly he felt better now. He would have enjoyed a bar of milk chocolate but the desire was not yet a craving. In the widest terms of life and death, all was not lost, and he was not going to allow himself to be put out by personal remarks from Special Branch cops. The flannel jacket and trousers seemed to have come from rival suits, the jacket being tight and the trouser legs resembling two floating balloons. Foley did not care. He would have to buy handkerchiefs when the Inspector was through, and pyjamas and razor and a new pipe and God knew what else, but at least he was insured for both baggage and body. Foley tried to recall the terms of his accident insurance. One item, he remembered, had been twenty thousand dollars "for death." Another was the same sum for some such mishap as 'total and irrecoverable loss of all sight in both eyes or total loss by severance at or above the wrist or ankle of both hands or both feet or of one hand and one foot." Or was it " of one hand or one foot?" He recalled no reference to blows on the head by blunt instruments but he was sure something of the sort must be there somewhere. The policy had been nothing if not comprehensive. There had been a fifty-dollar a week benefit for " temporary partial disablement." Perhaps he could claim the fifty dollars.

He was waiting two hours in an empty office before the guard ushered him before Inspector Sheridan. They were nice about it and at no time said that he must not leave the guard station. At the same time they made no suggestion that he take a stroll round the city. When he asked how long it would be before the Inspector arrived he was told in an unexpectedly friendly manner, "He'll be along presently." After an hour and a half reading ancient magazines in the empty office Foley marched out to the entrance hall and told the duty sergeant that he was going to buy chocolate, and would be back. The sergeant summoned a young guard. "O'Reilly will show you the finest confectioner's in town," the sergeant said. Guard O'Reilly had escorted him to a nearby shop which was as dingy as a roadmender's pocket. Then he had escorted him back to the guard station.

Inspector Sheridan said: "I'm sorry about this. I hear you took a nasty knock."

Involuntarily Foley raised his hand to his bandaged head. "It's okay," he said. "You should have seen the room."

"I've seen it," the Inspector said. "Have a cigarette."

Foley accepted a cigarette and leaned across the desk towards the Inspector's lighted match.

"Now," said the Inspector, "help me all you can. What happened, all over again. Who knows you here in Ireland, who knows you're here, everything you brought over with you, everyone you've met. If it's not important tell me anyway."

Inspector Sheridan spoke rapidly, toying with a ball-point pen and watching Foley closely as he spoke. His hands were restless, his rain-grey eyes as steady as two stones. Foley wished he could present the Inspector with lists of significant clues. He told him about Mr. Casey and the castle, and prattled on about his stolen baggage. He mentioned Parker and McCarthy, and Minton. Inspector Sheridan listened without interrupting. He looked fit as a footballer. He pulled open and slammed shut successive drawers in the unfamiliar desk, finally found a telephone directory and leafed through the pages.

"The Parker Tourist Service," he said, searching.

"Something like that. The Parker something-or-other."

The Inspector slid his finger slowly down a page. "He's not here," he said.

"He said he was."

"He's not. Are you surprised?"

Foley shrugged.

"Do you have Minton's address?" the Inspector asked.

"Why?"

"Routine."

"He wrote it on the back of a card. I don't remember it."

"Try."

"I don't think I even looked at it. We were drinking. I put the card in my pocket-book and the pocket-book's gone with everything else."

"Didn't you glance at the address? Take your time."

"No, I don't remember."

"Think."

"Hell, I tell you I didn't see it. Cork, he said. I know he mentioned Cork."

"Well, thank you."

"Okay, I'm sorry. But Minton was all right. I met him in the bar. We'd come over on the same flight. He was an executive or something with a Pittsburg drug company. I don't remember the name."

The Inspector made a note with the ball-point pen. He said: "The original folder you had from Mr. Hide in Chicago was exchanged for a new one by Mr. Dempster in New York. The new one was swapped again at Shannon by Parker and McCarthy. Right?"

"The way you put it, it sounds queer."

"Don't you think it's queer?"

"I guess so."

The Inspector gave him another cigarette. The interview extended on. Finally the Inspector pushed back his chair and stood up.

"Ring me from Bandon, will you? As soon as you get in. Where are you staying?"

"I don't know. It's about the only place I left to chance. I figured I might get an invitation to stay with Mr. Casey."

"Let me know as soon as you can. Contact me here. We'll ring your embassy and look after the passport."

"Have you any idea what this is all about?"

"Not yet."

"Is someone going to hit me again?"

"You've nothing left they could want, have you?"

"I couldn't tell you. I don't know I ever had. But supposing I had—you favour my going off on my own, isn't that right? That would give them another chance at me. If they wanted another chance they could have it. Isn't that it? That way you just might get something to go on."

The Inspector did not answer immediately. He walked

45

towards the door. At the door he paused and said: " I've something to go on already. But if you're asking me if I'm more interested in whoever wrecked your room than in your health, the answer's yes."

Nothing hypocritical about you, Foley thought. The Inspector opened the door for him and he walked along the corridor and through the entrance hall and out to the Morris. Foley was relieved to retreat into the street. The afternoon was cloudy and warm. He walked into a wide shopping street and bought a pipe and an ounce of tobacco. In a small hotel he had a beer and a mutton sandwich. He would have preferred a hamburger but the only alternative to the mutton sandwich was the set meal in the restaurant. He walked back the way he had come, stopping to look in shop windows and to buy a store of chocolate for the trip. He wedged his bulk into the driving-seat of the Morris and drove south along O'Connell Avenue. On his left he glimpsed a terrace of Georgian houses. In two minutes Limerick was behind him.

" If you ever go across the sea to Ireland . . ." he sang loudly.

The noise was more a gesture of defiance than honest exhilaration. He was in one piece, things might have been a good deal worse. Possibly, though he could not yet detect it, the day had an amusing side which might amuse him at a later date. For the present he was free. Signposts pointed him to Croom, Charleville, Buttevant and Mallow, unknown names opening new and conceivably even enjoyable worlds. Somewhere beyond Mallow was Bandon and Ballykilleen and his castle. On the map which Shanklin's had placed in the car Mallow seemed a sizeable place. He would stop there and buy pyjamas and a toothbrush.

Foley glanced over his shoulder at the back seat. No one was there. He had known no one was there but you could not be too careful. He was faintly perturbed that Inspector Sheridan had not more decisively pooh-poohed the suggestion that someone might hit him again. Foley frowned. Behind the heavy glasses his eyes grew worried. Come to think of it, the Inspector had not pooh-poohed the suggestion at all.

Chapter 6

The countryside undulated greenly. The fuchsias hung blood-red in the hedges, their colour overwhelmed by the white of the hawthorn. South of Limerick the road was straight, the landscape flat. After Mallow the fields became more rolling; some were almost hills, green and adolescent. Foley kept his right hand on the wheel and held in his left a half-eaten bar of milk chocolate. The wrapping hung down on his knuckles. If he ate any more he would feel ill. He stowed the chocolate reluctantly in the glove compartment and wiped his fingers on the balloon trousers. He started to hum to himself, then ceased. He was not yet in a humming mood.

If this were country where he owned a castle, maybe he would keep the castle after all. He might never again return to Ireland, probably he never would, but a stake in such grassy countryside would be worth possessing. When he was old, whiskery and a full professor, emitting wisdom and distinction like electricity, he would be able to tell his friends: " Have my castle in Ireland for the summer."

Could a gesture be grander? Foley began to hum again. Slowly because of arthritis he would dodder to the cupboard and take out an iron key thirteen inches long. " The portcullis jams, you have to bang it," he would say.

"My gamekeeper will sort out any problems. You'll find him at the gate-lodge. Name of O'Flynn—Brendan O'Flynn. Very loyal, been with my family nine centuries. Came over with Brian Boru."

Or did he mean Strongbow? And was gamekeeper right? Gamewarden, perhaps. Or beater, like the flunkeys in *Time and Life* pictures who went beating along with British prime ministers when they shot grouse in the grouse season. No matter, by the time he was a venerable old professor and more accustomed to owning a castle he would have his vocabulary right. From the gate of a whitewashed cottage by the roadside a woolly dog charged barking at the car. Foley covered the brake with his foot. The dog swerved at the last moment and chased insanely after the Morris. A mile farther on the ambush was repeated by another dog, equally woolly. Foley trod hard on the accelerator. Glancing in the driving-mirror he saw the dog racing after the car, yelping in anger and diminishing in size as the Morris drew away. The fawn-coloured saloon car which had been behind for six or seven miles also accelerated.

Foley drove faster. He cut a right-hand bend and swung the wheel to the left to avoid a car speeding towards him on the crown of the road. He kept his foot on the accelerator. The needle on the speedometer crept up to sixty . . . sixty-five. Foley kept the accelerator steady. He was a good driver but sixty-five on the left side of an unfamiliar curving road was as much as he dared risk. He looked in the mirror and saw behind him an empty road. When he looked again the fawn saloon was once more in view. So far as he could see, the saloon held only the driver.

At Crean's Cross Roads, Foley slowed down. Road signs pointed left to Cork and Blarney, right to Banteer, straight ahead for Coachford, Crookstown and Bandon. The Morris crossed the junction and gathered speed along the road to

Bandon. The fawn saloon had caught up and now was twenty yards behind. Ahead Foley saw cows, a dozen or fifteen healthy cows, entirely blocking the road.

To be rid of the need to make decisions was a relief. Foley shifted his foot to the brake. The cows straggled across the road from ditch to ditch. A drover with a stick was making an impressive show of trying to crowd the beasts to the side of the road.

"Ha!" the drover shouted, fetching a cow a hefty whack on the rump with the stick. The cow galloped forward then stopped and turned its head sullenly. The drover's efforts were more for appearance than from any burning desire to let the traffic through. Foley stopped the Morris with its radiator inches from the dewlap of a sleek Guernsey cow. A man appeared at Foley's window. "Dr. Foley?" he asked loudly through the glass.

Foley hesitated, then wound the window half-way down. Was this why the Inspector had not dismissed the notion that someone might hit him? Presumably no one would hit him while a cowhand looked curiously on. Foley wound the window fully down. The drover had given up his pretence of clearing the road and was leaning on his stick, watching. The cows trampled in confusion. The man from the fawn saloon stooped down and asked again: "Dr. Foley?"

Most of the head that appeared in the opening was nose, a protuberant pock-marked nose which bore itself like a banner in advance of the head. It occurred to Foley that though he had never in his life hit out in self-defence, he could hardly miss the nose.

"My name's Casey," the man said. "We've corresponded about a place of yours at Ballykilleen."

Foley opened the door and climbed out into the road. He gripped Mr. Casey's hand.

"Delighted to meet you," he said. "I've been getting hardened to surprises but this is the best yet."

A cow pushed its face between Foley and his lawyer, thrusting them apart. The two men edged away towards the rear of the Morris.

"Ho!" cried the cowboy, springing into activity and chasing the offending cow along the road in the wrong direction. Mr. Casey smote his jacket where the cow had brushed past, leaving a large dustmark.

"Bloody animals," he muttered. His nose was like a moving planet in the country road.

"I was in Limerick so I rang the Erin to see if I could give you a lift to Bandon," Mr. Casey said. He stared at Foley's bandaged head. "They told me the dreadful news. Dreadful, most dreadful. I called at the garda house but you'd left. They said you were heading for Bandon. I was returning home anyway so I thought I might catch you."

"I've been watching you. I thought I was in for another mugging."

"Another what?"

"I thought you might be going to club me."

"Dear me. I thought it was you because of the bandage and the Morris. I was waiting to see if you stopped anywhere. How're you feeling?"

"Better for meeting you. There'll be a bruise for a decade or two yet but the headache's gone—almost. My feelings about your country are mixed."

"They must be, a dreadful business. The gardai will find them, have no fear."

"When do I see my castle?"

"Your castle? Castleferry? This evening if you wish. We'll drive out. You must have supper with my wife and me."

The cowboy had set to work in earnest and succeeded in herding most of the cows into the hedge. Mr. Casey drove off first, steering cautiously between a pair of dithering strays. Foley followed. The convoy of two proceeded at a steady fifty. Foley finished the chocolate. He filled and lit his pipe without slowing, keeping the fawn saloon in sight except where the road curved. In Crookstown the saloon halted to give right of way to a pony and cart. Foley drew up just behind. Mr. Casey protruded his nose through the window, then his head, and waved at Foley Foley waved back. As they were leaving Crookstown the saloon stopped again, by a telephone box. Mr. Casey walked back to the Morris.

"I must tell my wife to expect us," he said. "Would you care to see Castleferry now? I have the key. We can be there in twenty minutes."

"Fine," Foley said. "Whatever you say. I can wait if it's not convenient. I've waited three months, another hour or two won't hurt."

Mr. Casey was fifteen minutes telephoning. He returned to the Morris and said: "Sorry but we'll have to postpone Castleferry. I've a client been waiting all afternoon for me and she'll sit there all night if I don't see her. The Irish are the most litigious people on earth. We sue in the way other nations drink wine or eat hot-dogs. Let no one tell you we're dreamers and poets who care nothing for money."

He took out a handkerchief and blew his mighty nose. Foley leaned back expecting an effect like an earth tremor but there sounded only a gentle purr.

"If you wish, I could show you the road to Castleferry and you could drive back to my place when you're ready," Mr. Casey said. "It's only a few miles. Supper won't be before eight."

"Fine," said Foley.

"You keep straight on through Ballykilleen. Carry on by the river and a mile the other side you'll see Castleferry on a hill to your left. You can't miss it."

Mr. Casey produced a bunch of keys and removed one of the smallest, a key for a Yale lock. He repeated the route to Castleferry and added directions to his own home in Bandon. The convoy set out once more. The sun had come through the clouds and Foley looked with pleasure on the sunlit cottages and farmhouses which dotted the green hills. Sheep grazed in some fields, cows in others. He noticed a signpost pointing to Ballykilleen and a turning to the left. The fawn saloon slowed and flashed its rear-off-side indicator. The saloon did not take the left fork but stopped a few yards beyond it. Foley waved and steered into the side road.

The road to Ballykilleen was twisty and the hedge on either side was so thick and high that Foley could see nothing but the road, the hedges and the blue sky. He felt in his pocket and his fingers touched the key. What kind of castle had a Yale lock?

Chiselled into the stone lintel above the front entrance was the inscription: "*Deus noster refugium 1790.*"

The door was large, the wood rotten, the Yale lock superfluous. A heavy kick would have ripped the door from its hinges.

Foley's immediate reaction was sour disappointment. Castleferry was no a castle but a mansion. There was no portcullis, no drawbridge, keep, towers or crenellated walls. Casey might have been more explicit, Foley thought. By eighteenth century standards the mansion was not even big. Foley walked back down the drive to see the three-story building in perspective and gazed at the mansion.

"The inheritance of the Foleys," he said to himself. He added a quiet bugle call: "Ta-ta-ta, tara-ta-ta."

The levity restored his humour. The old house was matchlessly sited and proportioned, and beautiful; useless until a fortune was spent on it, but beautiful. Foley did not have a fortune to invest in Castleferry, and he knew now that he would never return home with grand old world invitations to Aunt Rhoda and Uncle Jay and Oscar. As a holiday retreat Castleferry was a non-starter. But it was a handsome old house, dignified as a dowager, and it was his own.

He walked through a knee-high wilderness of weeds and grass which stretched parallel with the front of the house and once had been a lawn. The house stood on steep rising ground overlooking a broad river. From every angle the proportions were clean and simple. The Foley who had built Castleferry in 1790 had built it to last, with walls four feet thick and a roof of stone slabs supported by hand-hewn arches and beams. Time and neglect had not yet defeated it. Another century of decay would pass before Castleferry could fairly be classed as a ruin.

Foley picked his way over brambles and nettles to the back of the house. The windows were locked and shuttered from inside. Many of the glass panes were broken. Planks of wood had been nailed over a window which was totally wrecked. A door was overgrown with briars. On a wall in letters two feet high someone had painted: " Vote Sinn Fein." The paint had faded and ivy all but obliterated the " Vote."

At the main door was a bell with an ornate and rusty handle which Foley pulled, not for want of an answer but because the bell was his. The response was a scraping of iron and rust. He turned the Yale key in the lock and pushed the door; the door should have creaked in harmony with the decrepitude of the house but it swung open silently. Daylight preceded Foley through the door into a large uncarpeted hall. Directly ahead was a staircase with carved banisters. Foley stepped inside. The hall smelled of damp. An oak table with a leg missing lay on its side in a corner. Foley counted four closed doors leading off the hall and a fifth door under the stairs. He opened the first door on his left but could make out little except the outline of a dim empty room. He entered over floorboards which creaked as the front door should have creaked, groped across the floor and wrenched open one of the shutters, pinching a finger on the iron crossbar which had held it shut. Light flooded the empty room. There were no carpets, no furniture. By the fireplace lay a litter of crumpled newspapers. In the grate was an empty, rusty tin to which clung a scrap of label displaying baked beans. Foley examined the huge framed print which hung crookedly over the fireplace. In the foreground was a mêlée of soldiers with fixed bayonets and sweeping moustaches, and behind the soldiers a shell had burst causing horses to prance and toss their riders into the air and on the ground. The artist had loved every moment. Foley put his head six inches from the caption and read: " The Assault on Spion Kop, January 26, 1900."

Foley returned to the hall. He opened the door under the stairs and almost fell headlong down a flight of stone steps leading into total darkness. He struck a match and peered down and saw nothing. A cellar smell of damp and decay crawled up into his nostrils and clung there. He closed the door and walked upstairs.

On the landing were several doors, all shut. At the end of a corridor were more stairs. Foley felt he had seen enough, at least until such time as all the shutters and windows could be opened and Mr. Casey could give him the informed five-dollar tour. Even more than by the uncertain silence, which was not a total silence, he was made uncomfortable by the mansion's ancient stale odour. He put his hand in his pocket for his pipe. Somewhere a floorboard creaked which was not the floorboard on which he was standing.

Foley stood still and listened. Nothing. A shutter banged in a room downstairs, the room he had entered. Silence again, broken almost immediately by a twittering bird outside.

He tried a door on his right and looked into the expected gloom. He walked across the room, opened the shutters and looked through broken windows on to the overgrown lawn and the stony rutted drive. At the end of the drive lay the road to Ballykilleen and beyond the road stretched the river. The view was one of perfect peace but the sight of the Morris below pleased Foley more. He turned from the window and surveyed the room. It was empty except for a startling four-poster bed.

The bed consisted only of the wooden frame and springs. The canopy and curtains had been stripped away and one of the posts was slightly askew, giving the bed a limping unstable look. Foley stared stupidly. It was not the bed which mesmerised him but his new expanding suitcase. The suitcase stood open and empty on the springs, its contents piled neatly beside it. He recognised the hotwater bottle, his shirts and underwear. The Travel-Wide folder was there, and on it his passport, travellers' cheques, and a pile of brochures. They came in quickly and quietly. Suddenly McCarthey was closing the door.

"This will do as well as anywhere," Parker said. "Thank you for opening the shutters. We'll be needing the light."

Chapter 7

The late afternoon sun fell like a caress on Castleferry. Sunlight filtered diagonally through the windows of the bedroom on the first floor. The bald head of Parker caught the sunlight and shone like a china bowl.

"Welcome to Castleferry," he said. "You see we brought your baggage. Careless of you to misplace it."

Foley said nothing. He stood with his back to the window, frightened, uncomprehending. The sun warmed his shoulders. He could do nothing but wait, see what they wanted. McCarthy wore a grey polo-neck jersey under a sports jacket. His big shoulders leaned against the door, his ape arms hung loosely by his sides.

"Even more careless to misplace what we happen to want," Parker went on. His voice was gentle. "You're giving us a lot of trouble. Frankly we didn't expect it."

He paused as though assuming Foley would speak. Foley waited in silence. There was still nothing to say. Parker watched him appraisingly. "You're no hero, are you, Dr. Foley?" he said.

"If there's something you want why don't you ask?" Foley said.

"We're asking. Answer my question first."

"What question?"

"You're no hero."

"No."

It was true, Foley thought, he had never pretended to be a hero. He had never been in circumstances which required him to be a hero and he had no ambition to be thought of as a hero. He stood still, almost to attention, like an army recruit. Was Parker trying to goad him or what? They were two to one. What could a fat mathematics teacher do? The grey jersey by the door was by itself two to one . . . three to one.

"In fact you're a pasty coward," Parker said.

He picked up a handful of Foley's white shirts and arranged them as a cushion on the edge of the bed and sat down.

"A podgy American coward," he said.

"Better a podgy American coward than a bald-headed Irish slug," Foley said.

It was childish, but immediately he said it he felt better. A second passed and he realised that he had made a bad mistake. Parker's bony knuckles were white as he gripped the post at the corner of the bed.

"McCarthy," he said silkily. "Our friend is insulting your country."

McCarthy advanced across the room. Foley turned and looked quickly out of the window and saw the top of the Morris, the bumpy drive which carved through the jungle of green, the river, and the small green hills curving to the horizon. None of these offered help. He faced McCarthy again and edged away along the wall. He was in the corner when McCarthy reached him. McCarthy lifted his fist and hit Foley on the cheek. With his other fist, almost simultaneously, he punched Foley on the mouth. Foley slid down the wall. He put out a hand to break the fall and a splinter pierced his finger. McCarthy kicked him in the side. Foley lay on the floor, a heap of ill-fitting flannel suit. He heard a small continuing sound as though of a stream gurgling over rocks. He realised he was sobbing.

What time was it? The time seemed vital. Would Mr. Casey miss him and come soon to Castleferry and take him away to somewhere warm and safe?

Parker was speaking in a gentle voice. "In the first place I don't like this kind of thing," he said. "I don't like rough stuff. You can believe it or not, it's the same to me. It's just for the record."

Foley raised his hand to his eyes. The glasses were still there.

"Second, I'm not Irish, I was born in Lewisham, if you know where that is. McCarthy, now, he's Irish. Irish as the bogs. An expert on Irish prison life. An alumnus—isn't that the word? Even the Irish don't like McCarthy, do they, mate? He's misunderstood."

"Shut your gob," McCarthy growled.

McCarthy stood slouched against a corner-post of the bed. He was examining his knuckles. Foley raised himself on one elbow and looked from McCarthy to Parker and back to McCarthy.

"He talks," Foley said.

McCarthy's features were blank. Slowly a scowl spread across them. He grunted something incomprehensible and began to advance on Foley.

"Wait," Parker barked.

McCarthy halted. Parker's voice was soft again. "He has a quick temper, Dr. Foley, a nasty temper. You'd be unwise to upset him."

McCarthy resumed the scrutiny of his knuckles. Foley levered himself up to a sitting position. His bandaged head throbbed, his ribs ached. He had never been hurt like this before. He found his handkerchief and put it to his mouth. The handkerchief came away with blood on it. Blood had splashed on his shirt and tie. Foley traced his tongue over his teeth. They seemed to be all there. The splinter in his finger was as long as a pin. While Parker and McCarthy looked on in silence he found the splinter and pulled it out slowly and in one piece.

"We want the letters that were on your travel folder," Parker said. "The letters of your name."

"I know."

"Smart of you."

"I've only known for about the last five minutes. I'm not tuned in to this kind of world."

"What have you done with them?"

"Swallowed them."

"McCarthy," Parker said softly. "Hit him again."

Foley noticed that Parker turned his head away. The bully boy in the grey jersey moved forward.

"Hold it," Foley said, "I'll tell you."

"Certainly you'll tell us," Parker said. "Relax, McCarthy. Sit down."

McCarthy did not sit down. Above the polo neck a mouth leered. The grey jersey came closer. Foley shut his eyes. He sunk his head on to his chest, drew up his knees and wrapped his arms tightly over his head, tensing himself, waiting for the blow. A hand like a manacle clamped on his arm, under the shoulder, and dragged him to his feet. Foley kept his eyes shut. Just such a steel hand had clubbed him in his room at the Erin in the early hours of the morning. This very morning, Foley thought incredulously as he was swung off balance; only hours ago. Why didn't the brute hit him and finish with it? He heard Parker shouting, "Let him go!" The blow burst on the side of his face. Then the floor cracked against his head.

There was an unpleasant smell of dust, acrid big-grained dust which coated his lips and his nostrils. His cheek and the side of his nose pressed on the floorboards. Foley knew where he was and what had happened and wished that he was unconscious. He opened his eyes and saw two shoes. Above the shoes, trouser legs. He rolled over and lay spreadeagled on his back like a sunbather. High above he could make out several Parkers.

"Here are your spectacles," Parker said.

Something cold touched his face. He reached up for the glasses and let his arm fall to the floor again, the glasses in his hand.

"Is friend McCarthy——" Foley started to say, but he could hear nothing. He tried again, louder. "Is friend McCarthy fondling his beautiful fists?"

The words were far away.

"Since you ask, he is," Parker said. He was standing close. "Actually he's sucking his knuckles. I think you hurt him."

"Tell him," Foley started to say—the voice was clearer now, almost his own. "Tell him how sorry I am."

The words were fading again. He made a great effort. "Tell him if I really hurt him he can hit me again, hit me as often as he likes."

"You're a bloody fool, he'll do it."

"I don't care."

"I tried to stop him."

"So kind of you . . . such a sweet nature."

"Just tell us what you've done with those letters."

"What if I don't?"

"You will!" Parker shouted.

He was angry, impatient. Parker had smiled earlier, now it was Foley's turn. He stared mistily at the ceiling. There were several patches where the damp had seeped through.

"I think I was going to," Foley said. "I think I was. I'm not sure now. Your pal makes me stubborn. Tell me what you want them for? Who are you? And what the hell is this all about? If you hit me again I shall probably die and you'll never learn anything."

Foley closed his eyes. His speech had wearied him. "Where's McCarthy?" he managed to say.

"He's here."

"Good. You might like to know that I'm expecting friends here. I wouldn't like McCarthy to be absent."

"Who are you expecting?"

"My lawyer, for one."

"Really? What about those letters?"

"What about my questions?"

Foley braced himself for round three and a third knockdown, except that he was down already. Nothing happened. There was a long silence. He heard the squeaking springs of the four-poster as Parker sat down.

"We'll stay all night," Parker said.

"Suits me, my friend shouldn't be too long."

"You don't say."

"You don't believe it."

"Those letters please."

"Are you communists?"

"We dislike people called Foley."

"People like you are put away for thirty years. You should read the papers."

"Those letters."

" Suppose I tell you?"

" You can go."

" Maybe. And if I don't?"

" But you will."

" Go to hell."

The steel manacle forced Foley to his feet and flung him against the wall. He was picked up again and thrown full-length on to the floor. He heard a match striking.

" I've had enough," Parker said.

The voice was hoarse and tired. Foley remembered that Parker had been invading a hotel room the previous night and must be short of sleep.

Another match was struck.

" McCarthy will burn you until you speak."

" You wouldn't do it."

" No, I wouldn't. Personally I shall stand outside. McCarthy will."

Without a further word Parker turned and strode out of the room. McCarthy moved in swiftly. Foley felt an arm encircle his neck from behind, and a stinging heat on the lobe of his ear.

" Stop!" he squealed, kicking and punching.

McCarthy released him and he rolled over and lay panting. Somewhere he had lost his glasses. He heard Parker say, " Well?"

" They're at the Erin Hotel, most of them anyway. You bastards, you sweet bastards."

" Where at the Erin Hotel?"

" On the back of a photograph behind the bar, a photograph of a girl, signed Joy. There's some other writing—' All my love, Audrey.' Something like that."

" Joy and Audrey. Fat, stupid and a lady's man too. Unbelievable."

" You bastards, what did I do to you?"

" I leave you to imagine what will be done to you if this isn't true."

"It's true. I threw some of the letters away. They wouldn't stick. I don't know which ones. Most of them should be there. Now for pity's sake go and take your goon away."

"I'm going, McCarthy will stay."

Foley realised he was still clutching his glasses. He glimpsed the grey jersey in front of him and closed his eyes. He can't go on and on, he thought. The fist descended gratuitously. He lost consciousness.

Chapter 8

Foley heard a car starting up. He crawled towards the window on an everlasting journey over loose splintered floorboards, dragging himself inches at a time on forearms and knees, wondering how long he had lain unconscious. Probably not long, ten minutes perhaps . . . less. The sun had gone from the room but outside the evening was bright. Through the window Foley glimpsed blue sky and white dabs of cloud like cotton wool. His hand touched something soft. It was his bandage and he let it lay there. He recognised a pair of indestructible glasses on the floor a yard away and retrieved them and put them on.

He felt destroyed. He bit his lip in pain and anger and humiliation, the vision of a squeamish insistent Parker and a leering McCarthy before his eyes. He wondered which he hated worst: probably Parker . . . no, McCarthy. He did not know. Nor could he be sure whether the blood he tasted on his tongue resulted from McCarthy sadism or his own teeth biting into his lip. He felt no special pain in his lip. His head from scalp to neck was a battleground of pain, as though without anaesthetic twenty wisdom teeth had been pulled out.

He reached the window and hauled himself on to the window-seat in time to see a black Jaguar bumping away down the drive. He could not see who was at the wheel. Had the car been hidden among the trees and bushes when he had arrived at Castleferry? How long ago was that? An hour . . . two hours? He rested on the window-seat. He had not seen the Jaguar before. His own Morris, Shanklin's Morris, still stood by the front door, almost immediately below. Foley stared down from the window. To drop to the ground would invite a quick end from a broken neck and he was not yet ready for such a leave-taking. He had no rope, the four-poster bed had no sheets for knotting together. There were no drainpipes. Had there been a drainpipe Foley could not see himself shinning down it. At any other time the idea might have amused him. Neither could he climb down a sheer wall. He had no confidence in his ability even to climb through the window. A passing image of his paunch presented itself, a paunch jammed immovably between window-ledge and wall. They had fire-engines to cope with that sort of thing. He gazed out hopelessly on rural Ireland. The sun was low in the sky, the blue was changing to a milky grey. Wretchedly he brushed his eyes with the back of his hand. Robin Hood would have managed it, or Tarzan, or the Prisoner of Zenda, or the Three Musketeers, or Oscar . . . anyone capable.

If there was a way it had to be the door. Foley walked stiffly across the room and on reaching the door recognised with satisfaction that he had walked. He was more able than he had suspected; not much more, but improving. He tried the door. It was locked on the outside. He stooped and looked through the keyhole and saw brown peeling wallpaper on the wall opposite. The key had been taken away. Foley remembered a movie in which Alan Ladd, or Bogart, someone, had slid a newspaper under a door which was locked on the outside, then poked the key so that it fell on to the newspaper. By pulling the newspaper with the key on it back into the room, the prisoner had unlocked the door and fled. Foley stared blankly at the door. So much for movies.

"Hey!" he shouted, slapping the door with the palm of his hand. "Hey, there! Mr. McCarthy, are you there, Mr. McCarthy?"

As a start he must discover who was guarding him, if anyone. McCarthy had been ordered to stay. If he'd stayed, where was he? Where was Parker? All Foley could see as possible weapons with which to defend himself against McCarthy were shoes and the expanding suitcase, and he could not picture himself wielding either with any deterrent value. Could the hotwater bottle be put to use? Maybe if he had scalding water . . . Foley quietly cursed; or if he had tools for digging a tunnel, or an arsenal of bazookas, and a helicopter. He was becoming light-headed. He would achieve nothing from a brain clogged by wishes and fancies. He would have to play this by ear. He chose the heaviest shoe. Footsteps were mounting the stairs. Foley flattened his back against the wall by the door.

Outside the door McCarthy said: "Shut your noise. No one can hear you."

"You heard me," Foley called back.

He listened for the sound of the key in the lock.

"Shut your noise."

Foley held his breath. McCarthy tested the door handle. The door rattled briefly but stayed shut.

"Come on in, McCarthy. I want to talk to you."

"You'll get yours soon enough," McCarthy called back.

The footsteps creaked away.

"I want to talk to you," Foley shouted desperately. He beat on the door with the shoe. "I'll give you money."

The footsteps receded down the stairs.

"I'll give you money!"

The words reverberated round the bedroom. Then silence.

Foley sank to the floor. He was ashamed and relieved. McCarthy could have pushed the shoe down his throat had he wanted, bounced him round the room like a beach-ball. He sat on the floor for several minutes holding the shoe, thinking. If brains were all he had he must start to think about using them.

He rose, walked to the four-poster and transferred the luggage to the floor. The bed was heavy but he could raise it several inches off the floor. He lowered it again. One of the castors had fallen away. He lifted the bed, grunting, and at the second attempt replaced the castor. By pulling and pushing he discovered that the bed could be moved easily, noisily over the floor on its castors. The crooked post wobbled but held fast. He measured with his hands the width of the bed and the length of the window-seat.

He studied the floorboards. One by the door and three near a corner by the window were looser than the rest. He could have removed the one by the door with his hands but he ignored it. He wound the bandage securely round his right hand, then examined the window. From one of the broken panes he extracted a small piece of glass. He knelt by the narrow end of the loosest floorboard and drew the glass along the groove which separated it from the adjoining one. Dust and insect life down the ages had congealed into such a compact strip of filth that the process was like digging in cement. Foley succeeded in clearing a space large enough to insert the stem of his pipe. Using the pipe as a lever he prised upwards. The stem snapped.

He put the pipe aside. He tried to prise up the floorboard with a penny but the coin was too small. He unscrewed the metal plug from the hotwater bottle. The plug had twice the length of the penny, and a wing-shaped top which fitted into the groove between the boards. The fat cylindrical screw base of the plug straddled the boards. Fulcrum was the problem. For fifteen minutes Foley worked with the glass, shaving away the wood from the adjoining board until he had carved a space large enough to allow the plug to lean in the groove. He wedged the pipe stem under the plug, then brought his heel down sharply on the base of the plug. The loose floorboard splintered upwards fractionally above the level of the adjoining board. Holding the plug down hard with his heel he bent and gripped the free edge of the board, and pulled. The board rose another half-inch and Foley slid his fingers under it. Perspiring, he jerked again. The board was less loose than he had thought. Then it came away with a loud crack. A spider raced out of the darkness of the gap left by the board, scuttled over a joist and on to the floor and away over the floorboards. The board which lay alongside the gap was easy. Using hands and feet, Foley pulled it free.

The boards were about seven feet long. Foley placed them with one end on the window-seat, the other on the floor, parallel to each other and with the raised ends at the extremities of the window-seat. Before manhandling the bed over to the window he laid two padded trails of shirts and underwear on the floor to muffle the noise of the castors. Then he pushed and pulled the bed over the clothes until the head faced the door, twelve feet away, and the castors at the foot of the bed rested against the boards. Through all the creaking and scraping and jolting he was allowed to work undisturbed. He gathered the clothes off the floor and threw them in a corner.

Foley had thought the last part of the operation—the last but one—might be impossible. But he managed it. He adjusted the direction of the four castors, then he positioned himself between the sloping boards with his back to the window, gripped the base of the four-poster with both hands and tugged upwards. The two castors rose on to the boards. Foley rested, holding the bed steady. He pulled again, slowly, and slowly the rear castors continued upwards along the boards. He held the bed steady again and rested, the sweat dribbling over his face. Holding the base of the bed he manœuvred first his right leg then his left on to the window-seat, and squatted there. The weight of the bed seemed to have doubled and the strength in his arms was ebbing. He pulled the bed higher up the boards, raising his own body into a crouch as he pulled. The boards protested under the weight of the bed. He pulled harder. The rear castors were now level with the window-seat, the front castors squarely on the floor. Foley's arms shook with the weight of the four-poster. He could delay no more. If McCarthy could be coaxed into the room there was the faintest chance . . . surprise might tell.

Foley was not merely surprised by the foolishness he was trying to engineer, he was amazed. This was pulp magazine activity gone mad. If the plan was the outcome of a methodical, mathematical brain, better take up painting or languages.

He smiled grimly. He filled his lungs with air and lifted his head. "McCarthy, McCarthy, McCarthy!" he bellowed. "Slug McCarthy! Goon McCarthy! Goon, goon, goon!"

He let his head sag down. The sweat trickled faster. With numbed arms he held the four-poster poised. He lifted his head again.

"McCarthy!" he yelled, stamping his foot on the window-seat. "Mother McCarthy! Mother Machree McCarthy! Come on in, you slug McCarthy, fight it out! Fight it out, I tell you!"

There were leaping footsteps on the stairs.

"I'll fight you, McCarthy! Slug, slug, slug! You slug me and I'll slug you—you slug! You're evil, McCarthy. Did you know that? Come in, I'll fight you!"

The key was in the lock. Now it was all timing and

luck. "Good luck," Foley murmured beneath his breath.

The door burst open and for an instant Foley was staring at a snarling McCarthy framed in the doorway. With the remaining strength of his body Foley pushed the bed. At the same moment he released his grip. The four-poster careered down the boards and across the room.

McCarthy stepped back too late. The bed exploded into the door with a smashing and tearing of wood. Foley raced across the room behind the bed. "Hey-yea-yea-yea!" he shouted, louder than a pop singer.

The shattered head of the bed blocked the lower part of the doorway. Foley scrambled over the springs to reach the doorway. He looked for McCarthy but could not see him. He dropped from the bed to the floor, outside the room.

McCarthy lay struggling on his side in the doorway. The broken bed had pinned his foot against the frame of the door. His face was smothered in blood. He was swearing and moaning. Blood splashed down his grey jersey.

Foley stumbled across the landing and down the stairs. He did not look back. He ran across the hall, opened the door and plunged out of the house. The air was clean and fresh as a long drink. The light dazzled him. He fell into the driving-seat of the Morris. The key was in the ignition. He turned the key, put the car into first gear and started away. He accelerated, changed up, and reached the gate in fourth gear. He drove through Ballykilleen at sixty and slowed only when he saw the road to Bandon. He continued to brake. The needle retreated to twenty . . . fifteen. Though travelling slowly, the car started to swerve.

The Morris swerved slowly into the hedge and stalled. The petals of a hawthorn fluttered slowly on to the bonnet. Foley fainted.

Chapter 9

The air hostess was a disappointment. Mr. Casey should have warned him. "Willie, Willie, let's do the town," she whispered. She was eager only for the fleshpots. Air hostesses were all alike. He wanted to tell her about complex variables and orthogonal functions, he wanted her to listen while he talked of numerical analysis, which after all was his first love . . . was what he did well. He embraced her on the great four-poster but she struggled free. The bed was in the middle of a green field and he was on the bed, on vacation. A cow paraded past; printed on the side of the cow was an advertisment, Cow Hide. Behind the cow walked a bartender pushing a trolley. The bartender was Minton. Mixing a Martini, Minton said: "Enjoy your vacation." The bed started to move, slowly at first. The hostess had disappeared and he was alone on the bed. The field sloped steeply, the bed gathered speed. He stood erect like the captain of a ship, paunch forward, the wind blowing his hair. A drumming of hooves made him turn round. The cow was in pursuit. On the cow's back were two figures, and though he could not see their faces he knew they were Parker and McCarthy. They had sticks with which they beat the cow's sides. A speedometer on the bed registered one-hundred-and-ten. Suddenly, fifty yards ahead, he saw Inspector Sheridan, performing like a policeman on traffic duty, one arm above his head, the other horizontally outstretched . . . the bed would flatten him if he did not jump clear. Close behind trampled the cow. The speedometer touched one hundred-

and-fifteen, the wind tugged his thin hair. He was captain. "Fasten your seat-belts!" he shouted. Now the cow and the bed raced side by side. McCarthy was crawling along the edge of the bed like a spider. There was blood on his face. The field was a blur. He felt a hand on his back but he forced himself to disregard it, bracing his body for the collision with Inspector Sheridan. "Mother of God!" the Inspector said. "Holy Mary, Mother of God!" He felt the hand on his back.

Foley's eyes flickered open. He saw the base of the gear lever. His glasses had come unhooked from one ear. Cramp anchored his limbs.

"Arise, sir," the brogue urged. "Arise now. Mother of God, help the poor fellow."

Foley struggled up from the floor of the Morris and adjusted his glasses. Dusk had fallen. An old man in dusty clothes and a tumbledown hat was half kneeling inside the car, watching him anxiously.

"You've parted from the road, sir," he said. "Thank God there's life in you."

Foley was not sure he had heard correctly. The brogue was thick. But he could see he had parted from the road. The front of the Morris was buried in the hedge. He could not remember how the car came to be there. Everything else he remembered clearly. He also remembered the snug apartment near the campus, the smell of chalk in overheated classrooms, maples fringing the parking lot. Foley knew it was too late for remembering. He was in trouble, he must try to concentrate. He thought again of the classrooms and the maples. "But that was in another country and besides the wench is dead." Where had he read that?

"... terrible depredations," the old man was saying.

He said more but Foley missed it. The old man gabbled on, but though Foley listened hard he was unable to identify more than a word here, a word there.

"That's right," Foley said, the moment the old man paused for breath. "Could you tell me is this the correct road for Bandon?"

The question provoked an incomprehensible monologue. The man talked as though he had talked to no one for months in a lilting chatter that was unencumbered by consonants. Foley felt disconcerted, recognising without enthusiasm that this was his first encounter with a muscular Irish accent. He found the old man almost totally unintelligible. Each word poured into the next like honey. There were no gestures or pauses, just the honeyed, singing words, windy with aspirates. Foley thought he caught the word "Tipperary." Was he in Tipperary?

"Tipperary," Foley said, nodding his agreement.

He switched on the engine. It's a long long way to Tipperary, he thought, and at this rate of progress it will be an even longer way to Bandon. The old man backed out of the car and shut the door. Foley gave him an encouraging smile and waved through the window. He reversed the car out of the hedge.

"God give you a safe journey," called out the old man, standing well clear.

The headlights lit up the road ahead. After a mile they picked out a telephone box. Foley stopped the car, climbed out, and entered the box. He struck several matches as he fumbled through the directory. There were a score of Caseys but only one in Emmett Street. Beneath the office number was a home number. Foley struck another match, perused the instructions on making a call, and dialled the operator. The operator sounded so distressed to learn that the caller possessed only a sixpence for a threepenny call that Foley thought he was going to be given the call free rather than have to pay the extra three pennies. The operator asked him to put the sixpence in. Foley heard a woman's voice saying, "Hallo, hallo?"

The operator, suddenly irritated, snapped: "Will you

press Button A, caller? In front of you—are you blind? Button A, man!"

Foley found the button. "Mrs. Casey?"

"Hallo? Molly Casey here."

"Mrs. Casey, this is William Foley. I must apologise—I'm sorry I'm late, I'm on my way but I'm not sure where I am. On the Bandon road, I think. About a mile past the turning for Ballykilleen."

"Foley?"

"William Foley. You know—Castleferry?"

Mrs. Casey did not answer immediately. Suddenly she announced in triumph, "Dr. Foley. You're the American who inherited Castleferry."

"That's right, I've been looking over it. I thought I'd call——"

"I thought you were in America."

Foley shivered. He was about to learn something he did not want to learn. He tried to make his mind blank.

"I met your husband this afternoon," he said tonelessly. "He gave me the key. He asked me to supper."

"This afternoon?"

This afternoon, please lady, that's what I said, just don't repeat everything. He spoke in a rush: "On the road south of Mallow. He phoned you. Isn't he home yet?"

"Dick has been home all day. He's had 'flu."

Of course, 'flu. Now that it no longer mattered, his mind emptied. His body felt more than usually heavy, listless. He wanted to sink down on the floor of the telephone box and sleep.

"I'm sorry, I'm so sorry. Would you tell your husband I'm sorry?"

He replaced the receiver and stood in the telephone box with his forehead against one of the glass panes. There was no point going on. In this country he was everyone's toy. Everyone laughed at him, mocked, walked on him, said one thing, did another.

Who was Big Nose? Who cared? At least the real Mr. Casey—Old 'Flu Casey—he would not be going through life with a nose as big as Big Nose Casey. Real Casey . . . unreal Casey. Unreal country, too real for health, sanity.

His head was hot on the glass panel. He wondered how long he would keep his feet before he fainted again.

The sheets were crisp as paper and smelled strongly of soap. Another scent, flowery and agreeable, mingled with the smell of the soap.

Foley went over his plan once more. No plan could be simpler. He would stay between the sheets until the fastest transatlantic jet aircraft in the western hemisphere called for him personally and flew him non-stop to Chicago. Once in Chicago he would never again stir away. So far as he was concerned the Irish vacation was over. He had seen his Castleferry. Ireland could have it. He had seen Irishmen, and Ireland could have them too. A confused image compounded of sea-blue eyes and hanging black hair moved in his mind. Somewhere he had seen an Irish girl.

Whoever she might be, Ireland could have her also. If Ireland had proved a snare, an Irish girl would be a double snare, a snare squared. Whose bed was he in, anyway? God, but would he ever again argue about squares, teach the uses of the square root of minus two, examine problems of numerical analysis?

He turned his head and looked at a pot of marigolds on the bedside table. His glasses were by the marigolds. He put them on. The walls were distempered white. The single bed in which he lay had a white-painted iron frame, and on the wall facing the bed hung a water-colour landscape in soft violets, blues and greens. Red linen curtains drawn across the window failed to keep the daylight from the room.

Foley pushed the sheets back and rested his feet on a rug by the bed. He recognised the pyjamas as his own. On the carpet by the door was his expanding suitcase. His head started to ache, and raising his fingers he touched a new bandage, sticking plaster over his cheek, swollen lips. He moved his eyes cautiously in search of a mirror and succeeded only in intensifying the ache. The absence of a mirror was a relief. The face had never been spectacular, now it must be bumpier than a bus with a flat tyre. He stepped gingerly across the room to his suitcase, opened it and saw his possessions: crumpled clothes, a hotwater bottle without a plug, brochures screaming the joys of Ireland, travellers' cheques, a passport. He walked to the window and drew back the curtains. The sun shone on a narrow street. Among the parked cars below he identified a blue Morris. People and traffic were milling along the street in leisurely confusion. Two small boys were chasing each other on bicycles. A horse clopped past pulling a cart on which sat a man in ragged clothes. At the far end of the street, Foley saw cows and heard the shouts of farmers. Beyond the cows he glimpsed grass and a river.

The bedroom door opened an inch, then wide.

"Dr. Foley, you must stay in bed," a woman said severely.

Foley scuttled back into bed. He pulled the bedclothes up to his chin. The woman was tall with black hair and an apron which bore wet patches as though it had lately laboured at a sink.

"I don't know what's going on and it's none of my business," the woman said. "I do know you're to stay in bed. While you're in my house you do as you're told. Could you drink a cup of tea?"

"Thank you," Foley said.

He wanted to ask where he was. Instead he said: "I guess it's market day."

"It is."

"That's nice."

"There are two men asking for you downstairs. They say they're guards. I'll send them up—but you're to stay in bed now."

She went out, closing the door.

Stay in bed . . . market day . . . guards downstairs. Foley recognised the voice. Mrs. Casey would have made a formidable wardress. Or would she? He suspected that a softy lurked under the surface severity. He remembered little of what happened after he had telephoned Mr. Casey's number from a coin box in a country road, but he remembered being helped from a car into a house. There had been two or three men, cops maybe, perhaps a doctor. Someone must have been to Castleferry for his suitcase. Had they found McCarthy? There had been a girl with black hair, and hands smelling of disinfectant. He recalled her saying, "Keep still," and repeating, "Keep still, please keep still." He must have been a restless patient.

That was it—he had demanded to telephone Inspector Sheridan to tell him about Parker and McCarthy, and the letters on the photograph in the Shamrock Bar, and how the letters must be important because Parker and McCarthy had burned him with matches. No one would let him telephone. Someone had promised to phone for him. He remembered he had shouted and struggled and there had been a telephone in his hand; he had gabbled into the phone that Parker was from Lewisham and Mr. Hide was a communist. Someone had taken the phone from him. Maybe he had passed out again. He did not remember being put to bed.

The door opened and five people filed into the room. Mrs. Casey carrying a cup of tea came first, wearing her damp apron and the disciplinary look. Foley was glad he was in bed and not cross-legged on the carpet smoking his pipe.

After Mrs. Casey came Inspector Sheridan with expressionless eyes which told Foley the worst. He did not know the details of the worst, only that Parker and McCarthy were loose. Probably they had not found the miserable letters. Neither had the Inspector.

Chapter 10

Sergeant Burke lumbered in at the heels of the Inspector. He returned Foley's gesture of recognition with a grave nod. His place was in the shadow of the Inspector. He would keep his eyes open and speak when spoken to. He had been first on the case and was well pleased at being told to accompany the Special Branch man to Bandon. Trips into County Cork were all too infrequent. He stood aside to allow room for a girl carrying a basin. A man with grey hair followed the girl into the bedroom. The nose of the true authentic Mr. Casey was an every-day matter-of-fact affair, Foley noticed, slightly hooked but not sufficiently so to call for a second look.

"Dr. Foley," Mr. Casey said softly, approaching the bed. "Most distressing, Dr. Foley. A ghastly experience, truly ghastly. You must look on my home as your own."

"I'd not expected us to meet like this," Foley said.

Mr. Casey moved away from the bed and hovered in the background, fidgety and embarrassed by the minor drama which had come uninvited into his home. The girl had set her basin down beside the marigolds and was unwinding the bandage from Foley's head. Her eyes were wide-set and blue, her nose slightly hooked. She was about thirty.

Foley lay still while she dabbed his forehead with damp cotton wool. He smelled disinfectant.

"You mustn't worry about a thing," Mr. Casey advised from somewhere near the door. His voice was so soft that Foley had to strain to catch the words. Maybe he was still suffering from the effects of the 'flu.

"Dr. Hanlon said you would be grand, grand," Mr. Casey said.

"Dr. Hanlon is our doctor," Mrs. Casey explained. "A fine doctor. He saw you last night. Drink your tea while it's hot."

"My daughter is a qualified nurse and midwife," Mr. Casey interposed.

Foley raised his eyebrows. He caught sight of his host standing near Sergeant Burke, close to the door, looking as though he would be glad to make an unobtrusive exit. Whether the intelligence of the daughter's calling was offered from pride or from the belief that the patient might need reassurance, Foley did not know. As Mr. Casey opened his mouth to speak again, Inspector Sheridan coughed. After coughing he cleared his throat. The Inspector said nothing but looked ostentatiously out of the window. Sergeant Burke stared at the floor.

Mr. Casey backed farther towards the door. "We must have our talk about Castleferry soon," he said to Foley. "When you're well enough."

"I look forward to it," Foley said. "Thanks for everything."

"Please keep still," ordered the girl.

Her voice was as soft as her father's. She bound a clean bandage expertly round her patient's head. Foley lay motionless. The girl knotted the bandage and collected her basin. She worked with the economy of experience, wasting neither effort nor words. Her black hair was rolled in a neat chignon at the back of her head.

"Thank you, nurse," Foley said.

"You stay in bed now," she said.

Father, mother and daughter departed. Inspector Sheridan

sat on the end of the bed. He delved into an inside pocket, took out a photograph and passed it to Foley. Before he could glimpse more than a corner of the picture, Foley knew that it was not of Joy. He looked at a photograph of a bald-headed man leaning against a bar. He knew both the man and the bar. Behind the bar, which was largely obscured by the backs of the customers, hung a board decorated with faces. Also behind the bar, holding a bottle in one hand and a glass in the other, was a bartender who may or may not have been Sean. His head was turned away as though someone had called to him. The bald-headed man was in profile. He appeared to be holding a glass of stout.

" Know him?" the Inspector asked.

" Parker," Foley said. He handed back the photograph.

" I put a man in the bar after I'd left. He'd been there five minutes when Parker came in. Someone else was there before both of us. I suppose you've no ideas?"

" I'm not trying to guess any more."

" Presumably there was some sort of information contained in those letters from your folder."

" Microfilm?"

" The barman's no help. No one has asked him about the photo except me and Parker. He didn't know it was missing until I arrived."

" Where's Parker now?"

" He stayed the night at the Erin. For the past thirty minutes he's been on the road to Kerry. I've a man following him."

" This isn't Kerry here, is it?"

" Nearly. Not quite."

" I suppose you couldn't arrest him?"

" Not yet."

" Maybe you could try."

" I'd like answers not advice."

Foley put his hands to his head. The girl knew her

bandaging. His head felt safe inside the bandage. He reached out for the tea, trying not to hate the Inspector.

"I'm still your bait then," he said.

The Inspector looked Foley squarely in the eyes. He seemed to be assessing him, groping into the character of the overweight American tourist who had blundered into the thick of . . . what? A communist cell? Professional spy ring? What kind of subversion? This was Ireland, not a world power hugging to itself the newest in nuclear secrets. Amateurs? Trivial thugs paid by some crackpot with time on his hands and money in his pockets? There had been scares in Ireland before to-day, but this had an authentic smell. Supposing he brought Parker in, what could he expect to learn? Parker on the loose was a sounder bet than Parker behind bars, but risky. If only he had met Parker in person he might have an idea of what he was up against; but Parker was an unknown, a Londoner, possibly, not Irish, and armed with a muscleman named McCarthy, none of which helped much. McCarthy was known, a hired moron, and he might talk when found. By then it might be too late. Too late for what?

The Inspector scowled. He could hear the ticking of his watch. The photograph of Parker in the Shamrock Bar had been wired to Dublin and to Scotland Yard. But up to this moment the search through records had revealed nothing. They should speed things up with computers like they did in the States.

The Inspector had only his nose, the tail on Parker, and the fat American. His nose had smelled a cauldron of trouble after the unlikely attack on the American in the Erin Hotel, and he had talked with Dublin. The Deputy Commissioner had left with his wife for France on his first holiday for two years. The main concern of his immediate chief, Superintendent Joyce, had been that the Press should not corner the American. The Inspector saw the Super's point of view. When he rang the Superintendent with word of a second incident, the Castleferry incident, the point of view took on even greater validity. An American tourist who had been twice beaten up within his first twenty-four hours in Ireland would be meat and drink to the Press. But there was little to go on and nothing Dublin could do which he could not more effectively handle on the spot. He was on his own, he and the Sergeant, and young Croft on the tail of Parker.

"I wanted to know if I was still the bait," he heard Foley say.

"You make it sound melodramatic," the Inspector said.

"To me it's melodramatic. What about the bait?"

"That's up to you."

"Up to me?"

"I'll be honest. You're juicy enough. It's up to you."

Foley could not trust himself to answer. His only answers were untypically offensive. Up to me, he thought. Man-steak for the lions, a fly for the spiders. His bruised body recoiled from the prospect of being tossed once more into the jungle. He would not forget the "juicy." He shuddered at the nerve of the Irish police.

He said: "What happened to McCarthy?"

"Missing," the Inspector said.

Missing. Foley saw in his mind the grey jersey advancing into the bedroom at Castleferry, the tight fists, the close scrutiny of the cut knuckles. Missing. McCarthy had sense, he thought. He's not the only one who's going missing, it's the best place to be.

He told the Inspector: "The answer's no. I'm sorry, I've had enough, I'm for home."

The Inspector showed no surprise. Foley looked at Sergeant Burke. The Sergeant stood as though on parade, legs apart, hands behind his back.

"What use could I be?" Foley spoke hurriedly, justifying himself. "I've told them all I know. They're not interested in me any more. They don't want to go on knocking me about for the hell of it. I'm no good to them now."

He waited for someone to agree. From the street outside came the lowing of cows. "Anyway, I'm on vacation," he said lamely.

The Inspector made no effort to persuade him. "They can't be sure you've told them all you know," he said.

"No one could know less," Foley said eagerly.

"Perhaps I could. You told me some of it on the phone last night. Now I'll have the rest, everything, from the moment you left me yesterday."

Foley finished his tea. He told the Inspector about the phoney Mr. Cosey with the big nose and the fawn saloon, and about Parker and McCarthy, and their methods of extracting information. He gave only a few words to his cinematic escape. In retrospect his stratagem with the four-poster sounded more ridiculous than it had seemed at the time. He skated over it quickly. He tried to recall everything Parker had said. This did not amount to much. He could not be certain whether Parker had said he was a communist or not. This seemed important to Foley but the Inspector appeared to be indifferent. Sergeant Burke was writing on a pad. The telephone rang downstairs. Foley hesitated.

"Go on," the Inspector said.

Foley remembered that Parker had said McCarthy knew about Irish prisons, or something to that effect. That could be useful. Convicts could be found. He told the Inspector.

"We know about McCarthy," the Inspector said.

"I didn't know."

Foley felt irritated. What did these cops know and what did they not know? If they wanted information they would waste less time if they could bring themselves to tell him what they already knew. The Inspector seemed simply to want him to talk. Maybe that was cop technique.

Mrs. Casey knocked and entered. "Inspector Sheridan, there's a call for you."

"Go and answer it, Sergeant," the Inspector said.

Mrs. Casey collected the empty tea cup and left, followed by Sergeant Burke.

"Would you like a trip to Kerry?"

"Is that where Parker's gone?"

"It's the way he's heading."

"I'll stay here."

But full marks for perseverance, Foley thought. If Parker was on the road to Kerry, Kerry was where one American tourist would not be touring, not just at present. Bandon was too attractive an alternative. Bandon had clean whitewashed bedrooms, cups of tea, black-haired girls with bandages. Bandon would do fine until he boarded the plane for home. He must inquire about plane schedules. Kerry, for all he cared, could slide into the sea. If he set foot there, the way events had been going, very likely it would.

Sergeant Burke returned and said: "Headquarters, sir. Croft's been on. He's lost Parker."

The Inspector nodded, almost as though this was the news he had been expecting.

"Parker took the road to Tralee instead of driving straight on through Killarney. Croft lost him outside Tralee. There was a horse show and the traffic was jammed for two miles. He thinks Parker doubled back to Killarney."

"He thinks that, does he?" The Inspector stood up. "Get me Dublin. Ask Mrs. Casey if we can borrow her phone. I want Superintendent Joyce."

The Sergeant went out again.

"There's a government laboratory in Kerry; place called Caherdaniel, by the sea," the Inspector said. "I'd a feeling Parker might be heading there. Just a feeling. Now I don't know."

Foley wanted to say that was too bad. The Inspector walked to the door.

"I'll have a look anyway. I thought you might have enjoyed the ride."

"Some other time. I'm convalescing."

"I'll be in touch."

He went out and closed the door. Foley lay between starched sheets feeling sorry for Croft.

Sergeant Burke chose the road through Macroom. On a week-end drive with his wife and sons he would have taken the lower road through Bantry and Glengariff. Either way led to Kenmare, and from Kenmare along the southern stretch of the Ring of Kerry to the Marine Biology Station at Caherdaniel, but the lower road was more scenic. The lower road was also slightly longer, and Sergeant Burke judged that the Inspector would prefer speed to the scenery. The Sergeant had to make up his mind about what the Inspector wanted. Alone in the back seat, Inspector Sheridan brooded silently, his eyes staring out of the window as emptily as those of a blind man. He had withdrawn into a mood which did not invite questions on routes or on anything. Once, on the outskirts of a village, two boys with hurling sticks chased a ball in front of the car causing Sergeant Burke to brake violently. The tyres screeched and the Inspector had stirred into life, winding his window down and savagely cursing the boys. An hour later he spoke again. The car had crossed from Cork into Kerry and was approaching Kenmare.

"They're doubling the guard on the station," the Inspector said. "That'll mean two octogenarians instead of one."

"That's the Superintendent's orders, is it, sir?" the Sergeant asked.

He was not certain what the Inspector was talking about but he had to say something to show he was listening.

The Inspector made no reply. Sergeant Burke pondered whether or not to ask what the guard was guarding against. In the driving mirror he saw the Inspector gazing sightlessly through the window. The Sergeant decided to give his attention to his driving. He had considerable respect for the Inspector. Up to the previous day he had known him only by hearsay and from his reputation as a Scott Medalist. The Inspector had won a silver Scott Medal seven years previously for arresting, alone, two armed men in the grounds of the President's residence in Phoenix Park.

After Kenmare the road stretched like a narrow shelf along the flank of the mountains. To the left of the road the ground slipped away to the sea, sometimes abruptly, more often in gently curving fields. Walls carved the fields into squares and diamonds. Squat cottages with slate roofs or honey-coloured thatch stood cautiously back from the sea's edge. Headlands like black snouts probed the sea. In places the road swung inland and the sea vanished. Always the mountains were there, dark green, and brown and grey, their contours disfigured by rocks, dappled with heath. Beyond the mountains still steeper mountains lifted towards the sky. Somewhere to the north, lost in a barrage of rain clouds, rose Macgillycuddy's Reeks, and beyond the Reeks were gentler mountains, and again the sea. The garda car raced monotonously along the coast road unimpeded by traffic.

"Have you fished here, Sergeant?" the Inspector asked from the back seat. He looked through his side window at the sea.

"Once I did, back at Sneem. They've a small harbour there."

"Any use?"

"Very fair, sir, plenty of mackerel. My only success was a bass, a poor baby of a thing, no fish at all. It gave itself up."

"Bass should be plentiful around here."

"They should. Mine was no fish at all, that's the truth."

Sergeant Burke was happy of the chance to talk. He was drowsy, his eyelids insisted on drooping. Parknasilla and

Sneem were behind but another thirty minutes' driving lay ahead. He was glad to talk fishing.

"My brother caught a tope with a rod at Derrynane two summers ago and swore it was sixty pounds," he said. "He's a great liar."

The Inspector was silent.

"The tope's good off Derrynane," the Sergeant said. "It's grand fishing there. They say when the summer's warm the blue shark come in like ships, two-hundred pounders some of them."

Sergeant Burke glanced in the driving mirror. The Inspector had lapsed into his reverie. The Sergeant sighed and changed gear as he approached the brow of a hill. He looked out of the corner of his eyes, enviously, at the sleeping figure in the front passenger-seat.

Foley sat with his chin on his chest, snoring softly. With each exhalation his lips gave a gentle pop. He had fallen asleep at Kenmare.

Chapter 11

The sign on the perimeter fence said: "Caherdaniel Biological Research Laboratory. Government Property. Keep Out." On the inside of the fence sprawled an unimpressive group of sheds and low brick buildings. A one-room shed at the main gate bore a sign announcing: "Passes Must Be Shown." A schoolboy could have stood at the gate and thrown a stone over the road and the rough ground and shingle beyond, and into the sea.

Sergeant Burke stopped the car at the main gate. A

uniformed guard appeared from the shed and waited inside the gate, watching the car. Inspector Sheridan stepped into the road, slammed the door and walked to the gate. Foley awoke with a start.

"Are we here?"

"We are," the Sergeant said.

"Parker—have we seen Parker?"

"Not yet."

Foley rubbed his eyes. He had fallen asleep a few moments after ceasing to puzzle over what had prompted him to change his mind about Kerry. Civic duty? Curiosity? Thirst for excitement? The motive was none of these, least of all the last. Foley wanted to be where excitement lay in guessing whether the next cup of tea would be sugared or not, or whether it would be brought by Mrs. Casey or the daughter. His sense of duty, he was not ashamed to admit, ran a poor second to his instinct for self-preservation, and though he was curious he was not so curious as to risk being killed like the cat which curiosity killed. The safest spot, Foley had reasoned, even with Parker in the offing, was the narrow gap between the Inspector's shoulders and the Sergeant's shoulders. If they were for Kerry, he was for Kerry, potential Parker-bait or not. So long as he held on to the Inspector's hand he would come to no harm. Once the Inspector had gone from Bandon, Bandon would be a refuge no more.

Foley had shaved and dressed while the Inspector telephoned. He had presented himself downstairs with his tie crooked but his bandage straight. The sun was shining and he felt less frail than he had expected. In fact, he felt almost perky. He was to see Kerry in a fast car, an experience which might be worth a few light phrases at the Dean's cocktail parties. The gathering sense of well-being had been dispelled by the Inspector, who instead of being thrilled by his presence merely grunted: "Sit in the front." Mrs. Casey had turned on her heel without a word. Foley was upset to have proved so poor a patient as to have given offence, but relieved that only the mother had witnessed his exit. Father was at his office, daughter among the bedpans and progress charts at Bandon Hospital. One sharp word from the daughter, Foley thought, and he would have been back between the sheets with a thermometer in his mouth.

The Inspector was showing a card to the elderly official at the gate. The official pulled the gates open.

"Straight ahead, Sergeant," the Inspector said. "The building on your left."

The car slid through the gate and into Irish Government property. When the Sergeant parked by three other cars outside the brick building, the Inspector said to Foley: "We shouldn't be long. You can come along or stay here."

"I'll come with you," Foley said.

"As you please, but I don't expect Parker would bother you out here."

Foley abandoned a private resolution to try and like the Inspector. Inspector Sheridan was ready to use him to attract into the open a gang of seedy villains, equally ready to despise him for being a coward. Probably the Sergeant was the same. All cops were the same. These two knew well enough why he chose to accompany them. Foley followed the Inspector and Sergeant into the building.

They were expected. A commissionaire shepherded the trio into an ante-room which smelled of wet clothes and stale tobacco. He studied the pass which the Inspector had received at the gate, then lifted the internal telephone.

"Professor Holstein? Inspector Sheridan is here with Sergeant Burke and a Dr. Foley . . . Right, sir. Right away, sir."

The commissionaire led the visitors from the room, across the entrance hall, along a passage, and left into another passage. The building was impersonal, functional. No attempt had been made at adornment. The corridor floors were echoing plastic tiles, the walls red brick. Foley, walking in Indian file between the Inspector and the Sergeant, guessed that the building was for administration of a peculiarly dreary nature. It reminded him of some of the less spectacular blocks on his own campus, clerk-inhabited outposts of the fringe where no one was quite sure what went on. Whatever experiments with marine fauna and flora were being made at the Caherdaniel laboratory, there was no sign of their being carried out in this building: no white-coated workers gliding along the corridors clutching test-tubes of algæ, no fish-smells.

A stout woman emerged from an office carrying a basket filled with papers. She flattened herself against the wall to allow the procession to pass. The commissionaire stopped at the end of the corridor and knocked on a door. A plaque on the door read: " Dr. E. Holstein. Director."

" Enter," called a faint voice.

Professor Holstein was alone in his office smoking a cheroot. He sat hunched like an incendiary dormouse behind a huge desk. He was small and wrinkled with far-off watery eyes and copious white hair. Above jutting white eyebrows his forehead soared high and vertical until finally extinguished among the rowdy hair. The lapels of his suit were stained with food. His forefinger and index finger were brown with nicotine. His expression was dazed, remote. The old hooded eyelids slowly flickered. He seemed to be stirring from a long hibernation. As though to rid his mind of ancient preoccupations he shook his head, once to the left, once to the right.

" Please sit, gentlemen," he said, rising six inches in his chair.

The voice was hoarse with age and tobacco, the accent foreign. He sat, and gave his head a final shake. The expression remained bemused. Foley judged him to be in his mid-seventies.

"Dr. Foley? A doctor of medicine?" queried the Professor.

He stubbed out his cheroot. Though the only window in the office was open, the air was stale and thick. Except for a large graph on which "Maximum" and "Minimum" were the only words Foley could decipher, the walls were bare. On the desk stood a pile of books, scattered papers, an empty cup and saucer, a telephone, an overflowing ashtray. In a corner behind the desk was a table heaped with more books, in the other corner stood a safe.

"D.Phil.," Foley corrected. "I teach math."

"You're the American tourist the Inspector mentioned on the phone? I think you've had a bad time in Ireland."

"Not too good." Foley smiled. He liked the wizened old man.

"A pity. I had a good time in America—at first. I was at Columbia University for four years after the war." He paused. "After the war I needed a good time."

Again he fell silent. His eyes wandered to the open window. The pause lengthened. The Inspector was about to speak when the pale eyes lighted again on Foley.

"Columbia treated me well," the Professor said. "I had research assistants, my own laboratory." He rubbed his thumb against his wrinkled tobacco-stained fingers, indicating dollars.

"You have to be bright to attract the dollars," Foley said. "They don't throw them around."

"I was bright, but I was unlucky. The Russians and the Czechs were doing almost exactly the same work—especially the Czechs. I didn't know at the time. No one knew. Everything was so hush-hush then. The Czechs had a fine team in Prague. One of them I knew in Leipzig before the war. I was unlucky."

The gaze wandered again. Inspector Sheridan coughed but said nothing. Sergeant Burke alone remained on his feet, standing by the door like a sentry. His mind strayed to the subject of bass, hungry snapping bass as big as boats. Dr. Holstein lit a fresh cheroot and inhaled with little short breaths.

He talked partly to Foley, partly into space. "Luck," the Professor continued in a quiet croak. "Who's lucky? The Czechs produced a chemical from a green freshwater seaweed for industry and thought that was it—finish. They called it chlorophyn and sat back and said: "That's it. Finish. We'll get a Nobel Prize. They were first home with a useful new product, a wonderful new product, and for them the race was over."

He spread his hands expressively. Ash fell from the cheroot on to the desk. "So perhaps I was lucky," he said.

He talked dreamily, his eyes wandering from the window, to the desk, to Foley, and back again to the window. " I carried on where the Czechs left off. In America suddenly the dollars dried up. They thought I should have achieved what the Czechs achieved. Now I have something which can be used industrially, cheaply, for the manufacture of cattle-food, fertilisers, insecticides, drugs. A thousand things. I have——" He looked at Foley. "How should I put it? I have a jet aircraft compared with the Czech hot-air balloon. A megaton bomb to their spear."

The Professor paused and looked at Foley. Foley was listening with his mouth slightly open.

" It sounds fantastic," he said.

"Exactly, fantastic. There is something perhaps more fantastic. On paper my chloriodine had an amalgam of properties which together should be an effective antidote to radiation sickness; and at least a partial protection to radiation burns."

He paused to watch the impact of his words, an old man as conceited as a child over his success.

" I have not here the facilities to experiment, but the theory is sound. It should work. Chloriodine should work.

It would open another world to doctors and surgeons and X-ray technicians. It would open new worlds even to mathematicians such as yourself, Dr. Foley. As to the political implications——"

The Professor left his sentence deliberately dangling. Again he spread his hands.

"So who's lucky?" he said. "The Czechs—where are they now? And the Americans? I'll tell you—nowhere."

"I've never heard anything like it," Foley murmured. Cautiously he asked: "Let me get this straight. This chloriodine would make everyone safe from nuclear attack?"

"In theory," Dr. Holstein agreed. "And there's absolutely no reason why it should not be so in practice. It would cost money, but people have money. Governments have money. Of course no one would escape a direct hit. The only safety would be from fall-out."

"Of course," Foley said.

The Professor's gaze drifted to the window. "Fantastic," he said quietly. "I'd no conception."

His eyes focused on Foley. "A scientist cannot guess where his work may lead. You know that. Perhaps it leads nowhere, perhaps it just misses, or someone else is there before you. If I'd the choice again I'd do the same, just the same."

Throughout the two-way conference, Inspector Sheridan listened closely. His concern was security, not some hypothetical nostrum for nuclear fall-out, but the implications riveted his attention. The presence of the fat American was a stroke of luck. The Inspector had half-regretted inviting Foley to the laboratory, for the odds against his accomplishing anything by being put into the approximate path of Parker were so long as to be virtually worthless. But he proved an unexpectedly valuable audience for the Professor. Dr. Holstein, whose dollars had dried up, was in effect crowing before a symbol of the world's great dollar democracy. The inspector suspected that without Foley present, Dr. Holstein would have talked less freely.

"Most interesting," the Inspector said. He became businesslike, in charge, unrolling his patter like a scroll.

"Professor Holstein," he said. "We intend increasing security precautions here. I spoke to you of this on the phone and I'd be glad if you'd accompany me round the Station. Security reinforcements must be deployed to achieve maximum effectiveness. We've every reason to believe an attempt may be made to break in. The importance of the developments you describe speak for themselves. I'm sure there's no fear for your own safety but we shall take no risks. The position can be described as one of emergency. You'll be looked after until the emergency has passed. I'm sure it will be only temporary."

He took a breath. He was not absolutely certain that the Professor was listening. The old man with the stained fingers and the smudged lapels seemed withdrawn in a world of his own. His head nodded absently. He made no reply.

"Is there one place, Professor, where anyone could find the results of your work?"

The Professor's head was sunk so low in his body that his shoulders were almost level with his ears. He blinked. His watery eyes had no expression.

"Any particular——?" the Inspector began again.

"I keep all my paperwork in two boxes," Dr. Holstein interrupted, his voice like rustling leaves. "All that matters. If a cryptologist could decipher my writing——" The leaves stirred and swirled in a chuckle—"a biologist could interpret it."

"Where do you keep these boxes?"

"You're too late," the Professor said. "You ask all the wrong questions."

Slowly he pushed his chair back. The dazed expression swam in his eyes. Without rising from his chair he turned and reached out for the cold brass handle of the safe. The door was slightly ajar. Dr. Holstein swung it open to reveal a bare interior.

"You should have been here an hour earlier," he whispered. "Only an hour. Why couldn't you have been here an hour ago? Then my boxes were here. Now they are gone. My boxes are gone."

Chapter 12

The hour which followed was an interlude of controlled pandemonium. Dr. Holstein's announcement barely had time to sink home when the telephone rang. Superintendent Joyce in Dublin urgently wanted to speak with Inspector Sheridan. The Inspector took the phone from the Professor. Foley did not know what to say or do but he felt this was no time for staying seated so he rose and walked to the wall on which hung the graph. He stood by the graph, excited and a little frightened by the crisis.

Dr. Holstein had not been so shocked by the discovery of the raided safe that he was unable to do what had to be done. His first action had been to ring the Station security officer who occupied a room in the same building. There had been no answer; the security officer doubled as catering officer and was in the canteen, and the canteen line was engaged. Dr. Holstein then rang the guard on the main gate but this line also was engaged; at that moment the guard was telephoning the commissionaire in the administration block to say that a plain-clothes Inspector from Dublin, a Sergeant, and a third party for whom the Inspector vouched, were on their way with an appointment to see the Director. Frustrated at every turn, Dr. Holstein had called the guards at Waterville and was put through. The moment he replaced the telephone, it rang. The commissionaire had said: " Inspector Sheridan is here with Sergeant Burke and a Dr. Foley."

That would be the Inspector who had spoken to him earlier from Bandon. Shocked, in mourning for his stolen papers, the Professor had lit a cheroot with trembling fingers.

Waterville rang Cahirciveen and Sneem. Cahirciveen had a car at Ballinskelligs which would proceed immediately to Caherdaniel. Sneem rang Killarney and Dublin. Killarney alerted Kenmare. Killarney also rang Dublin. Superintendent Joyce was at home on his day off. He had taken tea in the kitchen with his wife and was back at work on his rose-trees when his office telephoned. He reached his office twenty minutes later.

Neither the Superintendent nor Inspector Sheridan was in an equable frame of mind. Each wanted to blame the other, but neither could see any real justification for doing so. Both felt a bitter sense of failure. They had acted, but too late. They spoke heatedly, then hung up on one another: the Superintendent to place calls to the Deputy Commissioner in Chamonix and to Colonel O'Regan, of Central Intelligence, at the Curragh; the Inspector to unleash his acrimony on the first fool to cross him, and to begin the investigation which he knew would keep him all night from his bed.

Before the Inspector had cracked down the receiver, two squad cars squealed to a stop at the main gate. A third arrived a minute later. One perspiring guard in uniform pedalled up to the gate on a bicycle. Guards, uniformed and in plain clothes, started to spill into the Director's office.

Foley edged along the wall into a vacant corner and sat

on a chair. During the subsequent hours he counted eleven milling men, most of them from the garda technical bureau, measuring, writing, photographing, dusting for fingerprints. One group scrambling round the safe, another round the Inspector—until his bark sent them backing away. The Inspector snapped out orders and made a dozen telephone calls. Sergeant Burke and two uniformed guards collected the laboratory staff into two nearby offices, requisitioned for interviewing purposes. Four times the Sergeant reappeared to beckon the Inspector into the interviewing rooms, four times the Inspector returned from the interviewing rooms to take telephone calls.

The Professor sat slumped in his chair behind the big desk, smoking cheroots. He waved away a suggestion from the Inspector that he retire to his own home, with a guard to look after him. No one spoke to Dr. Holstein after the brief interrogation by the Inspector. A Sergeant from Sneem tried and received no response. The Director sat stupefied.

Glowering, the Inspector snatched up the phone.
" Who's that? "
" Inspector Sheridan? "
" Yes. Who is it? "
" This is Captain Smith, Central Intelligence."
" Before you go any further, Captain Smith, I should warn you there could be fifty people listening to every word you're saying."
" Not on this line. We know what we're doing."
" Since when? I'd have thought you lot might have taken an interest in this place before now."
" We've taken an interest."
" Well, it hasn't done much bloody good, has it? "
" Look here——"
" Come to the point, man. We've work to do down here."
" Just before you allow me to come to the point may I say you sound as though you'd just heard your wife's

sleeping with the gardener? After listening to you, I wouldn't blame her."

"Good, very good, very acid. You've got five seconds, Paddy."

"Colonel O'Regan had merely asked me to see if you wanted assistance."

"Magnificent! What assistance had he in mind? Horses? Field artillery?"

"Why don't you calm down? We could send a man."

"A man? We'll have champagne ready."

"We could send——"

"Don't tell me. He'll introduce himself as Finnegan and have a copy of the *Catholic Digest* under his arm. Get this straight, I don't want him."

"You're a fool. I doubt if you've the slightest idea how big this is."

"I warn you, Smith, if any of your lot start messing things up I'll lock him in the nearest cell. I mean that."

"You ignorant copper—you realise I shall report every word of this to Colonel O'Regan?"

"Do that. Tell him to stuff his errand boys. That goes for you."

The Inspector trailed back to the interviewing rooms, working to control his temper by drawing deep breaths, one after the other.

The photographers and the fingerprinters had left. As swiftly as the Director's office had filled, it emptied. Last to go were two guards who had done nothing but stand and await instructions which never materialised. Foley found himself alone with the Professor. The Professor appeared to be asleep. His cheroot had fallen on the tiled floor and died there. Foley wandered into the corridor, returned, browsed through the books on the table and selected one titled, *Studies in Marine Entomology*. He retired with the book to his chair in the corner. Another twenty minutes passed. Sergeant Burke put his head round the door, looked first at Dr. Holstein, then at Foley, and withdrew. Outside, dusk was falling. Footsteps rang in the corridor. A young man in a raincoat appeared in the office. Foley had seen him before but for a moment could not place him.

"Is Sergeant Burke here?" the man asked.

"He was in one of the rooms down the passage," Foley said, and remembered Croft, the eager detective in his room at the Erin, Parker's tail. Probably it had been Croft who photographed Parker in the Shamrock Bar. Foley hoped so. Maybe the photograph would count in his favour. He would be in need of favours after losing Parker. Foley was suddenly apprehensive at the thought of Parker.

"Any news of Parker?" he said.

It was the wrong question. Croft misinterpreted it as sarcasm.

"Watch it," he threatened, pointing a finger at Foley. "You just watch it, or I'll have you. I've met your sort."

He glared, then turned on his heels and went out. Foley buried himself miserably in the entomological studies, but the words left no impression. Inspector Sheridan and the Sergeant entered. They looked tired. The Inspector touched the Professor's shoulder. Dr. Holstein stirred.

"We're leaving now," the Inspector said. "With your permission, Sergeant Burke will stay with you to-night. He only needs a chair downstairs."

"Whatever you say," whispered the Professor.

"Could you manage a quick drink and sandwich first? The Sergeant and I thought of finding a pub."

"There's a place along the road to Caherdaniel," the Professor said. "I've never been inside."

"Are you ready?" the Inspector said to Foley. The tone was abrupt, indifferent.

"Any news of Parker?" Foley said.

"I've sent Croft to look for him."

"Look for him where?"

"How should I know where? Probably where the chloriodine boxes are. Croft lost him so now he can find him."

Dr. Holstein had never had reason to enter Timothy Donnell's. Infrequently he drank a glass of medium sherry before supper, rarely anything more. Sherry was not in demand among the customers at Donnell's, which was in any case licensed only for beer and spirits. The house squatted picturesquely by the roadside, overlooking the sea. Mr. and Mrs. Donnell, an elderly couple who had ventured outside Kerry only once in their lives, to Dublin, for the wedding of their eldest son, ran the business respectably and hospitably.

Sergeant Burke parked outside the door. Two bicycles, a five-hundredweight van with a greyhound in the back, and a small mud-coated car testified to the popularity of Donnell's: an oasis in a depopulated area. In town or suburb the muddy car might have attracted attention, but on the Kerry roadside, outside Donnell's, it looked as natural and permanent as a tree. The Inspector led the way through the door and into a dark shop stocked from floor to ceiling with groceries, hardware and haberdashery. A staircase rose to two bedrooms on the second floor, a counter supported scales, a bacon slicer, jars of sweets and a few recent but not impeccably up-to-date newspapers. Wellington boots, buckets and strings of onions hung from the ceiling. Tinned foods, cereals and an assortment of rosaries, crucifixes and religious statuary packed the shelves. A wide area of the floor lay invisibly under cans of paraffin, sacks of potatoes, crates of apples and carrots. The Inspector strode through the shop and pushed open the door which gave into the bar. This was an even darker room, little larger than a pantry, with a tiny counter and a door leading on to a yard and an outside lavatory. Two farm workers, tieless in brown suits, stood with glasses of stout at the bar; three others, all older men, also with stout, sat shoulder to shoulder on a bench against the wall. Mr. Donnell was perched on a stool behind the counter. Everyone looked at the new arrivals.

" Good evening," the Inspector said in a clear voice.

The men in occupation nodded and murmured replies of welcome. They kept their eyes on the Sergeant. They did not know him and they were not overjoyed by his presence. Foley could not understand how the Inspector's party of four could fit into the bar but somehow it was managed. Mr. Donnell came from behind the bar carrying two stools, and the old men on the bench slid silently together to make room beside them. The Inspector bought three whiskies and stout for the Sergeant.

Dr. Holstein sipped his whisky without a word. His hooded eyes took in nothing of the surroundings. Foley noticed the Inspector glancing at the frail, white-haired man as though anxious for his health. Hardly a place to bring the Professor, Foley thought, even though he had suggested it himself. Mr. Donnell withdrew into the shop to cut rashers.

" I gather none of your present staff were working with you on this chloriodine?" the Inspector asked the Professor.

Evidently the interrogation was to continue.

" That is right," Dr. Holstein said. " Staff came and went. They were engaged on various projects, some helped with the chloriodine at different stages but for the past eight months I worked alone. I knew I had won, I needed no one else."

" In fact you're the only one with a coherent picture of your discovery?"

" Discovery and invention, Inspector, chloriodine is both."

" Only you'd know how to produce it?"

" Yes. And whoever has my boxes."

The Inspector toyed with the stem of his glass. Only an

hour before he had driven up to the Station with the Sergeant and the American there had arrived a man from the Ministry of Agriculture, so the man had said. Mr. Malcolm Martin, Technical Adviser to the Minister, bristling with credentials. This much the Inspector had discovered.

He could picture the elderly guard at the main gate saluting as the man drove out again, twenty minutes later, the two cardboard boxes on the back seat. The guard said the man had been a gentleman, polite with a smart appearance—" Just like a government person." He had worn a hat and might or might not have been bald. No one else had taken any interest in the Minister's technical adviser or even noticed him. Visitors to the Station, scientists or government officials, were not so rare as to prompt concern. The commissionaire in the administration block swore that no Malcolm Martin had passed that way. True, there was a rear door to the building, but it was awkwardly situated behind a pile of coke and nobody ever bothered with it. Coolly the man had entered the Director's office with a prepared apology and excuse for immediate withdrawal if the Professor had been inside, perhaps he had been ready to cosh anyone he encountered. More likely he had watched and waited outside the Professor's window until the office was empty. Whatever the details, luck had attended him. Luck and professionalism. Bitterly the Inspector gave credit for the professionalism. He swallowed his whisky. Sergeant Burke swept up the glasses and set them down on the bar. He opened the rear door and looked out. He went through the door and after a minute returned and stood at the counter waiting for Mr. Donnell to refill the glasses. Foley had to stand and squeeze against the Sergeant to allow Dr. Holstein to push past and proceed through the back door. It was like being pushed by a butterfly.

" Where do we spend the night?" Foley said.

" Sergeant Burke is staying with the Professor. I'm driving to Kenmare. You can stay where you like."

"I'd like to fly home to-morrow."

"Out of the question. I can take you as far as Kenmare. I suggest you go back to Bandon."

"When can I go home?"

"I'll let you know."

"Don't hurry yourself," retorted Foley, angry but not daring to sound too angry.

Even with the second whisky sliding down his throat the Inspector was in an ill mood. Foley began to suspect that the Inspector disliked him as much as he disliked the Inspector.

They should have put this in the brochures, Foley thought, looking round the dark miniature bar. The old men on the bench were pure unspeaking drinkers. The two younger men at the counter were murmuring in an unknown tongue which Foley presumed to be Gaelic. They cast frequent uncomfortable glances at the ill-assorted group which included a uniformed guard sergeant.

Foley preferred not to guess how long he might have to stay in Ireland. More than anything he wanted to return home. He listened to the Gaelic murmuring. A car started up outside. Foley's whisky slopped over his hand as the Inspector rose urgently and bumped against his arm.

"Sergeant," the Inspector snapped. "Get the Professor!"

Inspector Sheridan and the Sergeant moved to the back door and into the yard. The murmuring at the bar ceased. All eyes turned towards the swinging back door and the darkness outside. The Inspector raced back through the bar into the shop, and out through the front door. Foley followed.

In the shop a late customer with muddy shoes who had been thrust aside by the Inspector half-lay against the sacks of potatoes.

"What is it?" he asked as Foley appeared in the shop.

The road outside was empty. The Inspector ran back into the shop.

"Which way did they go?" he demanded, gripping the customer's arm.

"They went east."

The reply appeared to throw the Inspector momentarily off balance. His face was angry. Two vertical wrinkles appeared above the bridge of his nose.

"What happened?" he demanded. "Did you see them?"

The customer was not to be hurried. "This fella pushed the old man into the back of the car," he said. "He was out cold, the old man. The drink must have been on him."

"The other fellow—was he tall, bald?"

"He was. Was he a pal of yours?"

Chapter 13

The chase was fruitless; they found nothing to chase. Sergeant Burke stamped on the accelerator and projected the car through the night as though he were making up time on the Monte Carlo Rally. The headlights pierced the dark like spears.

They travelled east on the Ring of Kerry road along which they had driven, at a more gentlemanly pace, that afternoon. This time the Inspector sat in front, Foley at the back. The Sergeant flashed his indicator, touched the horn and raced past the few stray cars which also headed east. None was the black Jaguar described by the eye-witness at Donnell's.

Foley had chimed in to say that it was a black Jaguar which he had seen leaving Castleferry. The Inspector answered with a grunt and Foley resolved not to speak to the Inspector again unless spoken to. He was glad the Jaguar had several minutes' start, partly from fear of a fight should the two cars meet, partly out of resentment towards the Inspector. The start would have been less if the eye-witness had not become uncommunicative when asked for his name and address but by the time the Sergeant had elicited these particulars the Jaguar could have been three or more miles away. Inspector Sheridan knew he would not catch the Jaguar but he had no choice but to go through the motions of trying. Other garda cars might have better luck, though even this the Inspector doubted. He was not a pessimist, but a sixth sense told him that the whole wretched business would get worse before it got better.

The boxes were stolen, the Professor kidnapped. Probably the only scientific discovery of consequence ever to have been made on Irish soil had been sneaked from under his nose. If he could have got hold of the photograph in the Shamrock Bar he might have learned how and where to act, but it was too late to worry about that. He had been outwitted, outmanœuvred, and all he had to show were descriptions of a car and a bald-headed Londoner somewhere in the night ahead of him. Somewhere also were the convict McCarthy and a shadowy, improbable character with a big nose. Where they were and what they were up to, heaven alone knew. Over the short-wave radio the Inspector asked that all cars be alerted and a watch put on harbours, railway stations and the airports at Shannon, Cork and Dublin: purpose, urgent, to bring into protective custody Dr. Ernst Holstein, repeat Holstein, Director of the Marine Research Station, Caherdaniel, and to apprehend one Parker, repeat Parker, wanted for suspected espionage, kidnapping and assault; description of Jaguar, black, registration unknown: description of Parker, tall, bald, slight cockney accent, possibly wearing white raincoat: description of Holstein, elderly, white hair, German accent.

At the word " espionage " Foley pricked up his ears. He

tried to recall if ever he had heard the word spoken outside the cinema. His bandage needed repairing. He wanted to go to bed and sleep, but though tired he was not relaxed. He tried to unwind by conjuring up an image of a girl, any girl, but he saw only Parker, stolen boxes, seaweed, cars racing through the Kerry night, a half-forgotten thug named McCarthy, with hands like hammers.

Outside a hotel in Kenmare the Inspector abandoned Foley with instructions that he return to Bandon the next day and remain with the Caseys. If the Caseys did not want him he must find a hotel in the town, and if the hotels were full he must report to the Bandon gardai, who would fix him up somewhere. He must in any case, wherever he stayed, contact the gardai and keep in contact. Any orders or information the Inspector might have for him would be conveyed through the gardai. Foley heard the orders with mounting irritation. He would have liked to ask the Inspector where he and the Sergeant were going and what they thought they were going to do, now they had given up the pretence of seeking the black Jaguar. He said nothing, honouring his promise not to speak to the Inspector unless spoken to. True, he had been spoken to, but curtly, off-hand. Rudeness did not count. Foley walked into the hotel without saying good-bye.

The only glimmer of activity was an old night porter reading the racing results in the evening newspaper. The porter made no attempt to disguise his suspicion of someone without luggage who asked for a room at midnight, but the American voice seemed to soften him. He led Foley up to an airless room with a double bed and a cracked washbasin. Foley gave him a coin.

"Good night now," the porter said, and shambled away.

Foley locked the door and jammed a chair against the door so that the back of the chair was wedged under the door handle. He washed, and as there was no towel he dried himself on the counterpane. Then he climbed into bed in his underwear and slept for eight hours.

Next day he sat for eight hours in buses and bus stations. He reached Bandon in the early evening. There were no taxis. After losing himself in the town he reached the Caseys' house hungry and fatigued. The blue Morris stood where it had been parked two nights previously.

He had telephoned Mrs. Casey from Kenmare to say he would be returning that day to pick up his suitcase and move out to a hotel. Mrs. Casey had replied that so long as he was in Bandon he would not move out to any hotel, he would stay where he was. In spite of the invitation, Foley fancied that Mrs. Casey sounded slightly cool, perhaps still smarting from the offence of his unruly departure. He had thanked her, privately determining to move out anyway, and trouble the Caseys no more.

Mrs. Casey came to the door. She pretended not to notice his bus-soiled condition. Her manner was forgiving, motherly. She asked no questions about Kerry beyond inquiring if he had enjoyed himself. Foley said Kerry was a fine part of the world. He might have returned from a stroll round the park.

"You'll be wanting a bath?" Mrs. Casey said. "The water's hot. There'll be a drink in the sitting-room in half an hour."

Wallowing in the bath, twisting the hot tap with his toe, Foley decided he would stay that night with the Caseys, then move out. He would have liked to stay up to the moment he would be allowed to leave Ireland, whenever that might be, but he recognised that the presence of a foreigner who had become involved with the police on one side and heaven knew what kind of criminal on the other must be a strain on even the easiest-going family. He would buy a bottle of something for Mr. Casey, and flowers for Mrs. Casey, or perhaps a book, and he would go. Maybe he could take them out for a meal. Should he get something for the midwife daughter? There were other children in the family, somewhere, but for all he had seen of them they were in hiding. Foley manipulated the tap with his toe. He was beginning to feel more civilised than at any moment since he had left Chicago. When he dressed he put on the tweed suit. A small boy rushed into the room and said: "Mammy says will you bring down any laundry when she does the washing to-morrow?"

The boy fell silent and looked round-eyed at Foley uncertain what to do next. Foley thanked him and said he would see what he could find. The boy backed out of the room keeping his eyes on Foley and closing the door with intense concentration so that it would not bang.

He nursed a tall chinking whisky in the sitting-room. Though the evening was warm a turf fire burned in the grate. Mr. Casey talked about the legal intricacies of tail male, interrupting his lecture from time to time to sweeten the whisky of his guest and client. Foley felt more guest than client. They were a friendly family, and if they were inquisitive about their oddly-connected house-guest they kept their questions to themselves. He was chastened to think that once, reading Mr. Casey's letter, he had suspected the lawyer of having an eye for the fattest pound of flesh which might be carved from an American client. Possibly he still had. Foley did not mind. The fire and whisky were good value. If this was the real Ireland he was content.

Mrs. Casey said: "The guards phoned you twice, and there was a call from Cork. He left his number and asked if you'd ring him. A Mr. Minton. The number's by the telephone."

Supper in the dining-room was salmon of a flavour and freshness which Foley had never before tasted. Telephone calls could wait. Until Mrs. Casey spoke he had forgotten the existence of Minton. He ate his plate clean and agreed to a second portion. He would have agreed to a third had he been offered a third but he was not. The last portion lay pinkly on the plate.

Mr. Casey asked in general terms about Kerry. Had the weather been good? Foley discovered that he wanted to talk. He found that his narrative made small sense without the background of the black travel folder, so he told the tale from the start, from the moment he opened Aunt Rohda's letter and read of Mr. Casey and Castleferry. Though he told it lucidly, as one accustomed to a captive audience, he was rewarded by blank puzzlement on the faces of his host and hostess. He understood the feeling. Even clearly expressed, the tale was confused. There were a multitude of loose ends, and Foley was not always sure what was important and what was insignificant. He was aware that in a context of world affairs the theft of a formula for a safeguard against the effects of nuclear fall-out might be of vital importance, but of more immediate and personal concern were his experiences at the hands of Parker and McCarthy. He reached the point where Dr. Holstein revealed that this discovery had been stolen when the telephone rang in the hall.

Mrs. Casey answered it. She returned to the dining-room and said to Foley: " It's the guards again. They want to speak to you."

Foley murmured an apology and went into the hall. The voice on the other end of the line announced that Sergeant Murphy was speaking from Bandon garda house to confirm that Dr. Foley was staying with Mr. Casey. Was that Dr. Foley speaking? Inspector Sheridan would like Dr. Foley to keep in touch. Foley replied that he knew what Inspector Sheridan wanted. Was there any word of Parker? That was not for Sergeant Murphy to say, the voice replied. How about Dr. Holstein? asked Foley, wondering why he bothered. Sergeant Murphy had not been authorised to make any statement, sir.

Thick cop, Foley thought, inclining his head so that he could read the name "Minton," and a telephone number, on a pad by the telephone. As he hung up, the back door slammed and the daughter hurried into the hall, out of breath and pretty as paint in her starched nurse's uniform.

"Hallo," Foley said.

"You're back then," the daughter said, pausing at the foot of the stairs.

"This evening."

He liked the sight of the daughter in the trim uniform and wanted to say: "That's a pretty uniform." He refrained. Perhaps in Ireland a compliment of this sort would be tantamount to a proposal of marriage, as the exchange of coloured beads or a handshake in the South Seas or darkest Africa were supposed to be a preliminary to the nuptial straw bed.

"You shouldn't have left like that. You weren't well," she said.

"I'm sorry."

She leaned forward from the foot of the stairs, one hand on the stair rails. She was seeking to locate the bruise on his head.

"Where's your bandage?" she demanded.

"I had to take it off. It got grubby."

"You'll have to have a new one."

"Thank you."

"You should never have taken it off," she said, professionally stern. "You don't deserve to be well."

Foley watched her disappear up the stairs.

While I'm here I might as well phone Minton, he thought. He dialled the number, vaguely surprised that so small and rural a country should have an effective automatic dialling system. A girl's voice said: "Lee Hotel, can I help you?"

"Have you a Mr. Minton staying?"

"Hold on please."

The delay was of a few seconds.

"Hallo," said the Ivy League accent.

"Is that Mr. Minton?"

"That's right. Who's that—Foley? Dr. Foley?"

"Hi there, you've been trying to get me. How're Pittsburgh Pharmaceuticals?"

"That's psychic—I wanted to ask you a favour about those very people. I was going to work round to it gently but you're forcing my hand."

"Good. How did you know how to get me?"

"Your Mr. Casey's in the book. You told me about him."

Did I? Foley thought. He could not remember.

"How's touring?"

"Okay. A long story. It's good to hear English spoken again."

"I thought you might feel like that. Listen, are you busy?"

"I'm not too sure. I don't think so."

"If you're heading back to the States in the next week or two I wanted to ask a favour. For me and the company. I was going to say come to Cork to-morrow and I'll buy you some of that Gaelic coffee, then I was going to work round to the favour over the liquor. Have you a tight schedule?"

"Not any more. I've no schedule at all. It'd be good to see you."

"You mean that?"

"How far's Cork?"

"Twenty miles. Drive slap through the centre of the city and over St. Patrick's Bridge. I think it's St. Patrick's Bridge. We're on the right along the quay—St. Patrick's Quay. Anyone will tell you. Have you a pen?"

Foley wrote the directions on the pad, beneath the scrawled telephone number. He heard a movement on the stairs and looking up saw the daughter. She had changed into a pale blue frock. She came down the stairs and went into the dining-room.

"I'll be in most of the morning," Minton said. "Try and make it for lunch."

"What's the favour? How crooked is it?"

"Sorry, it's not crooked. Competitive, a straightforward courier job. We're hoping to get a beat on our foreign rivals—businesswise. I need to get a parcel back to the States."

"A parcel?"

"There's a threat of a post office strike," Minton said. "The mails are risky and I could be stuck here longer than I expected." The Ivy League accent hesitated, then added: "The competition's wise to me anyway."

Foley said: "Do I get a commission?"

"Yes."

"I do? Hell, I was kidding. What's in this parcel—gelignite?"

He waited for the denial but heard nothing. At the other end of the line was silence.

"Hallo?" Foley said. "Hallo—are you still there?"

Minton said: "You could call it gelignite—paper gelignite, from Caherdaniel."

Foley felt cold. He shut his eyes. The fear clung.

"You'll be all right," Minton went on, his voice no longer casual. "I thought they'd have killed you by now but you're a natural survivor."

"This parcel—I've changed my mind."

"You haven't. You've no choice. Make it easy for yourself."

"I'm staying here."

"If you don't come to me, I'll come to you. Be sensible. There's nothing to it. They're not interested in you any more."

"I see."

"It's for Uncle Sam."

Foley could find no reply. If it was for Uncle Sam that made it easy. He felt himself shivering. His hand on the phone sweated.

"Not a whisper, Foley, not the police, no one. You're an agent now, one of McCone's boys. You'll get your commission. Be here by one o'clock. Room eighteen."

Chapter 14

With calculated carefulness, like a drunk man, Foley dropped two lumps of sugar into his coffee. Though his hands sweated he felt cold. The turf fire no longer warmed him.

He was an agent. A secret agent, by the sound of it, and he had barely been given the chance to say no, thank you, not this trip.

If he was a secret agent, he reasoned, he must be a spy. Surely they were the same. Applied to himself the terms were equally ludicrous. Maybe an agent merely carried boxes of stolen formulae from one country to another while a spy actively spied on people. If that were the difference, better an agent. He should have held out more steadfastly against Minton, told him to be his own courier. But Minton seemed to get what he wanted and if it were he who had so smoothly lifted the chloriodine formula from the Professor's safe he must know his business. Minton's business, Foley argued, was presumably on the side of the angels. Presumably he was a true red-blooded nephew of Uncle Sam; a goody, in short, not a baddy.

The complications which stemmed from any notion that Minton might be a baddy, not a goody, were too appalling to contemplate. Foley decided that for the time being he would " play it by ear," an expression which he had read and liked without quite understanding what it meant. He would proceed for the present on the hypothesis that Minton was a goody and that the task in hand was simply to collect from him the loot and fly back with it to the States. With any other hypothesis, madness lay; with the thought, for instance, that the formula rightly belonged not in the States but here in Ireland with Dr. Holstein and the Irish Government. Where was Dr. Holstein, anyway? Did Minton have him under lock and key in Room 18 at the Lee Hotel in Cork?

Foley's head swam. He stirred his coffee, slowly, carefully, as though it might be combustible and careless stirring would induce an explosion. From now on, he realised, every action had to be watched, guarded, calculated. He was an agent. A spy. A reluctant spy, but none the less a spy. The appellation fitted him so preposterously that suddenly he wanted to laugh. Ours not to reason why, Foley quoted to himself, ours but to be a spy.

" Share the joke, Dr. Foley," Mr. Casey said.

Foley started. He looked at his host blankly. " Joke?" he asked, clumsily passing the ball back to Mr. Casey.

A bright start to scheming, he thought; five minutes after being recruited as a spy to be caught inanely grinning about it into your coffee. Had they already guessed? Was he as obvious as if he were wearing in his buttonhole a badge announcing: " I Am a Spy?" Mr. and Mrs. Casey were watching him across the coffee cups, smiling. The only one not smiling was the daughter. She was occupied with the last portion of salmon. Little wonder the last portion had been held back. He would have to tread warily, cerebrate, play the tourist that he no longer was.

" It was Minton," he said. " He's witty, lots of gags. We were on the same flight from New York."

No harm there that he could see. Truth was safer than

falsehood. He would in any case have to explain his absence to-morrow from Bandon.

"He suggested we have lunch together in Cork to-morrow. He'll show me the city. I've heard so much about Cork."

Foley had never heard a word about Cork. No sooner had he spoken than he began wondering why he had tossed out such an unnecessary lie. He was not normally a liar.

Mrs. Casey and the daughter exchanged glances. Foley intercepted the glances and wanted to stand up and run. He remained in his chair, waiting. If challenged now he might earn a footnote in the espionage textbooks as the spy with the five-minute spying career.

Mrs. Casey leaned forward. "Will you be driving the Morris to Cork?" she asked.

"Yes," answered Foley.

Was there a trap? What else would he drive?

"My mother's asking if you'd give me a lift," the daughter said. "It's my free day and the buses are so poor. There's a summer sale starting. I need new shoes."

Foley awoke in the night with a familiar constriction in his chest. He lay still for a few minutes, panting and unhappy.

He sat up, took the eiderdown from the end of the bed and folded it behind his head as an extra pillow. He lay back in a half-propped position, breathing heavily. For the twentieth time in four days he wished he had not left home. When ill-health visited, home was the place to be.

His asthma attacks lasted sometimes a day, sometimes three or four days, and at this initial stage there was no telling how long a bout would last. He cursed and counted his inhalations and exhalations, working to make the latter long and steady.

"One two," he counted, "One two-o-o."

The sensation was of shortness of breath. When he had

suffered his first attacks as a child he had thought he was suffocating. He had believed he would die before morning. He had lurched out of bed, thrown open the window and fought to gulp the night air into his lungs. The doctor had told him he did not have too little air but too much, that people with asthma lived to be a hundred-and-six. The patient should lie still and try to breathe regularly, the doctor had said.

"One two-o-o," counted Foley, propped on the pillows and the eiderdown. Several minutes of counting and regular breathing passed before he remembered with a shudder that he was a spy.

The recollection, added to the onset of asthma, left Foley wanting to weep. Certainly he would sleep no more to-night. In the short time since he had awakened, the floral pattern on the curtains had grown faintly visible. He could see the dark square of the water-colour landscape on the wall, but not the colours. Foley switched on the bedside light and looked at his watch. Whatever the time, it was better knowing than not knowing. Knowledge of the exact hour was always a reassurance. His thoughts slid back to his new role. Minton had warned him not to utter a word to anyone, not even the police. That included Inspector Sheridan.

"The hell with it," Foley muttered.

He climbed tediously out of bed, stumbled across to his suitcase and took from it a paperback history of Ireland which he had bought in Chicago and not yet opened. At least he could read. This was the first chance to read since he had stepped off the Boeing at Shannon. The movement to and from the suitcase exacerbated the breathlessness and by the time he was back on the pillows his breathing was quick and harsh. He opened the paperback.

"The Gaelic-speaking Ormonds, Desmonds and Kildares ruled over far wider territories than the meagre English settlement of the Pale. The great Earls of Ormond were originally the Butlers of Kilkenny and supreme in the land until their power passed to the Earls of Desmond, a branch of the Geraldines, who in turn lost the leadership to another branch of the Geraldines, the fighting Earls of Kildare."

If only Mary Casey had not asked for a ride into Cork he could have taken his suitcase with him, collected the parcel from Minton, and driven direct to Shannon Airport, making a flight reservation on the way and thumbing his nose at Inspector Sheridan, Ireland, Parker and the entire lost vacation as he boarded the plane for home. Now he would have to bring Mary back to Bandon. To surrender her to the buses would be inexcusably unchivalrous.

Perhaps a spy was not required to be chivalrous.

Mary . . . it was a good name. Plain as any name could be. She had good looks, nothing plain about her looks . . . a nice figure. Top marks to Old Mother Nature.

"Acting as though it were the one true government, the Catholic Confederation at Kilkenny pressed ahead under the slogan, *Pro Deo, pro Rege et Patria, Hibernia Unanimis.* The Duke of Ormond, chief of the King's loyalist forces, entered into negotiations with the Confederation which resulted in a brief truce."

A thrush, rowdy as a boy, was first to break the stillness. In another minute the peace was irredeemably shattered by the clatter of the dawn chorus.

Asthma on top of his enrolment as a spy were complications sufficient to complete the shredding of a vacation long in tatters; but as though some remnant of holiday spirit might have survived, Foley arrived downstairs for breakfast to find on his plate the final insult—not breakfast but a letter.

He came into the empty dining-room breathing with difficulty, pausing at each step, and he spotted the letter from the door. His first wild thought was that the Dean was throwing a cocktail party and had nosed him out in darkest Ireland. The second thought was that the letter must be something far worse. He regarded it with distaste but without touching it. There was no mistake. His name, "Dr. William Foley," had been scrawled on the envelope hastily but legibly. The stamp was Irish, the postmark Cork. The date on the postcard was five forty-five on the previous evening. Before I was a spy, Foley calculated. Unless Minton had me enlisted before he told me I was a spy.

Mrs. Casey put her head round the door. "Good morning, Dr. Foley." She wore her apron. "Your breakfast won't be a minute."

"Thank you," Foley said.

Mrs. Casey withdrew. Foley sat down and rested. His chest and shoulders heaved from the effort of answering.

He picked up the envelope and thumbed it open. At five forty-five Minton could only have been writing to get in touch, nothing worse than that. He would have written after speaking with Mrs. Casey on the phone. Foley took from the envelope the photograph of Joy.

The photograph had been bent double so that it would fit into the envelope. The Hide Travel Bureau letters which had been stuck to the back of the photograph were gone. The only writing was that which had been there before: the signature "Joy" and across the neckline "To Sean, with all my love Audrey.' Attached to the photograph by a paperclip was a green raffle ticket, No. 219, and a scrap of paper on which had been scrawled JZB 745. Foley turned the ticket and the scrap of paper to see what message Minton might have put on the back. There was none. The only clue, in microscopic print along one edge of the raffle ticket, were the words: "Cork Printing Ltd."

Some clue, Foley thought glumly. He contemplated the photograph of Joy, the raffle ticket and the scrap of paper. Maybe they were going to raffle Joy. Minton was clearly a busy man. He had lifted not only the Professor's boxes but also the photograph from the Shamrock Bar. So much for that mystery. Minton must have returned to the bar and seen the foolery with Sean and the photograph. Or maybe he had never left. Foley could not remember. What needed no doubting was that a picklock who could open a safe would have had no difficulty entering the Shamrock Bar after it had closed for the night. Now Minton had returned the photograph together with a raffle ticket. What was a learner-spy to deduce from that?

"Good morning."

This time it was the daughter, dressed in a cherry-red costume and smart high heels. She wore a trace of lipstick. Her black hair caught the light and glinted and shimmered. The daughter sat down at the table.

"Did you sleep well?" she asked.

"Fine, thank you."

"Breakfast shouldn't be a minute. My mother's just coming."

"Fine."

"Dad had to leave early. He's in court at Skibbereen to-day. Rory's left for school."

She chattered without seeming to listen to what she was saying. She was watching Foley curiously.

"My head's completely repaired," he said, falsely gay.

He wished success and happiness to the diversionary tactic. If the daughter noticed the asthma there would be a tiresome lecture. He struggled to control his breathing, silently counting. "One two-o-o."

"I think we'll leave the bandage off," he said.

Mary eyed him doubtfully, dissatisfied. Mrs. Casey arrived carrying a tray of bacon and eggs, marmalade, toast and tea. Mary rose and kissed her mother on the cheek.

"Did you get your letter?" Mrs. Casey asked her guest.

"Yes, thank you kindly."

He had got it. Anyone else was welcome to it.

"It's going to be warm to-day," Mrs. Casey said.

She poured tea into three willow-patterned cups. One

of the cups had a chipped saucer which she kept for herself. She handed cups of tea to Foley and Mary.

"You must show Dr. Foley Castleferry from the road," she told Mary. "Perhaps he'd like to stop and take a picture."

Mrs. Casey turned to Foley. He was frowning into his bacon and eggs. "You can see Castleferry across the river about a mile out of the town," she said.

Foley continued to look at his plate, oblivious. He was thinking that when someone asked if a letter had been received they were not interested in whether it had been received but in the news it brought. To ignore the implied question might not only be churlish, it might provoke suspicion.

"My friend, Minton," he explained. "Just a note suggesting a drink."

He sank his fork into the egg. Warming to the explanation he continued: "He wrote it before we spoke on the phone, you see. It was just an ordinary note. Of course, if he'd known he could have reached me by phone he wouldn't have written."

Mrs. Casey looked at Foley in puzzlement. The speech had upset his breathing which quickened and grew almost audible. Mary Casey shot him a worried glance then lowered her eyes to her tea.

Foley did not notice. He rotated the fork in the egg, smirking to himself in satisfaction. How was that for lying? Slick as a salesman's hair. There were times when circumstances compelled a spy to lie. Any spy worth his salt knew that. Maybe he would make the grade after all.

Chapter 15

"You're very silly. You should be in bed."

"I know. I can't help it. I can't spend my vacation on my back."

"I should have guessed at breakfast. Won't you let me drive? You could lie down in the back."

"I like driving. Don't worry about me, it'll pass."

"Well, you're very silly."

Foley had answered this already and had no new reply. He negotiated the car along the narrow main street.

"Is it bad?" Mary asked.

"Not too bad. It's good to have a nurse along."

"I'm sure. A lot of use I am. If I'd any say you'd be in bed. Are all Americans such shocking patients?"

"Famous for it. We can't afford to be sick."

Bandon was left quickly behind. Foley stepped up the speed. The road wound through wooded hills following the course of the River Bandon. The river was wide and slow, the winding road almost empty of traffic. Foley touched the horn, pulled out and overtook a tractor that rattled along at a spanking pace. He kept one bespectacled eye on the road, the other pleasurably on the river. He breathed with difficulty. He would have enjoyed smoking his pipe but tobacco and asthma did not agree. He enjoyed instead the climbing sun and the low green hills, the river moving on his left like a fat slow snake, the imagined river-smell of reeds and rushes, and the cold water on cold polished pebbles. The smell in the Morris was of upholstery, petrol fumes and scent; only a suggestion of scent and apparent only when he turned his head to the left, towards the river and Mary. She sat with her handbag on her lap, her hands on the handbag. Foley caught the scent again. Better than disinfectant, he thought. He did not know one perfume from another but this one was splendid—flowery, unsophisticated. An Irish perfume, maybe, if they made perfume in Ireland: Celtic Mist, perhaps, or Irish Coffee, or Come Back to Erin. What was the Gaelic toast—*Sláinte*? That would be something to take back to the Dean's cocktail parties. " *Sláinte*, Dean, the cocktails are swinging to-day." In his mind, Foley tested for sound possible names for an Irish perfume: Galway Bay . . . Colleen . . . Aer Lingus. They sounded as much like racehorses as perfume. How about Paddy's Sin? Or Harpy? Foley liked Harpy. Harpy was either good or totally inadmissible.

A yellowhammer swung out of the sun across the road in front of the car and swooped away towards the river.

" Slow down or we'll miss Castleferry," Mary said.

No great loss, Foley thought, treading lightly on the brake. He wanted whatever price he could get for Castleferry. A dime would do. He did not want Castleferry. He did not want ever to see the house again. The old Georgian mansion recalled only violence and ignorance, a smashed four-poster bed, McCarthy's blood on the floorboards in the bedroom doorway, his own blood on the bedroom floor.

" There it is—look," Mary said, pointing through the window.

Foley stopped the car by the side of the road. At first he saw nothing but the picturesque landscape with the river in the foreground. Then he recognised Castleferry in a clearing on the other side of the river. Even at a distance, and with much of the building screened by trees, Foley found the house uninviting. The sun had crept behind a puff of cloud, leaving the grey stone of the mansion dark and cold.

Foley drove off.

"Wouldn't you like to take a picture?" Mary asked.

"I didn't bring my camera," Foley said.

He drove fast for a mile before allowing his feet to ease up on the accelerator. The view of Castleferry had spoiled a mood which had promised to be cheerful in spite of everything. Castleferry had been the cause of everything. The house had caused him physical anguish. Now he was a spy. That was a joke bad enough to be funny for anyone who enjoyed that kind of clowning. For all he minded, Castleferry could crumble into dust.

"It's such a terrible shame," Mary said in a quiet voice. "I'm so sorry, I really am sorry. I don't know what's happening but I know you've had a bad time and I do hope it's over. I do hope you can have a good time now. Ireland's such a lovely country."

Foley kept his eyes on the road. It had turned away from the river and was turning and twisting as though alive.

"I'm sure you'd be happy here but for——" She hunted for the right word. "But for those men," she concluded helplessly.

"I'm sure I would," Foley said.

He did not want to talk about it but he felt touched. Mary was painfully sincere. If she had not had a soft heart probably she would not have gone into nursing in the first place, into the rooms of ill people and rooms reeking of anæsthetics. Now she occupied herself with other women's babies. Maybe she had known unhappiness in her own life—like a date with McCarthy, Foley thought hilariously. Seats in the circle with the goon McCarthy. Who knew? Maybe McCarthy was a local lad, making bad.

The fancy was unfair. Still, he had learned that nothing was impossible in Ireland. He stole a glance at his passenger. Mary was looking through her side window and he saw only the curve of her cheekbone and the black hair furled in a chignon. He felt sad for Mary Casey because she was a midwife in Bandon, unable to afford a car, and smelling sometimes of disinfectant, sometimes of scent. Bandon for all its charm was a dead town, a town for summer anglers and for tourists to sigh over as they drove in at one end and out at the other. What did Bandon do in winter? He saw Mary, neatly uniformed, clutching her satchel of baby ointments and powders and scales, pushing a bicycle up snow-buried hills, pedalling along slushy boreens to deliver the babies of the farmers' wives.

"How do you get about without a car?" Foley asked.

"I have a bicycle."

"It sounds like hard work."

"See that?" she said, pointing. "That was built by Barry Oge, hundreds of years ago."

Foley looked through the window and saw the ruined castle. The road had rejoined the river and the castle stood serenely and impotently by the dark water which once it had guarded. The castle was the fourth or fifth he had noticed since leaving Bandon. They were not castles as he and Oscar had imagined castles. None had been elaborate constructions quivering with battlements and towers and massive crenellated walls from which archers could shower arrows on invading horsemen in armour and floating plumes. They were all as elementary as upturned shoe-boxes and seemed to have grown like trees from the soil. Their tops had crumbled unevenly away and stood in jagged relief against the wooded hillsides, their four walls were partly bare mouldering stone as old as Ireland, partly green with moss and ivy.

"Who was Barry Oge?" Foley asked.

"He was a great warrior chief."

"A sort of Irish Sitting Bull?"

"He was not. He was a great good man. He robbed the rich and gave to the poor."

" That doesn't sound like Sitting Bull, more like President Roosevelt. Who did he rob?"

" I don't know, I really don't know a thing about him. Probably his family. I'm sure he was a terrible old villain really with a big black beard."

" He'd get that from drinking Guinness."

" You must ask my father. He'll know."

" Did you know Sitting Bull was an Irishman? He came from Boston, one of the Boston Irish."

" He must have been a grand man then."

The road had left the river again. It stretched between high hedges drenched with fuchsia and wild roses, then between even higher walls almost wholly concealed under lichen and ivy. Long grass, ferns and nettles hid the base of the walls. Pigeons, harried by the approaching Morris, fluttered in worried groups from the undergrowth. Once a brown rat scuttled from the ditch, raced across the road and disappeared into the ditch on the other side. A ragged platoon of cows scrambled blindly from one side of the road to the other and back again as the car slowed behind them and came to an enforced halt. Foley touched the horn.

" Cows have right of way in Ireland," Mary said.

Foley asked about Rory, the youngest brother, and about two older brothers away at boarding school. Mary asked about Chicago and gangsters. He told her that Al Capone had been an Irishman from Tipperary—the first Irish place-name to come into his mind.

They drove through Inishannon, and on the other side of the village slowed once more, this time behind a battered car travelling at twenty miles an hour on a stretch of road too narrow and twisty for overtaking. When finally the road straightened and Foley drew out to overtake, the car in front without a signal of any kind swung out and made an awkward, slow right-hand turn across the road and into a farm drive. Foley jumped sharply on the brake. He swore and gave an angry blast on the horn.

"That's not the first time that's happened," he said. "Is it against the law to signal in Ireland?"

"It is not, but you have to guess what the opposition is going to do. It's like a game."

"What kind of game?"

"You have to be a good driver in Ireland."

"I've noticed."

"You mustn't be cranky, you didn't hit him."

"I didn't try hard enough. Next time I'll know what to do."

They drove on. Foley began to grin. "I've never met anyone like the Irish," he said.

"Aren't we the best people?"

"You know, I'm almost beginning to think so."

Some of you anyway, he thought. You, Mary, and the independent-minded man in the battered car, and Barry Oge, and Mr. and Mrs. Casey and the night porter in Kenmare and Sean in the Shamrock Bar and maybe Sergeant Burke. Possibly they were tougher, less innocent, in the big cities, in Dublin, Cork. Probably he would never know. He did not greatly care that he would never know but he felt sad that he would never know Mary better. He realised that he was not noticing her scent as he had noticed it before. Either he had grown accustomed to it or it had faded away. It could not have been an expensive scent.

From the crests of the switchback road Foley looked out over mile upon mile of countryside. The green fields were a score of different shades; some nearly black like the sea at night, others as pale as if they had been washed, rinsed, washed again and left to bleach in the sun. Others were dark brown and ploughed, some were yellow with hay. In a ploughed field close by he saw a farmer with a plough treading behind a horse. He was reminded of a painting, though he was unable to think exactly what painting or where he had seen it. There was a poem, too, about a ploughman homeward plodding his weary way, but it was an English poem, not Irish. The road dipped down between the high hedges which cloaked the road in shadow, and the high walls behind which lay estates with big houses.

The miles on the signposts to Cork diminished from double figures to single. Foley would have liked the drive to continue, with no Minton awaiting him at the other end, but the road grew wider, traffic heavier, and rows of graceless houses with slate roofs and lace curtains in the windows replaced the hedges and ancient walls. The dogs, he noticed, were tame. They did not fling themselves at the car but lolled on the pavements.

" Could you direct me?" he said. " I'll drop you wherever you say."

" It's not far from your Lee Hotel. Straight on at these lights."

" Why don't I pick you up again this afternoon. We can drive back together?"

" Not at all, you make a day of it."

" I'll make a lunch of it, then meet you."

" Keep in the right-hand lane."

" How about it? Say three o'clock."

" Nonsense."

" Humour me. I've asthma and I'm supposed to be on holiday."

Mary made no reply. Then she said: " All right, thank you very much. But only on condition we drive straight home and you go immediately to bed. You're not well at all."

" We'll see. I was going to move out to-day. I can't live off your parents for ever."

" You're not moving anywhere. You're not well enough."

" You've still told me nothing about Barry Oge. We can have it on the ride back."

" I'll think something up."

" Three o'clock at the main post office."

"No, at the Victoria."

"Where's that?"

"Over there. And there's the Lee Hotel—look, over the bridge, to the right. Where the cars are parked. You can drop me here."

"Get some nice shoes, Mary. American-style."

"Irish-style."

She opened the door and stepped out.

"Good-bye," she said. "Take it very quietly now. Promise."

"Sure, count on it."

Foley smiled at her and watched her cross the road, weaving between the unhurried traffic, the sun on her hair. He drove to the Lee Hotel and past the hotel and up a side turning before he could find a gap in which to park.

As he walked slowly back to the hotel his breathing grew harsh, but less so than during the night and at breakfast. Maybe the bout would be brief and mild. Foley prayed so. He deliberately expunged Mary from his thoughts, reminding himself: "I am a spy."

Silently he repeated: "I am a spy." The statement was an attempt at orientation. He repeated it a third time. He was a working man. The doorman on the steps of the Lee Hotel touched his braided cap. Foley nodded. Room 18, he told himself.

He wondered whether a spy would announce himself at the reception desk or go straight up. He would go straight up, Foley decided. There was no benefit in knowing the room number if he did not go straight up.

The hotel was new, pervaded by an odour of carpets and polished wood. Without difficulty Foley found Room 18. On the doorhandle hung a sign: "Please Do not Disturb."

Foley tapped on the door. There was no answer.

He looked at his watch. Twelve-thirty. Minton had distinctly said, "By one o'clock." Foley tried the doorhandle. It turned, the door opened. There could be a trap. Foley had wondered what to do if there was a trap but had come to no decision. Parker could be waiting for him, with McCarthy. If they were in the room there was nothing he could do about it. He hoped for the best.

Foley entered the room and closed the door behind him. There was no trap. The room reminded him of his own at the Erin after Parker and McCarthy had paid their night visit. Everything was everywhere, smashed and scattered, with drawers open and the carpet torn up and the clothes from the bed thrown in a corner. No one was in the room except Ivy League himself.

He lay face upwards, if it could be called a face. Foley had never seen so much blood.

Chapter 16

There was a chair near the door. Foley walked over to it and sat down. At first he thought he might be all right. Then he leaned forward, spread his knees apart, and was sick on the carpet.

For several minutes he sat humped forward with his head in his hands, elbows on knees, like a student after a party. He sat up, took out his handkerchief and dabbed his mouth. He removed his glasses and breathed on the lenses and rubbed them with his tie. When he had replaced his glasses he looked again at Minton. The body wore pyjamas with a blue-and-white stripe. The head was recognisably Minton's but it had been smashed in. The blood was not red but had dried to a dull, dark brown. The same dullish brown discoloured the base of a bedside lamp which had rolled against a leg of the bed. This was the first dead man Foley had seen. He stood up, picked up the chair and carried it across the room away from the vomit and from Minton. He sat down again.

"Oh, God," he said.

He wanted to say a prayer. The immediate need was for a priest, he thought, though the time was too late for a priest, and no priest seemed likely to arrive unless he called one himself. He searched his mind for the right words.

"The Lord gave and the Lord taketh away," Foley said aloud, staring at the wall. "Blessed be the name of the Lord."

He did not know if they were the right words or if they were cowboy words. He remembered them from a western movie in which someone had died on the trail and the trail-boss had scattered earth into the grave, saying the words. The scene had left him blinking moistly behind his glasses. He had never forgotten the prayer of the trail-boss.

Foley knew he must now go—get out, and without being seen. He tried to think, biting his bottom lip as he searched his mind to discover what must be done first, and fast, now that the prayer had been said. Certainly he would not find the parcel here. The room and the body bore the mark of a McCarthy; and therefore less directly of a Parker, and for all anyone knew of a Big Nose, if Big Nose was one of their company. They would not have left the Professor's boxes behind.

On the other hand, whoever had visited Minton had turned the room over searching for something. If the search had been for the two boxes, possibly they had been found, and possibly they had not been in the room. Foley stood up and went through the motions of scouring the room for the parcel. There was no private bathroom, only the room itself, strewn with clothing from Minton's suitcase and with a few sticks of Swedish-designed furniture. Foley abandoned the hunt after a few seconds. The parcel was not there; if there had been a parcel.

One last act before he ran: someone must be told. Minton could not be left to lie there. The police should know. Foley grimaced. He had no intention of facing a new involvement with the guards. The last man in the world he wanted to speak to was Inspector Sheridan; or almost the last. The alternative was the management. Let the management call the guards. What should he tell the management? A telephone lay on the floor with the receiver in place. Did he lift the receiver and say: "Pardon me, you've got a body in room 18?" Just like that?

Foley dithered. He heard a light knock on the door.

"No!" he breathed. He froze, foolishly staring at the door.

The door opened. A plump chambermaid with a broom in her hand looked at him.

"Hallo," Foley said, starting for the door.

The chambermaid saw beyond Foley into the ravaged room. She stared at the wreckage and at Minton sprawled on the floor. Disbelief spread across her face. She did not scream. Her mouth opened but no sound came from it. She stood motionless, gaping, gripping her broom.

"It's all right," Foley stammered, pushing past the chambermaid into the passage. "I'll look after it."

He ran along the passage the way he had come, waiting for the chambermaid to shout after him or scream or give chase. He heard nothing and he did not look back. At the top of the lushly carpeted stairs which led down to the lobby he stopped and leaned against the wall.

"God," he moaned.

His breath rasped like a saw. He gulped air into his lungs with small audible gasps. A porter was mounting the stairs with a suitcase in each hand. Looking straight ahead, Foley walked down the stairs past the porter and across the lobby towards the revolving doors and the steps which led out to the street. He had almost reached the doors when he noticed beside them a counter which gave on to an alcove, and a sign saying: " Cloaks."

There was a chance which had to be taken. Once outside the revolving doors he would never voluntarily return to the Lee Hotel. Uncle Sam or no Uncle Sam.

He halted gasping at the counter. He was aware of the presence of several people in the lobby but he did not look round. He dug in his pocket for the envelope from Minton and took from it the photograph of Joy with the green ticket and the scrap of paper attached. He slid the ticket from under the paperclip and held it out to the boy behind the counter. The boy wore a page's outfit with a high collar and a row of silver buttons. Foley took a step back from the counter, watching the boy's eyes, ready to race for the doors the instant the boy betrayed ignorance of the ticket.

" Two-one-nine," the boy said crisply, taking the ticket.

The boy retreated into the recesses of his cloakroom, holding the ticket. He shuffled his hands among the shelves which lined the wall, jerking his head up, down and sideways as he searched the tickets on the assorted cases and coats.

Foley leaned on the counter, struggling to regain his breath. The boy took down an umbrella, compared the ticket on it with the ticket in his hand and returned the umbrella to its shelf. He scavenged some more, then walked back to Foley.

" What exactly was it you left, sir?"

" A parcel," Foley said, and looked away to signify that he had no more to say.

He noticed two clerks excitedly talking to each other behind the reception desk. One had a telephone in his hand.

" When did you bring it in, sir?" asked the boy.

Foley thought hard. In the lobby over his shoulder he

heard scuffling footsteps, noisy chatter. Someone called out: "Desmond, come here!"

"Well, it was this way," Foley began ambiguously. "Last night I had to wrap up this parcel..."

He paused. The boy interrupted.

"That would have been the night attendant, John. He's on nights. I'm here till five, d'you see. Then John comes on."

Foley glanced over his shoulder. Half-a-dozen people had clustered round the reception desk. A man in the hotel's uniform and a man in a light flannel suit ran up the stairs together. Someone else barged through the revolving doors and into the street. Foley could not see the chambermaid.

"Something's happening," the boy said, his attention diverted to the growing confusion in the lobby.

"The President's arriving," Foley said. "He'll be here any minute. Do you have my parcel?"

"The President?" The boy's eyes grew round. "Is that right? Here?"

"Please, would you find my parcel?"

The boy moved reluctantly to the shelves on the other side of the alcove. Foley looked again over his shoulder. He saw the chambermaid. She was with a group of men at the foot of the stairs, talking and gesticulating and searching the lobby with her eyes. The men were also searching and as their eyes looked this way and that the group advanced slowly through the lobby. Foley snapped his head away and faced into the alcove. He squared his back to the lobby and lowered his head. The boy stood in front of him with a large brown paper parcel from which he was unpinning a green ticket.

"What's he doing here then?" the boy asked.

"Lunching. Having lunch. Thanks."

Foley slapped a half-crown on the counter. He took the parcel in both hands and walked to the revolving doors with his head to one side, away from the eyes in the lobby. He pushed through the doors, hurried down the hotel steps and started half walking, half running along the pavement towards the side turning where he had left the Morris. Before he reached the turning he halted to take a long look at a car parked across the street. The car was a black Jaguar.

A thousand and more identical black Jaguars must have been on the roads of Ireland, but this one he suspected he had seen before, driving away from Castleferry. Big Nose had driven a fawn saloon but Big Nose was beside the Jaguar, hastily retreating inside it, into the passenger seat, his eyes on Foley. They looked at each other across the street.

Foley reached the corner panting. He glanced back again. Big Nose was in the Jaguar, trying to inch it out into the street. Another figure was beside him and there was a movement in the back, but the interior of the car was dark and Foley could not make out the faces. Farther back, on the steps of the Lee Hotel, he glimpsed a gathering of people. They were looking along the pavement in his direction. One of the group shouted. Another raised his arm and pointed at Foley. The Jaguar, parked against the flow of traffic, was fighting its way into the road, impeded by a cavalcade of traffic travelling in the opposite direction. Clutching his parcel to his chest, Foley ran up the side turning.

For once his luck was in. The car behind which he had parked had gone, leaving the space in front of the Morris free for a quick start. Foley stumbled up to the Morris. There was no time for putting the parcel in the boot. He placed it on the roof of the car while he fumbled with the keys. The first of the two keys failed to turn.

"Please," he breathed.

He had inadvertently left open the window above the locked door but it was not sufficiently open for him to reach inside to the doorhandle.

The second key turned in the lock. Foley opened the door, grabbed the parcel from the roof and fell into the driving-seat. He slammed and locked the door and heaved the parcel on to the empty seat beside him. As he turned the first key in the ignition, fingers, not his own, touched the hair above his right ear. Then the top of the ear. Foley jerked his head away as though tickled by a razor. His side window was open three inches and McCarthy had thrust into the opening his hammer hand and wrist. The forearm above the wrist was too thick to penetrate farther into the narrow gap. The fingers splayed out wriggling to reach Foley's head.

"Open it!" McCarthy ordered.

In spite of the sunshine the young thug wore the blue duffle-coat over his polo-neck sweater. His eyes squinted through the gap in the window. With his free hand he squeezed and tugged the locked doorhandle. Foley groped for the handle to the window. The bald head of Parker loomed up over the shoulder of McCarthy.

"Give us the parcel and you can go!" Parker shouted, stooping to make himself heard through the opening in the window.

Foley found the window handle and wound it hard away from him, anti-clockwise. It was the wrong way. The window lowered and McCarthy's arm reached farther into the car. Foley reared out of range as the hand snatched for his thin hair. He twisted the handle towards him and the window wound up and jammed McCarthy's elbow against the rim of the window frame. Behind the faces of McCarthy and Parker, parked alongside the Morris, Foley saw the Jaguar.

Foley wrenched the handle harder towards him. McCarthy screamed, his face contorted by the pain in his trapped arm. The fingers of his free hand slid up the outside of the window and curled over the edge of the glass, striving to prise the window down. Trembling, Foley pushed the handle away from him. As McCarthy dragged his arm clear, Foley wound the window fully shut and let in the clutch. The Morris bounded forward.

The Jaguar moved faster. Big Nose catapulted the Jaguar forward across the path of the Morris. Foley braked and braced himself for the inevitable collision. His front fender crunched into the side of the Jaguar. His path was blocked. The only way to go was back.

Parker side-stepped to safety as Foley reversed with squealing tyres. McCarthy, hugging his arm, stood in pain in the road. Two girls watched open-mouthed from the pavement. Foley swivelled in his seat and reversed rapidly down the turning. He saw the group from the Lee Hotel striding up the turning towards him. Two guards led the group. The chambermaid, unable to keep up, was being helped along in the rear by an elderly man of military bearing in a short-sleeved shirt and yachting cap. One of the guards pointed at Foley and called out as the Morris backed past him and into the street along the quay.

Foley changed gears and sped past the Lee Hotel. The boy in the page's outfit was holding forth like an agitator to a gathering on the steps. He talked so enthusiastically that he failed to notice the subject of his yarn sweep by in the Morris. A guard endeavoured with outstretched arms to shepherd the gathering off the steps. At the end of the street, at the junction with the main road, Foley turned left without slowing, cutting in front of a laundry van and forcing it to swerve into the middle of the road. He crossed the bridge and stopped behind a lorry too cumbersome for overtaking. He was in the centre of Cork and the traffic was heavy. Through his side window he saw a bronze statue with the inscription. " Father Mathew 1818-1878." The driver of the lorry was leaning from his window asking directions from a youth with a bicycle. Foley rested his forehead on the steering whel, wheezing and gasping with asthma.

He lifted his head and looked back across the river. On the quayside outside the Lee Hotel were a dozen people, some running, others standing and waving their arms and pointing. They were too distant for recognition but some wore guard uniforms. He glanced at the parcel on the seat beside him. Somewhere a car siren started wailing. Where did a spy turn now? Who could help a spy?

The lorry driver was waving a grudging farewell to the youth and moving off as slowly as possible. Foley crawled after. In the driving mirror he saw the Jaguar barely a yard to the rear, following. Big Nose was at the wheel. Parker sat beside him, crouched forward, his bald head almost touching the windscreen as he fixed his eyes on Foley in the Morris. McCarthy was slumped in a corner on the back seat.

Chapter 17

The lunch-hour traffic honked and fooled like a carousel in slow motion. Cars halted without warning in the middle of the street. Some gave unknown signals as they double-parked at shops and restaurants. They reversed trustingly into the uncertain flow of traffic, crossed St. Patrick's Street at right-angles, stalled at junctions, stopped when they might have been expected to start and accelerated at moments when motorists of more conventional driving habits would have used both foot and hand brakes. Foley saw an opening among the swirl of cars and slid into it. At the end of St. Patrick's Street he swept round to the left, speeded along Grand Parade, and swung left again into South Mall. In the driving mirror he watched the Jaguar clinging to his rear fender.

He made another left turn into a street cluttered with parked vans and cars, and steered on to the pavement to avoid a man with a wheelbarrow. An old woman with a black shawl over her head and a shopping basket on her arm tottered backwards into the refuge of a doorway. Approaching an intersection, Foley thought: I'd never get away with it in Chicago.

In Chicago by now he would have had a screaming patrol car down his throat. In Cork, Foley discovered, traffic tended to move vaguely, unpredictably, as though unsure of the way. At least, he thought, driving was something he could manage. He had driven cars for a quarter of a century. Fear, flabbiness, myopia, falling hair and the acid taste in his mouth did not impair this small talent. The engine roared as he raced over the intersection, forcing an almost equally hurried car arriving from the right to brake hastily. He heard a clang behind and saw in the driving mirror the tangled fenders of the impatient car and the Jaguar. He found himself in St. Patrick's Street again.

Some time later, a year later maybe, and in another country, as far from Cork and fear as he could be, he would rejoice. He would even relax. Not now. Foley drove at a sedater pace across the broad shopping street and into a long alley where the immediate attraction was darkness and obscurity. Cars stood parked along the entire length, leaving space for a single line of traffic. A car confronted him five yards away, the driver leaning out of his window and waving. Foley wound down his window and put his head out.

"One-way street," the man in the car called out.

Nothing was to be won by argument; perhaps the man wanted an argument and would have been happy to argue the entire lunch-hour away. The Fighting Irish, Foley reflected . . . best back down.

He reversed fiercely into St. Patrick's Street, drove

forward, and cornered into the next alley to the right. This one seemed to be one-way in the correct direction. He passed a shop with a notice announcing: " Dungarees for Professional Men." At the end of the street he rounded into a wide road by the quays. He did not know where he was but he could not see the Lee Hotel. He saw a sign, Lavitt's Quay, then Coal Quay . . . Kyrls Quay . . . Bachelor's Quay. Along Bachelor's Quay were mellowed Georgian houses. He certainly was seeing Cork, he thought, even without Minton's company. The parcel on the passenger seat bumped against his hip as he pulled out into the middle of the road, skirting past a lorry which without warning had started away from the kerb. The Jaguar was nowhere to be seen.

He reduced speed to a rate which would not prompt second looks and cruised aimlessly among a maze of back streets. His sense of direction had vanished as comprehensively as Parker, McCarthy and Big Nose. He watched for the Jaguar. The streets were busy with idlers. Women gossiped on corners or wheeled prams in which groceries had been stacked at the baby's feet. A post office messenger boy on a bicycle had halted at the kerbside and was sitting on the saddle with his feet in the road. He picked his nose as he surveyed the passing show. Foley found himself once more in Grand Parade.

He looked at his watch. Ten minutes past one. Forty minutes ago he had walked into room 18 at the Lee Hotel. Now all the police in Cork would be hunting for the fat American in the blue Morris. The chambermaid and the boy in the cloakroom, enthralled with themselves, would be giving the guards loquacious descriptions: glasses, chubby cheeks, tweed suit, transatlantic accent, wheezes, everything. Probably the boy would embellish: killer's eyes, lips curled in a snarl, shoulder holster, sawn-off shotgun. The police would not hear the embellishments. Possibly already they had added, subtracted, consulted their Orders of the Day, and telephoned Inspector Sheridan with information of an Unexpected Development. Possibly even now the Inspector and Sergeant Burke were roaring along a road into Cork.

Foley pulled up at a row of petrol pumps. He sneezed. His shirt, damp with sweat, clung to his chest.

" Fill her up, will you?"

He marshalled his alternatives. They were not enticing. Sit in a movie and wait for three o'clock and his appointment at the Victoria? Cruise the streets?

He could find the post office and mail the parcel to himself somewhere: care of the Caseys in Bandon, or to be collected at the Erin Hotel, or to his apartment near the campus. That way, if Parker and his stormtroopers caught up with him, they still would not catch up with the parcel.

But Minton had mentioned a threatened post office strike. If Minton could have posted the parcel he would have done so sooner than entrust it to an unknown fellow-American, a tourist he had met casually in a bar. Casually? Foley muttered a sceptical, "Huh." If Minton had worked for the C.I.A. he must have had both eyes on the fat tourist with the plastic travel folder ever since Kennedy Airport; more likely, ever since the tourist was still a potential tourist dreaming through travel schedules in the Chicago office of the Thomas Hide Travel Bureau.

The attendant had grey hair and smears of oil on his forehead. He leaned on the open window, looking at Foley. Foley handed him a five-pound note.

Non-stop to Shannon for the first flight home? He would not progress far without his passport. To Bandon for passport and baggage—if the Inspector had not yet impounded them—then to Shannon?

He took his change from the attendant and drove off. He would wait for Mary and collect her at three o'clock as he had promised. He did not want to break the promise.

He saw no advantage in fleeing immediately from Cork. If the police were after him they would find him as readily on the country roads as in the city. More so.

He noticed a signpost: " Aerphort.' If the word meant what it looked as though it meant, the immediate problem was solved. One airport would make bookings as effectively as another. To book his flight home would be to do something constructive.

Cork Airport stood on elevated ground four miles south of the city. The road was broad, open and climbing. Foley drove fast, paying no attention to the panorama of everlasting hills.

Every few moments he looked in the driving mirror. A Mercédès crept up behind him, overtook at eighty, and sighed ahead with the sound of a breeze. Foley held the needle on sixty-five. He had no logical purpose in driving fast. His nerves dictated it. To drive fast seemed somehow more secure than to dawdle. As he turned into the approach to the airport, an Elizabethan aircraft rose from a runway and lifted into the sky. Foley slackened his speed. The Elizabethan nosed into the blue. Gradually it diminished to a silver speck.

Wherever it's going, I wish I were on it, Foley thought.

He ignored a large car park and stopped outside the glass-fronted entrance to the airport building. The building had been constructed in recent years. It was low and compact and could have been placed in a corner of Kennedy Airport and never noticed. High over the building fluttered a tricolour flag of green, white and orange.

Foley gathered up the parcel and stepped out of the car. Few people were about, but on the pavement outside the glass doors stood two men in uniform, watching him. Their eyes followed him as he carried the parcel to the boot of the car. Foley looked at the men and looked away. He was unsure whether they were some kind of airport police or flunkeys with an hour off and nothing to do. As he unlocked the boot he glanced at the men again. One continued to watch him, the other was lighting a cigarette. Police didn't smoke in uniform, Foley reasoned. Whoever the pair were, there was nothing he could do.

Placing the parcel in the boot, Foley looked closely at it for the first time. He saw little that he had not seen when he received it from the boy in the Lee Hotel. It was heavy, nearly as wide and deep as his suitcase. The wrapping of brown paper and string were anonymous. The string was tightly tied but not so tight as to prevent the contents of the parcel from sliding, fractionally, one box on top of the other. Foley found that when he pushed, through the brown paper, one cardboard box would shift and slightly overlap the other. The boxes were of the size and shape of shirt-boxes in men's shops. He locked the boot, then the car door. He looked back along the approach road: no guard cars, no Jaguar . . . so far.

Averting his eyes from the two men in uniform—he decided with disgust that they were chauffeurs—Foley walked through the entrance into an active and spacious lounge. People were seated in mauve chairs, their hand-baggage at their feet. Two small children pursued each other between the rows of chairs. A huddle of men descended the stairs from the restaurant carrying canvas bags and fishing-rods. The check-in and reservations counters were to the right. Ahead, Foley saw the sign: Toilets. He walked to the door marked " Men " and into the men's room. Finding himself alone he leaned his back against the tiled wall and tried to recapture his breath.

He counted: " One two-o-o, one two-o-o." The asthma might have been worse.

His face in the mirror was streaked with grime. Where the grime came from he could not guess. He washed his face in cold water and rinsed his mouth. A young priest entered. You should have been in room 18, Foley thought accusingly, and walked from the men's room resolved to be master of the asthma.

Near the men's room were two shops, the first displaying newspapers and books, picture postcards, tobacco and confectionery, the second chin-deep in handwoven tweeds, Aran Island jerseys, ties and hats, glassware, umbrellas, leprechaun ashtrays and Celtic crosses. He surveyed the postcards and bought four. They displayed untroubled aspects of Ireland: one was of sunset over Killarney, another was of a dame in a black dress and rosy cheeks crouched over a spinning-wheel, the others showed rustic views of cottages and donkeys with turf-baskets slung over their backs. Foley put the cards in his pocket-book, handed over an additional sixpence for the *Irish Times,* and took the newspaper to one of the lounge chairs.

He sat down. Before unfolding the newspaper he looked round the hall. The children had chased each other into a corner and were wrestling on the floor. So far as he could tell, no one showed any interest in him.

"Attention please," declaimed a girl's voice over the loudspeaker. "Will Mr. Mulcahy, passenger to London, please call at the reception desk."

Foley frowned, worrying whether he could have misheard what had sounded like "Mulcahy." He sat up and looked cautiously around. The words vibrated and echoed with the inaudibility of all announcements over loudspeaker systems.

"Mr. Mulcahy please," repeated the voice.

Foley unfolded the newspaper. He had learned that the *Irish Times* was not an evening paper. Therefore it could have no reference to the murder of Minton. But he sensed that somewhere the newspaper would hold something which he had no wish to see. He looked at the headlines. "Taoiseach Surprise in Pig Debate. Dáil Uproar Over Pig Subsidies."

Good, Foley thought, good. Farther across the page he read: "Mobile Libraries for Leitrim, Sligo, Roscommon."

There were stories about a trial in South Africa, a win by an Irish golfer, and a call by the Pope for peace and understanding. He turned the page and instantly recoiled from items headed: " Shamrock Rovers Defy Augury," and " O'Connor Swims Home—3, 3, 2, 4, 3."

He turned another page. A familiar lined face with a cloud of white hair stared at him from the grey bog of newsprint. The photograph carried an extended caption:

" Gardai were still searching last night for Professor Ernst Holstein, who has been missing since Tuesday from the Marine Biology Research Laboratory at Caherdaniel, Kerry. Dr. Holstein, director of the £120,000 M.B.R. Establishment, disappeared shortly after gardai from three counties visited the establishment to investigate a reported theft of documents from his office. Gardai would neither confirm nor deny reports that Dr. Holstein had been kidnapped.

" Harbours and airports have been alerted and roadblocks set up on routes leading into Shannon and Dublin. Two men held for questioning at Rosslare were released after one hour. Gardai are understood to be seeking a black Jaguar car.

" Dr. Holstein, aged 74, is a naturalised American citizen. He was born in Leipzig and came to Ireland from Columbia University, New York, seven years ago as head of the Government's new marine biology station. He is unmarried."

Foley folded the paper and stood up. He walked across the lounge to the reservations desk and waited while the young priest from the men's room finished a discussion with an even younger and strikingly handsome booking-clerk.

" It will be my fourth time to Lourdes in five years," the priest was saying.

The clerk wore an impressed expression. He was dressed in a black uniform and a white-and-black peaked cap. Round his cuffs were two gold rings. The pair talked unhurriedly about Lourdes. Then the priest said, "Good day," and walked off.

"Can I get a flight from Shannon to New York first thing to-morrow?"

The clerk was despondent. The corners of his mouth drooped. Foley wanted to advise him that he was wasted at the airport, that he should have been on the stage. The clerk acted as though he had just heard that his family and savings had been wiped out in an unspeakable disaster.

"I'm sorry," he said. "I had the same question earlier to-day, you know? There's nothing till Sunday afternoon."

"Nothing at all?"

"Nothing. There were two vacancies on a Pan-American flight this morning but they've been taken. Everything else is fully booked for the next three days."

"Why's that?"

Even as he put the question Foley was aware that he did not want an answer. He paid no attention to the clerk's explanations. That's that, he thought. He was virtually a prisoner in Ireland. He might as well have been handcuffed. To try now for a sea passage would be too involved, and too slow. Anyway, he did not have the money. Inspector Sheridan need have no anxiety that his chief witness might vanish from the country.

"I could put you down for a cancellation," the clerk was saying. "There's quite a short waiting-list. We telephone you the moment there's a vacancy."

Phone me where? Foley wondered bitterly. A prison cell? A public call-box? Care of Spies Anonymous?

"Thanks, no. I'll think about it," he said.

He walked away from the counter and towards the glass doors. Outside the doors he saw his parked Morris. A guard was peering in the windows.

Chapter 18

Foley hesitated only for a moment. Without the car he was lost. If the guard thought he had found the car belonging to Minton's murderer he would be unlikely to let it out of his sight. If he was admiring the design he might continue to admire it indefinitely. Either way, a bull-headed approach seemed as likely to succeed as any other. Foley had almost reached a point where he did not care what happened. He put his hand in his pocket and took hold of one of the two car keys. He hoped it was the one for the door, there was no way of telling. If the cop clapped a hand on his shoulder and said: "I'm booking you, Mac, first-degree murder," or whatever it was that cops said in Ireland, there would be an instant in which he would not expect an attack: not from a fat and short-sighted asthmatic who breathed like a steam-engine. Foley wondered whether he would be able to bring himself to lash out, kick, butt his head into the guard's face. If he did so successfully he might win a second instant in which to open the car door.

If the cop hit him first . . . well, he had been hit before. It could be no worse than being hit by McCarthy.

As he walked to the car Foley thought again, identifying frontal attack as bravado of an infantile kind. He could no more attack the guard than swim breast-stroke back to New York. The guard watched him approach. He was young and handsome; neither so young nor so handsome as the booking-clerk, but leather-skinned and well over six feet tall, in every way a tougher proposition with shoulders like a wall.

"Would this be your car, sir?" the guard asked in a voice soft as air.

Foley drew in his breath. He knew it was going to be parking nonsense, it was going to be all right.

"I've hired it. I'm just leaving. I called by to check my flight."

"I see. You're American, are you, sir?"

"Yes."

Foley sucked in a long, harsh breath. He felt the pricking of tears behind his eyelids. His nerves were going but he had to last out. The hue and cry had not yet reached the airport but it might do so at any moment. He tried to concentrate on what the guard was saying.

"You'll be touring, then? Or is it business?"

"Touring, officer. I've been here only a few days."

"Is that so? I'm sorry the weather has not been better for you."

"To-day's okay."

"Yes, it's grand to-day. But it's changeable you know, to-morrow could be terrible."

"Do you think so?"

"Ah, it could. It's very changeable. June is always very changeable."

"I should have come in August."

"August can be changeable too. June is a grand month. You don't have the same crowds in June. August is busy."

"Is that right?"

"August is terribly busy."

Foley battled to supress a mounting sense of unreality. He had a feeling of participation in a cross-talk act without being certain whether he was the comic or the stooge. He feared that any moment he would forget his lines.

"Do you happen to have the time?" he asked. It was the first thing that came into his head.

"Between two and three exactly," replied the guard, neither hesitating nor looking at his watch.

"I'm late. If you'll excuse me, I must hurry." Foley said, struggling to retain the final tatters of his sanity.

The guard tried to open the car door but it was locked, as it had been when he had tried it five minutes previously. Foley opened the door with the key and climbed into the car.

"Next time perhaps you'll use the car park, sir," the guard said. "This space is for setting down and picking up."

"I will, I will. I'm sorry, I didn't see any sign."

"The sign's there, sir."

The guard pointed to a notice on the kerb in front of the Morris: "Set-Down, Stop Only."

"It won't happen again."

"Don't let it bother you. Don't let it bother you at all."

From a Chicago cop that could only have been sarcasm. Foley glanced apprehensively at the guard. There was no trace of sarcasm.

"Thanks, thanks," Foley said.

"That's all right, I hope you have a grand holiday. Go safely now."

Foley drove off. As he turned into the main road to Cork he recognised a garda car approaching on the opposite side of the road. Two guards sat in the front seats and two more in the back. Too late, Foley raised his arm to mask his face; the guards' faces were already turned towards the Morris. If they were not yet positive, they were suspicious. The driver produced a blast on the horn. Foley accelerated hard.

That wretched guard at the airport will be court-martialled, put to the torture and shot, he thought. He gave the Morris all it had . . . sixty . . . seventy . . . seventy-five. . . . The garda car performed a U-turn and found itself behind a lorry carrying a carthorse in its trailer. The car overtook the lorry and sped down the hill after Foley, its siren wailing.

Monotonous, Foley thought grimly, monotonous. He careered along the open road, the siren at his back. He had a start of more than a hundred yards. Unless his judgment failed or the engine blew up he could keep his lead.

The needle touched eighty. For quarter of a mile Foley raced on the wrong side of the road, blowing his horn. He left in his wake a succession of meandering cars. With the siren at his back he could hardly escape attention. He might as well blow his own horn and try to clear the road.

Monotonous, he thought miserably. A crisis a minute. He was neither thrilled by the pace of the chase nor so frightened as before. His brain had almost ceased to function and was turning over feebly as though anæsthetised. The flight from his new pursuers was instinctive, not reasoned. Reasoning had got him nowhere. The object was to travel as fast as possible and escape. He would do his best, he could do no more. He had to keep going, fast.

The siren wailed. On the outskirts of Cork the traffic built up and Foley was compelled to brake. The siren fell silent, then it broke out again, but at a distance. Foley saw a road off to the right and judged that he might just reach it through a gap in the oncoming traffic. He swung across the road, lurched into the turning, and drove between rows of tidy council houses.

Had Foley been in livelier condition, physically and mentally, he might have congratulated himself on a small triumph. Wherever the garda car was, it no longer followed behind. His shirt was sodden with perspiration, the pricking behind his eyelids quickened. He allowed himself to sob quietly as he drove through the wasteland of houses. His hands on the wheel trembled with nervous exhaustion.

He kept on and by circuitous routes reached the city centre. He found a parking space off St. Patrick's Street. The time was nearly three o'clock. For a moment he could not remember why he was back in Cork, what he aimed to do.

Mary, that was it. Mary, Mary, quite contrary. Mary the Midwife.

Now the cops were after him. He had lost them but they were after him. He had supposed they would be, sooner or later. Now it was confirmed. They had been quick. In Chicago they would have been no quicker.

Foley walked weakly into the Victoria Hotel. He entered a lounge off the lobby and saw straight ahead of him, comfortably seated round a coffee-table, talking, discussing horse-racing, the price of petrol, life, how best to murder a man, Parker, McCarthy and Big Nose. Parker spotted Foley and spoke to the others. The three men rose together and came towards him.

The jungle instinct of the hunted took over. It had only been a question of time. Foley stepped back into the lobby and looked right and left. He could have either the street or the hotel. Both were populated. So long as he stayed among people he might have a chance. Parker and his pals would not risk their rough stuff in the full public gaze. He chose the hotel. If he had to run, or fall, or die, he would do so on carpets, not concrete. He looked again to his left. Among the illuminated signs was one which directed towards the bar.

They followed him into the bar and crowded in on him at the counter as though he had inherited money and was about to spread it around. Parker pressed against him on one side, McCarthy and Big Nose on the other. Seven or eight men were in the bar, some sitting, some standing at the counter talking. They talked among themselves and with the barmaid, disregarding the newcomers. Foley puzzled over how he might turn the customers and the bar to his advantage. He could think of nothing. The barmaid presented herself.

"Whisky," Foley said.

"Four whiskies," the girl said.

"One whisky," Foley corrected.

"The parcel," Parker hissed into his ear.

Foley said nothing.

"We want the parcel," Parker said. "We want the parcel, not you. Give us the parcel then go home, clear out, forget everything."

Forget everything? Foley sipped his whisky.

"I'm giving you a chance," Parker said in a low voice. "You know me. I don't want you dead. All we want is that parcel. It's no use to you. Be sensible."

"Go away," Foley muttered. "Why can't you go away and leave me alone."

"We want that parcel and we shall get it."

Impatience had crept into Parker's voice. His mouth was inches from Foley's ear. A tempest of laughter arose at a far end of the bar, then subsided.

"The parcel's not yours," Foley muttered. "Go away, can't you? I'm not well."

He stared at the bottles aligned on shelves at the back of the bar. His pleading was unlikely to impress. He tried to conjure up a more convincing approach, some excuse, or denial of his identity, or a ruse which would allow escape. Nothing occurred to him. His mind stayed empty. He wanted to shift away from Parker but McCarthy hemmed him in on the other side. Big Nose was asking the barmaid for three whiskies.

"You're a stupid fool," Parker said. He smelled not unpleasantly of after-shave lotion. "For God's sake be warned. If you don't give us the parcel you'll be killed."

"Like Minton?"

Parker said nothing.

"I said like Minton."

"Exactly."

"Bastards."

"McCarthy'll do the same for you. He'll kill you. He hates you."

"He's mental."

"The parcel!"

"They'll get you, you know, all of you. They're looking for you."

"No. They're looking for you."

Foley caught the barmaid's eye and asked for a second whisky. As he paid, a thought came to him which was so obvious and shocking that he reacted with a tiny gasp.

Why not give them the parcel? Parker was right, it was himself the police were looking for. McCarthy, breathing on his cheek, had killed and could kill again.

Foley rejected the idea before it could take shape but it clung, weakly kicking in the recesses of his mind. To hand over the parcel would be to become a traitor . . . but no one would know he was a traitor. No one knew he had the parcel except the three thugs at his sides, and Minton, who was dead.

Everything was so much more complicated than first appeared. The boy who handed him the parcel knew, and the boy would have told the world. In fact everyone knew. Foley felt again the pricking behind his eyelids. His brain had become an incoherent tangle of half-truths, errors, unreason. He was, God help him, a spy, and he could not afford errors, but he was sprinting desperately through glue, as in the bad dreams of boyhood. At the end of every avenue lurked dragons. He was helplessly alone.

"C'mon," he said, gulping the whisky. "It's in the car."

"You'll not regret it," Parker said.

Big Nose went first, then Foley, with Parker at his side. McCarthy started out at Foley's other side, then fell strategically behind. Foley noticed that McCarthy walked with a limp. He had not limped when strutting and showing his muscles that evening in the bedroom at Castleferry. A post-fourposter limp, Foley decided.

A foot trod heavily on his heel. In front, Big Nose

opened the door of the bar and strode through, the pock-marked nose advancing ahead like a blighted vegetable. Foley had not heard Big Nose speak since the encounter on the Mallow-Bandon road. They walked along a short passage, past toilets.

"What have you done with Dr. Holstein?" Foley asked Parker.

"Just take us to your car," Parker said.

"I suppose you killed him too."

Parker did not answer. They had reached the lobby. A chattering coach party filled much of the lobby and crowded the entrance. Foley felt Parker's guiding hand on his sleeve and the breath of McCarthy on his neck. Big Nose walked in front. Without asking himself precisely what he intended to achieve, Foley swung his heel backwards at McCarthy and felt it strike against bone. McCarthy cried out. Foley jerked his arm free of Parker, twisted away and ran up a flight of stairs into the hotel.

Parker and Big Nose melted discreetly into the throng in the lobby. McCarthy, with his limping leg, arm mangled by the Morris window, his shin freshly inflamed with pain, followed up the stairs. He had neither discretion nor restraint. His temper was gone. He followed in fury and on the landing stumbled and sprawled over the carpet. He was up in an instant. Someone in the lobby shouted. Foley mounted another short staircase, tiring fast and hugging the wall for support. At the top of the stairs he fell gasping to his knees. McCarthy trampled close behind.

Foley did not see how he could escape. He tore off his glasses and stuffed them into his jacket pocket. He heard McCarthy on the stairs below, scrambled up on to his feet and lurched down an empty passage, holding the wall and feeling in vain for a picture, fire-extinguisher, anything with which to defend himself. Doors leading into bedrooms stood at intervals on both sides of the passage and Foley fell against one and groped for the handle. Before he had the door open more than an inch, McCarthy reached him.

Foley was aware only of pain. He crashed into the bedroom with McCarthy berserk on top of him. He heard shouting not far away as though others had followed along the passage, then McCarthy was kneeling over him, punching. Foley wanted to raise his arms to push McCarthy away but he could not find them . . . he tried to lift his arms but nothing happened. He wished it would end, he did not care how.

He passed out. Then he found he could move his arms. The weight above him was gone, the punching had stopped. The fighting had shifted elsewhere. He heard shouts and scuffling, and when he raised his head he saw McCarthy struggling with two men. Each held an arm. McCarthy silently lunged and kicked and bucked in his efforts to free himself. He fought with the concentrated endeavour of a madman. Foley propped himself on one elbow and felt in his pocket for his glasses. One of the sidepieces had snapped off at a hinge. He held the glasses to his eyes and forced himself on to his feet. Blood flowed down his face. One of his eyes was closing. Somewhere close by an Irish voice said: "Easy now, will ya take it easy?" People were at the door and looking in, watching the battle. McCarthy tore an arm loose and slammed his fist into the face of the man holding the other arm. The man reeled backwards. McCarthy charged through the door scattering the onlookers. The power of his bullock shoulders knocked a smartly-outfitted female guest on to the passage floor. She dropped like an apple, her features frozen in astonishment.

"He's stolen my money!" Foley called out before anyone could ask questions.

The unknown man whom McCarthy had punched in the face sat on the floor holding his head in his hands. Someone knelt by the woman on the passage floor. Others galloped not too hastily along the passage in pursuit of McCarthy. Foley stumbled along with them, holding his glasses to his eyes. With a handkerchief in his other hand he tried to sponge the blood from his face. His head throbbed as though from a series of electric shocks, his mouth was cut and starting to swell. A man took his arm and tried to slow him down but Foley shook him off mumbling: "Money, he's got my money."

The mob nearly tumbled over one another in their progress down the stately stairway. Someone was hysterically shouting: "Stop thief!" In the lobby, McCarthy was nowhere to be seen.

Neither were Parker and Big Nose. Some of the pursuers ran into the street, others into the lounge. Most of the coach party were congregated in the centre of the lobby, blankly watching the confusion. A guard called for calm, another guard had stationed himself at the hotel entrance and was striving to prevent people from entering or leaving. Foley saw Mary standing alone near the doors. He hurried over to her.

"The car's waiting," he said. "I'm sorry I'm late."

Mary gazed in horror on the wrecked face. "What's happened?" she stammered.

Foley put his ruined handkerchief in his pocket without answering, gripped her arm and steered her through the door. As they stepped into the street the guard at the door called out: "Hey—you two!"

Others were pushing in and out of the entrance and the lone guard was unable to cope.

"Please, what is it?" Mary implored in a frightened voice.

Foley walked fast with his hand on her arm. His other hand steadied the glasses.

"Cork," he said, "I've been seeing Cork. Don't look round. Keep walking. I hope you got your shoes."

Chapter 19

Mary had let herself go at the sales, buying not only shoes but a costume, a hat, two lengths of dress material and two blouses, one of which she had been busy regretting while she waited with her parcels for Foley. She took the wheel and drove out of Cork and on to the Bandon road.

Foley lay on his side on the back seat with his knees tucked up to his chest. He was not trying to hide; the Morris would be instantly recognisable to anyone searching for him. He was exhausted. He closed his eyes but not to sleep. His mind raced, his cut and swollen face burned.

It could have been worse, of course. He could have been dead . . . dead . . . dead. The word beat in his mind until it became meaningless. He listened to the wheels purring over the road. The smell in his nostrils was of upholstery. He had detected perfume when Mary had helped him into the back seat, for she had renewed herself with a dab here, a dab there. Now he smelt only upholstery. The taste in his mouth was blood.

She was a sweet sad woman, he thought. He could depend on her. Everything would be all right . . . he was lucky to be alive, if it was lucky to be alive. Lucky to be a spy, with such opportunities as few ever had for serving his country right or wrong by the dawn's early light. Unlucky marching into the hotel lounge and the arms of the three creeping stranglers . . . that had been bad. They had not expected him yet he had turned up like a waiter. "Tea for you three gentlemen? Irish coffee?" Probably they had been marking time while a garage fixed the Jaguar, lamed in the chase round the city. Ignorant drivers. It would be good to drive Mary round Chicago, show her the lights on Lake Michigan . . . by the dawn's early light.

He lay like an embryo, listening to the purring wheels, the swish of passing cars. Mary seemed to be doing okay, steady forty . . . forty-five. She should have her own car. What sort of life was it, pushing a bicycle up hillsides to the farmers' wives? What sort of life was spying? Even as a temporary spy, a kind of vacation-job spy? Where did he go from here? He had the parcel. He had checked the parcel in the trunk of the Morris before they left Cork, wishing it were a present for Mary. Somehow he had to get it back to America. He had to get himself back.

The broken glasses had slid off his nose. They lay below him on the floor of the car. If he opened his eyes he could see them. He kept his eyes shut. He opened them and levered himself up into a sitting position, leaning forward with his arms on the back of the passenger-seat.

"I'll have to drop you in Bandon," he said. "I'd like to go back to your place but I don't think I can."

"We're going to hospital," she said.

"No. I wish I could, but you don't understand."

"If you told me, I'd try to understand."

"I can't go to hospital. I can't go anywhere like that. I'll be all right."

"You're in a terrible state."

"I wish I could have a bath."

"Have you had anything to eat?"

"I'm not hungry."

"Please, let me take you to hospital. I know them in Bandon. Let them look at you."

"I daren't. Where are we now?"

"Nearly at Inishannon."

Well clear of Cork, he thought. He wanted to ease up, cease running, find a dark safe corner.

"Maybe we should stop somewhere off the road," he said.

"I thought you were in a hurry."

"We should be all right if we can get off the road, just for a while."

One spy, he thought, American, in poor shape, flogging on, flogging on, but wanting to get off the road, just for a while.

He sat humped in a corner of the back seat while Mary slipped into a shop. A large new car like a palace, its green paint all but obliterated under mud and dust, drove slowly by along the street. Foley watched it go past. On the back seat crouched a pig, pale pink and fidgety, its snout against the window. Foley held his glasses to his eyes. The pig's eyes were two beads. Foley could not be sure whether they were watching him or not. He thought they were. Mary was away only two minutes. She ran back carrying a small wrapped packet and a bag of oranges.

A short distance beyond Inishannon she said: "I suppose we could try here."

She turned off the road and into a winding, rutted boreen. The Morris bounced on its springs and Mary changed to a low gear. The tyres churned over caked mud and stones. They parked on a patch of nettles. The view was bounded by the boreen in front and behind and hedges on either side. Foxgloves spiked upwards from the foot of the hedges. The sky had clouded over.

"Stay where you are," Mary said.

She climbed into the back seat with the small packet in her hand. From the packet she took a bottle of TCP and cotton wool. She washed Foley's face in TCP while he clenched his fists, pressing his nails into his palms. The TCP stung in the cuts in his mouth and cheeks. One eye was purplish-black. After she had bathed the cuts she used the TCP to try and clean the blood from his collar and the front of his shirt. She smells of disinfectant again, Foley thought. We both smell of disinfectant.

"Would you like a bandage?" she asked, taking a bandage from the first-aid kit.

"You say. Not unless I have to."

"I think you're beyond bandages."

"Save it for the next time."

"At the present rate your next bandage will be a pall."

"Smart answer."

"Smarter than you."

He grinned. Mary smiled at him. She smiled with her mouth and eyes. Foley wanted to reach out and touch the black hair. He remained still. He was not smart but he was a spy, and spying was proving to be as much as he could manage without attempting to entice Mary into his life. God knew it was no sort of life any more, not if the past twenty-four hours were typical, and he guessed that Mary would not be easily enticeable anyway. But she had smiled at him.

She was smiling again. The smiles of other women he had known had meant anything, good or bad. He would keep celibate until he ended his spying. If the spying ended him, still, for evermore, he would keep celibate, and so be it. He wished he had met her at a different time, in another country, before all this.

"What have you got there?" he asked.

"Oranges," she replied, rising and bending over the passenger seat to reach the bag of oranges.

Foley looked out of the window so that he would not see the curve of her body, which was all he wanted to see. He looked at nettles, foxgloves, thick grass, a dense hedge.

While he peeled an orange, Mary burrowed in her handbag for nail scissors. She took a roll of adhesive tape from the packet and snipped off a piece of the tape.

"Let me have your glasses."

He handed them to her together with the snapped

sidepiece. He believed her whole concentration was on the running repair but she said: " I wish you'd tell me about it."

Foley told her all he had told her mother and father on the evening of whisky and salmon, before she had returned home from the hospital and the farmers' wives, before he had telephoned Minton. He did not tell her that Minton had made him an agent, but he described how he had found Minton dead and how the police were after him from one direction, a posse of criminal delinquents from the other. He told her of the near-mayhem in the bedroom at the Victoria, and of the parcel which she had seen when he checked the boot and which he had to take back to America. He admitted that he did not know where in America—Washington, presumably. The parcel, he said, contained the formula for something called chloriodine, and if the formula did not go to America first it would go behind the Iron Curtain. The only other source for the formula was its creator, Dr. Holstein, and he was dead, or probably dead. Dr. Holstein had not given the opposition the formula because he would not, or without his books and notes and diagrams he could not, or he had forgotten it, or died of heart failure before he could speak. Alternatively he had written the whole thing out for them. Whichever way, the opposition badly wanted the parcel. Whatever they had or had not elicited from the Professor, they had no intention of allowing the parcel to reach the States.

" That's about it," he concluded. " Don't ask me any questions. I don't know the answers."

Mary had listened without interrupting, winding the tape round the glasses at the hinge where they had snapped, her eyes on the join.

" You should tell the police," she said in a husky voice.

" I can't. Not now."

" You didn't kill Minton."

" No, but they might try and hold on to me until they found who did. It would be too risky and complicated."

The glasses were temporarily mended. She handed them to him.

"I suppose you're a sort of spy," she said.

Her eyes were filled with tears. Foley was admiring the mended glasses. He did not see the tears. He adjusted the glasses on his nose.

"Perfect," he said.

He looked gratefully through the glasses at Mary, then he looked away and began gathering up the orange peel. Having collected the peel he did not know what to do with it.

"Don't cry," he said.

"I'm sorry."

"I'd give you my handkerchief but it's got troubles of its own."

"I have one somewhere."

"You mustn't worry. I'll drive you home."

"They might have killed you."

"I suppose so."

"It's so unbelievable." Her voice trembled. "This is Ireland not—well, not anywhere else. It's so horrible. It doesn't happen here."

"Doesn't it?"

"What will you do?"

"I don't know."

"Suppose I drove you to Shannon? We could be there in a few hours."

"I couldn't let you, you'd land yourself in endless trouble if they ever found out. You shouldn't be with me at all. It's my fault. Anyway I've tried and it's no good. There are no seats for three days. And the place would be crawling with cops."

"Could you go to Castleferry?"

"The last place. If I go back there it'll be to commit arson."

"You've got to go somewhere."

They were silent. Foley put the orange peel in the bag with the oranges.

"I don't know anywhere. They'll turn Bandon over looking for me. Maybe I'd be safest in Dublin."

She watched him anxiously.

"I daren't risk a hotel. I've got to hide somewhere."

"I've an uncle with a summer cottage on the Old Head of Kinsale," Mary said. "Sometimes we go for week-ends but there's no one there now because he phoned the other day and said it was empty if we wanted it. No one would look for you there."

"I'm grateful, but I can't. I'll find somewhere."

"No one would know. If you'd let me tell my father I'm sure he'd find some way out for you. I know he's a country solicitor but he's sharp and he knows several people—and he likes you."

"You're not to bring your father into it." He hesitated. "But if you're sure about this place at Kinsale...."

"I'm quite sure."

"Where's Kinsale?"

She drew a sketch map and told him about the cottage. They realised at the same moment that they were holding each other's hand. At what moment their hands had met, neither could have said. They looked at each other. They did not release their hands.

"Not far," Mary said softly. "About thirty minutes' drive."

They sat in the back of the car, not speaking, no longer looking at each other, but holding hands like teenagers and breathing the pungently disinfected air. The afternoon had grown cool and gloomy. Rainclouds blotted out the blue sky. The first drops of rain detonated on the roof of the Morris.

"Can't we stay here?" Foley said.

"You're codding."

"I am."

"'I am'," mimicked Mary, on the brink of laughter, "You should say: 'Yeah.' 'I am' is an Irish answer. Like 'I do not' and 'I cannot'."

"I know, it's catching."

"Say: 'Yeah man, reach for the sky or I'll fill you full of lead'."

"You say, 'Begorrah'."

"Begorrah, William," she crooned in an impossible brogue, "a treacherous day it will be, with the rain spilling like milk from a pail and the heron crying on the green lake and I, an old widow-woman with only my shawleen and the rags you see me in, walking the bogs and the back roads seeking fuel for my fire and a potato for my pan, and near destroyed with the cold, begorrah."

Foley laughed. "I'm not sure about the final 'begorrah.' Top of the class though. Just like the Irish in Chicago."

"Really?"

"No, not really. I was codding."

"You're learning, you old codder. We'll make an Irishman of you yet."

Mary gave him a quick smile, but she was not sure that she had said the right thing. He smiled back.

"What's that 'Sláinte' you all say? What does it mean?"

"Good health."

"Can you speak Irish?"

She did so, two or three quick sentences like a party-piece which she had said before.

"Really," he said.

"That means: 'Here's health from wall to wall and if there's anybody in the corner, let him speak'."

"The Irish are great on toasts."

"There's another goes, 'Health and long life to you, land without rent to you, a child every year to you, and may you die in Ireland'."

She drew away her hand. It was not her afternoon.

"We should go," she said.

Foley smiled at her again. He made no attempt to recover her hand.

"Would you do one more little thing for me, one last good deed? I'll never ask for anything else."

"Yes?"

"I like your perfume. Put some more perfume on."

They parked near a no-parking sign, by a telephone box, half a mile from the Caseys' house. There were shops but not people in the street. The rain fell in torrents.

He hurried into the telephone box and tore a corner off the photograph of Joy. He copied the telephone number on to the back, returned to the car and handed the tiny triangle of paper through the window to Mary. He unlocked the boot, took out the parcel, and gave Mary the keys.

At the window he said: "Try to find my raincoat."

"Ten minutes," she said.

He ran back into the telephone box and watched her drive off.

He rested the parcel on the floor at his feet and took out his pipe and a tin of tobacco. The asthma had subsided, at least for the time being. One day, he thought, should he live so long, he might be fully mended. His mouth was tender and raw and he could feel his pulse beating in the cuts in his ravaged face.

The minutes passed. She should be home now. The tobacco, unfamiliar but agreeable, made him cough, and smoke quickly filled the telephone box. He pushed the door ajar to allow the smoke to escape. From his pocket he took the envelope in which the photograph and cloakroom ticket and scrap of paper had arrived from Minton. On the back of the envelope Mary had sketched for him a map of the Old Head of Kinsale. The map was a second attempt, occupying the lower part of the envelope. The first attempt was on the upper part and had gone so badly out of proportion that Mary had scribbled over it in disgust. A cross marked the uncle's cottage, another cross and a large letter L indicated a lighthouse. There were other lesser crosses, and arrows, and short squiggly lines which represented the sea. Mary had explained that this was the way she had been taught to show the sea at school, in geography lessons. Foley looked gloomily at the map. All it lacked were the points of the compass, a galleon sailing on the sea and somewhere the words: "Treasure buried here." He returned the map to his pocket.

Ten minutes ... fifteen ... twenty. She drove quite well, she could not have crashed. But he began to be anxious. Something was keeping her. He laid his pipe on the coin-box.

The floor was filthy with cigarette-ends and toffee-wrappings and a page from the telephone directory. The directory was in rags, the pages torn and loose. He lifted the receiver and listened to a continuous burring sound. He would give her another five minutes, then telephone her. If the wrong person answered he could hang up. She should have been home long ago. The rain drummed on the roof of the telephone box. No one arrived wanting to make a call. The pavements were deserted. Small shops lined the street and the rain had driven pedestrians into the doorways of the shops. Puddles spread along the gutters and encroached farther and farther into the road. As he looked again at his watch the telephone rang out.

He picked up the receiver. Now he would hear not Mary but the Inspector, he thought ... that was the pattern of things, that was how it was to be a spy.

"William, you must go quickly!" he heard Mary say.

Her frightened words fell over each other. He stared at his beaten face in the mirror above the phone.

"William?"

"What is it?"

"You must run, they're here, they've just left in a car, a second ago—the Inspector, two others. They made me tell them—they made me, William, they recognised the car. They'll be there in a second. You must run, hide, I'm so sorry——"

She was crying hoarsely.

" I didn't tell them about the cottage——"

Foley dropped the receiver, lifted the parcel by the string and barged open the door with his shoulder. The receiver fell, jerked on its cord, swung with a crack against a pane of glass in the kiosk wall, and went on swinging.

Embracing the parcel he ran down the street. His run was more of a waddle. He was very tired. The rain splashed on his bare head and hands and made fat wet stains on the parcel.

Chapter 20

The asthma had not subsided so completely as to make running simple. After twenty yards Foley was so out of breath that he was compelled to walk. His tweed suit was quickly soaked and began to release a pungent smell.

At the end of the street he looked right and left, undecided. He wheezed noisily, trying to judge which was south, towards Kinsale. He could not see himself walking to Kinsale but he was determined so far as possible to point in the correct direction. He looked behind him and remembered that he had left his pipe in the telephone box. Beyond the telephone box, at the far end of the street, a black car swung into view.

Foley turned abruptly and continued walking. He chose the street to the right. The bicycle was on the pavement on the opposite side of the street. It leaned unguarded against the wall between a butcher's window and a tobacconist's.

He crossed the street. Water had come through his shoes and at every step his feet squelched. A group of people stood sheltering and gossiping in the butcher's shop. The bicycle rested in solitary isolation against the wall, an errand-boy's bicycle, heavy and slow, with a big iron basket built on to the front of the handlebars. In the basket were packages tied with string, and on the packages, sopping with rain, lay an evil-looking cloth cap. Foley put the cap on his head and balanced his parcel on top of the basket. He wheeled the bicycle off the pavement on to the road, one hand holding the parcel steady on the rim of the basket. He mounted the sodden saddle. His foot slipped on the greasy pedal and he nearly fell, bringing the bicycle and parcel down on top of him. He tried again, poised astride the saddle, one foot on a pedal. The bicycle wobbled forward along the road, the front wheel swayed and Foley swayed with it. Resolved to sink or almost literally swim, he pedalled through the middle of a wide puddle. He waited for angry shouting to break out behind him. The only sound was of pouring rain.

A yellow car sped past on the other side of the street. Foley steered precariously into the first side-turning to which he came and pedalled down an alley that was removed from the sight of the butcher's and tobacconist's shops. Though he wanted to cycle faster he was wary of falling. He could see only a few yards through the gloom. He steered with one hand on the handlebars, the other holding the parcel steady on the rim of the basket. At the end of the alley he curled his fingers round the brake and squeezed. The bicycle halted more sharply than he had anticipated and his belly jolted forward against the handlebars. With one foot planted squarely in the road, the other in readiness on the pedal, he looked both ways along another empty shopping street. The cap was greasy and far too small for his head. He pulled the peak down as far as it would go and started away again, pedalling determinedly, his head bowed into the rain, his vision restricted to the three or four yards in front of the leading wheel. The bicycle was ungainly but solid. Foley resisted an impulse to test the big bell on the handlebars. He would ring it only if anything came in his way, he decided, and then he would ring it like the bells of hell. Meanwhile he would keep pedalling, trustingly. A black car approached noiselessly, its windscreen wipers beating from side to side like silent metronomes. Foley glanced up, glimpsed the profile of Sergeant Burke, and immediately looked away.

The car swished past, throwing a spray of water over his leg. Head low, he pedalled harder, his body tensed.

They were not looking for a man on an errand-boy's bicycle, he reasoned, not yet. They would hardly have recognised him under the cloth cap; and though he might not look like an errand-boy, neither did he look like William Foley. They might have identified the parcel. They could not have missed seeing it if they had been looking his way.

His feet ground round on the pedals, his eyes were half-blinded by the rain on his glasses. Hot with sweat, he pedalled on with the melancholy desperation of a gross outsider in a Sunday afternoon bicycle rally.

He realised that the shops and houses had gone and that he was cycling up a hill. He had not the least idea where he was, but there was no sign of the garda car. The hill was not steep but his legs ached and his back was stiff. He thought of Mary, cycling up hills to visit the fertile wives, perhaps up this very hill. Near the brow of the hill in spite of intensified efforts to keep the pedals rotating, progress slowed to less than walking pace. Attempting to stay in motion he tried tacking, then he jerked the front wheel first to one side, then the other. Only yards short of the top of the hill he became irredeemably becalmed. He stumbled off the saddle and into the road, barely succeeding in keeping upright on his feet. A little red Volkswagen climbed smoothly up the hill behind him and swept past with a friendly toot on its horn. Still no garda cars. Foley pushed the bicycle up the road. On the crest of the hill he looked back and saw Bandon.

The town lay below like an advertisement for country butter or home-fed chickens of Ireland of the Welcomes—except for the rain, which at last was slackening. Foley gazed on the huddled agglomeration of grey slate roofs and dark trees and the still darker water of the River Bandon. Somewhere in the town were searching guards, somewhere else his baggage, passport, the car hired from Shanklin's . . . Mary. Beyond the town was Castleferry. He wondered if ever he would see any of these again. The passport was important. He found himself caring only for Mary.

He turned away and looked ahead towards rolling, interminable hills. The rain had eased and was falling lightly. The road reached down on the other side of the hill, then up again.

He pedalled south. He did not know he was heading south until the clouds to his right parted like slow curtains, revealing the sun. Even then he was not sure. He recognised that the Irish sun, if consistent with the Ireland and the Irish of his brief experience, might well be consistently unpredictable, even deliberately, artfully perverse, capable of setting in the east. Where the sun rose and where it set would depend, in Ireland, on how the sun felt. To-day it had chosen the west.

He stopped by the roadside, dismounted, and wheeled the bicycle on to the grass verge. He laid the bicycle on its side and placed the parcel beside it. Then he took all the packages from the basket and removed the string which had been tied round each one. Before replacing the packages he peered inside two: one contained liver and kidneys, the other six pork chops. He knotted the pieces of string together and tried to bind the parcel on to the basket. The string was still too short. He removed his tie and knotted it on to one end of the string. The additional length enabled him, puffing, blowing, to secure the parcel on to the basket.

Before setting off, he looked both ways along the road. No one was in sight. He placed his thumb on the bell and pressed down. The bell rang out like an alarm, frightening a blackbird out of the hedge. He clamped his hand over the bell, muffling the clamour.

The sun shone too late and too weakly to forestall his shivers. The rain seemed to have seeped even into his blood for his limbs worked as weakly as the sun and only the physical effort of pedalling kept his blood circulating. Any moment, he feared, cramp would set in. A new hill confronted him. Grunting like a sow, he rose up in the saddle and lunged hard on the pedals. At the top of the hill he climbed off the bicycle and rested, panting. A solitary van drove past. Reflecting that at last he had committed a crime—he had stolen a bicycle—he wiped his face with his dirty, bloodstained handkerchief. If Joy could have seen him, he thought, or his students, or Aunt Rhoda, they would have summoned an emergency meeting or sent off a worried letter to the authorities. He suspected that his appearance had never been so grotesque; a drowned toad, limply astride a bicycle in the heart of nowhere, cloth-capped, tieless, heavily bespectacled, with leaking shoes, first-aid plasters decorating his mouth and cheek, a black eye, and a dripping parcel overlapping the handlebars. If spies worked under camouflage, he was well camouflaged. He might be taken for advance publicity for a travelling circus, or for an eccentric millionaire. No one could possibly see in him anything so mundane as a spy.

He cycled on between impenetrable hedges. Rounding a bend he came upon five children walking in the road. A girl of about ten was bouncing a big rubber ball, and a small red-haired boy was aiming at stones with a hurling-stick as tall as himself. One exceptionally small boy whom Foley realised was probably not a day over two padded along with brisk steps in an effort to keep up. Foley hailed the party, deliberately avoiding the moment's reflection which might cause him to think twice and possibly decide that an encounter even with children carried risks.

" Pardon me," he called out.

He squeezed the brake and again fell forward against the handlebars. He stood in the road astride the cross bar, one hand on the parcel. Though tied, the parcel swayed with every movement of the bicycle. The children stopped at the sound of his voice. They looked at him impassively.

" Could you tell me if I'm right for Kinsale?"

The girl stopped bouncing the ball and held it against her hip.

"I'm touring," he explained when no one answered. "I've just arrived from Tipperary and I'm making for Kinsale."

The children stared at him. They had not seen so interesting a figure since the caravan of tinkers had passed along, the previous week. They were not frightened, and they looked as though at any moment they might answer, but none spoke.

"Would you mind telling me if this is right?" Foley asked patiently.

The children stared, exchanged glances with one another, and said nothing. Foley wondered if he was making sense. In an instant of inspiration he realised they might speak only Gaelic. The only Gaelic he knew was " Sláinte."

" Sláinte!" he said.

The boy with the hurling-stick took a step back. No one else moved.

" Kinsale—Kin-sale," he tried again. A forlorn note had crept into his voice.

"Kinsale is on a way," said the girl with the ball.

"Good!" He was in luck. He plunged into his idea of an Irish accent. "The Ould Head of Kinsale."

No reply. Maybe they thought him an Irishman with a speech defect. But nothing was to be gained by parading his American accent. Children talked to their parents, parents talked to everyone. He tipped the repulsive cap on to the back of his head with what he hoped might pass for Tipperary nonchalance. The silent children were beginning to unnerve him. He looked from one to another. They gazed back.

"The Ould Head of Kinsale," he said despairingly.

"It's on farther," the girl said.

"Thanks a lot."

How much farther on? Foley wanted details, precise directions, but he judged that he would obtain them only at disproportionate cost to his already unsteady nerves. He seated himself on the saddle and steadied a squelching shoe on the pedals. As though suddenly loath to see him go, the children moved forward and clustered round the bicycle.

"It's on south," the boy with the hurling-stick said.

"Through Kilbrittain," the girl said.

"Is it far?"

"It is not. It's just a step."

"You can go on the small road."

"Where's the small road?"

"Just along, on this side."

"This side?"

"It is."

"This small road will take me through Kilbrittain?"

"No, Balinspittle, Kilbrittain is straight."

Foley determined to leave before his mounting confusion developed into utter rout. The two-year-old was stroking the spokes of the front wheel and muttering incantations. A little freckled girl with a scrubbed face was trying to insinuate her hand under the parcel and into the basket.

"I appreciate it," Foley said, and pushed down on the pedal with his foot. "Good-bye."

"Good-bye now."

The small road was small only in width and in the time and trouble which had been spent on its surface. It was not small in length or character, which was both cunning and picturesque, like a favourite politician. Unsignposted, it started furtively as little more than a gap in the hedgerow. Foley pedalled through the gap because he considered he would be safer away from the main road and the sooner the better. Until he came to a crossroads, several miles farther on, and a signpost directing him to Balinspittle, he had no notion where the road would lead him. He was little wiser when he saw that he was heading for Balinspittle. The girl had mentioned this unsavoury-sounding spot but how reliable she was remained to be discovered.

Two children and a man on a tractor were the only human life he encountered for four miles. Foley pedalled faster past the children but waved to the tractor driver and received in return a courteous salute. Birds and beasts abounded; small and furry wild life, grey and brown, scuttled across the road at his approach, birds gabbled in the hedges and trees and flapped over the road and away across the fields. Foley conjectured that if he cared to stop and seek he would find even fish, for at intervals along the road lay lakes of rainwater like waterjumps on a steeplechase course. He had ample time for conjecture. The inferior road, which as a tourist in a limousine he might have delighted in, wound, straightened, twisted again, climbed and fell, and eventually grew monotonous. Thoughts of chloriodine, conspiracies and murder swirled in his mind, and though for a brief time he laboured to expunge them with feats of mental arithmetic, he abandoned the attempt as hopeless and gave free rein to consideration of his appalling predicament. What if he found the cottage? Did he sit there, on the parcel, for three days, waiting for Mary to mail him his passport? And what good to him, at an airport jammed with watching police would be a passport bearing the name and photograph of William Foley?

His arms pressed numbly on the handlebars, his legs rotated mechanically. Waterjumps swamped his ankles. Three times he stopped to rest, stretching full length at the roadside.

He cycled past the signpost to Balinspittle and half an hour later reached the village. He looked at his watch; five minutes to seven, cocktail time. Foley realised he was hungry. He had eaten nothing except an orange since breakfast, liquid intake had been two whiskies. He propped the bicycle against the kerb outside a murky shop and arranged the cap squarely on his head. The cap was especially bizarre and he was in two minds whether to shed it. He left it on. Conceivably it gave him the air of an all-weather golfer.

"I'd like a bag of those." He pointed to a jar of chocolate drops. "Would you make it two bags?"

The old woman behind the counter stirred from her chair with a rustling of shawl and skirts. She had bristles on her chin and moved with the speed of a slow handclap. She unscrewed the lid from the jar of chocolate drops.

"It's been a soft day," she said.

"It has," Foley said.

He bought an iced-bun and two elongated doughnuts which had been sliced along the top and wedged with synthetic grey cream. The old woman, politely disregarding her customer's farouche appearance, tucked the purchases into an enormous paper bag as though they were dynamite. He bought an ice-cream cornet, a chocolate ice wrapped in silver-and-blue paper and a screw-top bottle of a beverage called: "Fizz: Ireland's Raspberry Cream Soda." The old woman's frown multiplied the already numerous wrinkles in her brow as she set to work with pencil and paper, adding up the score. She checked and cross-checked like Einstein on the track of an original discovery.

"That will be four-and-threepence," she said doubtfully.

Foley handed her a ten-shilling note and there followed further delays while the woman dipped her gooseberry chin into the till and fingered the coins, passing pennies and sixpences from one palm to the other, replacing some in the till, dscovering others, changing her mind, muttering, and eventually surfacing with an assortment of small change.

"Am I right for the Ould Head of Kinsale?"

"Keep left by the church," she said, and came to the door of the shop to point the way.

"God give you a safe journey," she said.

She watched him wobble off, the Fizz protruding from his jacket pocket, the ice-cream and paper bag resting on the parcel.

He stopped under a hedge a short distance south of Balinspittle and sat down by the bicycle, using the cap as a cushion. He spread his purchases in front of him. He started with the ice-creams because they were on the point of liquefying, and moved on to the cream doughnut. The Fizz made him belch and the doughnuts and the iced-bun were stale, but his sweet tooth was pacified and he ate hungrily. By the time he had eaten the first bag of chocolate drops he was wondering whether he felt better or worse. He put the second bag of chocolate drops into his pocket, pushed the empty bottle of Fizz into the hedge, and resumed his journey with a sick feeling in his stomach.

The sea was on his right. Then the sea was both to the right and the left and he was cycling along a high spit of green land broken only by the road, occasional walls, and here and there cottages and a windblown tree. In places the cliffs fell sheer to the sea. When he saw the lighthouse ahead, and beyond the lighthouse the sea, he halted and took out the sketch map. He studied the map and searched the headland with his eyes. Mary had said that the cottage stood on its own, a hundred yards back from the road, and just before the road met a stone wall with a rust-coloured iron gate. The gate was to keep sheep and goats inside the field behind the wall, she had said. Beyond the gate the road wound up a slight rise to the lighthouse.

He pedalled on and came to the rust-coloured gate. A hundred yards to his left, exposed and isolated in a world of green, stood a cottage. The dark blue sea stretched like glass below and beyond the cottage and the surrounding fields. Foley tucked back his cuff: eight-thirty, and he had arrived, he had done it. Fatigued, shivering, ill from a score of maladies, he almost fell from the saddle. There was no traffic, no life. The Old Head of Kinsale stood silent and still as a church. Faintly the ocean boomed at the foot of the cliffs.

He gazed through travel-smudged glasses at the distant cottage. So far as he could see it was deserted. No smoke came from the chimney. He wheeled the bicycle off the road and started to push it over the field to the cottage.

Chapter 21

She had said she had not told them about the cottage. He was sure she had said that. He had been in no position, cramped in the telephone box, to wait for details, but she would not deceive him about the cottage. She was the only clean page in the entire grisly history of his Irish vacation. The moment he doubted this, suspected the truth might be otherwise, he could give up, he could give himself up, or walk into the sea. He had been unforgivably wrong to lead her even ankle-deep into his new and private world of chicanery and murder. She had been no more educated to the dark side of the world than he had. In woods where plots and counter-plots sprouted like weeds, where murder was done, and dragons prowled in every path, they were two equal, innocent babes. The others had experience, methods, and they had twisted out of her or tricked out of her his whereabouts, in the telephone-box. They had crowded her, probably threatened her, but she had not talked of the cottage. Perhaps in time she would be cheated into doing so, but not yet.

Foley leaned the bicycle against the cottage wall and tried the door. It was locked and he had no key. The door was in two parts, like a stable door; either section when unlocked could open and shut independently of the other. Recently they had received a daub of white paint. A rough path, at an angle to the unchartered route along which he had pushed the bicycle, led from the front door and across the fields to the road. Among the brambles and nettles at the foot of the cottage walls swayed daisies three feet tall.

He walked backwards over the trodden earth and gravel outside the door and surveyed the cottage. He judged it to be a hundred years old and decided that thatch was quaint but ridiculous. One gale from the sea and presumably the thatch would be whipped into the air and away into the next county. He made a reconnaissance round the four walls. Against the back wall was a lean-to shed with a broken door. Inside the shed was a pile of whiskery, chocolate-coloured turf and a stack of logs. He tested every window. All were locked from inside.

He peered through a window at the back of the house, near the shed. Somewhere he had seen a way of breaking a window noiselessly, or almost noiselessly. What movie was that? The technique had called for Plasticine or sealing-wax, something of that nature. Foley wrapped his fist in the cloth cap and gingerly struck it against a pane of glass. The pane held fast. More vigorously he swung again. The glass shattered. His arm, protected by the sleeve of his jacket, disappeared through the hole as far as the elbow. Glass tinkled to the floor inside the cottage. Foley withdrew his arm, removed the cloth cap from his hand and released the window-catch from inside. As he climbed into the cottage he murmured: " Crime number two."

He stood inside the cottage and took the change from his pocket and counted it. There was over a pound. He placed the coins in three neat piles on the window-ledge, among the splinters of glass. He wished he could also have left money for the butcher who owned the bicycle.

The room occupied almost the entire ground-floor space. It was living-room, dining-room and kitchen combined. He explored. One door led into a light though primitive lavatory, two others opened into cupboards. He walked into the centre of the room and looked about him.

The only other door was that which gave on to the fields. The walls were distempered white, the stone floor was scrubbed and swept. Furnishings were functional; there were no pictures, and an old carpet, dyed brown and reaching over most of the floor in the living space, was one of the few concessions to the soft life. Grouped round the fireplace were a rocking-chair, two worn arm-chairs and a scarred coffee-table. The fireplace, by far the most dominant feature of the room, extended along nearly the whole width of the wall and in the centre was laid with crumpled newspaper and kindling wood. Above the wood and paper hung a large blackened kettle, suspended on an iron chain which was attached to a hook somewhere out of sight inside the chimney. In a corner of the fireplace rested a pile of logs and a square turf-basket filled with turf. At the opposite corner stood an ancient turf-wheel. Foley regarded the turf-wheel blankly.

In the middle of the room were a wooden table and around it four upright chairs with rough wooden frames and seats of coarse string. By the window through which he had climbed was a low bookcase. At the other end of the room was a second table, and against the wall, reaching to the ceiling, a Welsh dresser crowded with crockery. Pots, pans and jars were arrayed on shelves which had been screwed on to the walls. On one shelf was an assortment of oil lamps. Two paraffin stoves stood with assorted buckets, a broom like a witch's besom, and a large tin bath. In one of the wall cupboards was another broom made of twigs tied round a stick, and a shelf of tinned foods.

Foley reconnoitred tentatively, as though afraid of being interrupted. He sought in vain for a tap. Mary had not mentioned water.

He climbed the uncarpeted wooden steps to the upper floor and came upon three small bedrooms, thinly partitioned from each other by unpainted hardboard. The ceilings would have brushed the hair of anyone over six feet tall. Blankets on the iron beds were folded with military exactness and arranged squarely on the mattresses. On each pile of blankets lay a pillow without a pillowcase. Each bedroom contained an upright chair, two had chests of drawers. The chests had been scraped bare of old paint but no fresh paint had been put on. Foley opened one of the drawers and saw sheets and pillowcases, some laundered, others creased as though already slept in. In another drawer lay clothing which resembled poor pickings from a jumble sale. Behind each door were hooks. There were no wardrobes, cupboards, carpets or pictures; there was no bathroom.

Foley walked back along the narrow landing and down

the steps. Each step creaked under his weight. Cleanliness pervaded the cottage. The rooms gave an impression of having been furnished partly with pieces reclaimed from out-houses and junk-rooms, partly by a schoolboy with an average talent for carpentry, and then handed over to an energetic charwoman. The smell was a mixture of carbolic soap and peat.

Foley unbolted both sections of the door, wheeled the bicycle into the cottage and closed and bolted the door. He stood the bicycle against the whitewashed wall. He was hungry again and thirsty but even more he was fatigued. He wanted to lie down on the stone floor where he stood and close his eyes and sleep.

Wearily he dragged himself up the steps. He gathered the blankets from the three bedrooms and shut himself inside the smallest bedroom. He prepared the bed with two blankets to lie on and six to cover him. He stripped off all his clothes, wrapped a blanket tightly round his wet, white exhausted body, and folded a second blanket round the first. He lay down and pulled the six covering blankets up to his chin.

Somewhere outside, over the sea, gulls called. Foley shut his eyes. If they wanted him, he thought, they could come and get him, all of them . . . the whole grinding crew of them, cops, crooks, dragons . . . but so much the better . . . the better . . . if they left it for eight hours . . . nine hours . . . a month. . . .

They came for him in the silence of the night, making no sound on the stairs, entering his room in Indian file, Inspector Sheridan and the Sergeant first, a faceless young detective named Croft, then the baddies, Parker, McCarthy, limping, and Big Nose, whose nose had swelled to such proportions that he carried it like a baby in his arms. Mary waited outside on the landing, too wretched to enter the infested bedroom.

"They made me tell them," she sobbed. "They made me."

Foley sat upright with a jolt and opened his eyes.

Outside, dawn was breaking. The early light crept like an assassin through the uncurtained window. Foley saw his clothes in a squalid heap on the floor. He lay back and closed his eyes. He was sticky and hot. The air he breathed was clammy as though a mist from the sea had percolated into the room. He threw off all but two of the blankets. He looked at his watch but the hands had lodged at nine forty-five and were motionless. Working to focus his thoughts on Mary, he fell asleep. When he awoke again the light was bright and he did not know whether it was morning or afternoon.

The sun shone all day. No one came for him. Foley walked six miles to Balinspittle and six miles back. The only sentences he spoke were routine requests for provisions. No one looked at him twice.

His clothes were still wet and on rising he had hung them over the back of the chair and on the hooks behind the bedroom door. He had dressed instead in a selection borrowed from one of the drawers: corduroy trousers stiff with mud and years, tartan shirt, an enveloping off-white jersey, and roomy shoes which looked as though they had last been used for trench warfare. More than anything, Foley wanted to bath and shave. He wandered round the outside of the cottage and over the fields and back to the cottage in a profitless search for a well. He untied Minton's parcel from the bicycle and put it in the cupboard with the broom and tinned foods.

If he could not wash, at least he could eat. Mary's uncle, or the uncle's wife, or housekeeper, or whoever was in charge of the cottage equipment, had provided everything from coffee and cutlery to matches. Foley chose the kidneys from among the variety of meats in the basket and fried them in a pan on the paraffin stove. After the kidneys he was still hungry so he fried two pork chops and a slab of liver. The only liquid refreshment he could discover was a half-bottle of undiluted orange squash. He drank sparingly from the bottle but the saccharine sweetness interested his palate and he drank again. He would have traded ten bottles of undiluted orange squash for one cup of hot black coffee but there was no water for coffee. He put the bottle to his lips again. When he took the bottle away the squash was gone. He decided he must replace it. He could leave the money but a new bottle would be an excuse to step outside the cottage. A visit to Balinspittle would pass the day. He could either cycle or walk.

He chose to walk. By now, Foley reasoned, the police might be looking not for an American in a hired blue Morris but for an American on an errand-boy's bicycle. The bicycle was his only transport but it might prove more dangerous than useful. The reasoning pleased him. He had cycled enough, he preferred to walk. He transferred his pocket-book from his jacket to his trousers pocket and set out.

The crinkled sea glittered. From the position of the sun, Foley judged that the meal he had eaten had not been breakfast but lunch. He trudged along the side of the road and raised his hand when a solitary farm worker walking on the other side of the road nodded as he passed and said, " Hallo." Traffic barely existed. Foley walked steadily, meditating with mingled fondness and regret on Mary. He should have met her in some saner place and age, he thought. What did they say in the movies? " Things might have been different." An image of Minton, murdered on the carpet of the wrecked hotel room, edged Mary from his thoughts; then Parker and McCarthy swirled in and he summoned back Mary, smiling as he tried to recall the cod of the old woman in the shawleen, looking for turf.

He stared up at the sun and shielded his eyes with his

hand. He was hot in the engulfing sweater. He wondered what the few people he passed must think of the unshaven derelict with the black eye, kitted out like a fisherman but with a paunch and a patched city face which were on familiar terms only with fish served on a plate.

His feet began to ache and he was starting to regret not having cycled when he came to Balinspittle. He entered Malone's Bar and asked for beer. The bar was empty except for the youth behind the counter. The hands of the clock pointed to four thirty-five. Breakfast had been a late lunch.

He bought two packets of potato crisps and a bar of milk chocolate and borrowed a pen from the youth. He set his watch, retired with his food and a pint of beer to a circular table by the window, and took from his pocket-book the picture postcards which he had bought at Cork Airport. Sunset over Killarney was appropriate for Aunt Rhoda.

"An interesting country," he wrote, "which lives up to expectation." The pen remained poised above the card. What next? "Wish you were here?" "You may be amused to know that I have been made a spy and people are trying to kill me?" He swallowed a mouthful of flat tepid beer.

"At present I am near a place called Kinsale and the sun is shining. I have had some interesting adventures. Will tell you about them when I get back. The castle was not a castle but a house. Probably I'll sell it. My love to Uncle Jay and yourself, Willie."

On the back of the card which showed the dame at the spinning-wheel he wrote in similarly non-committal language to Oscar. "See you in the cellar," he concluded, wondering if ever he would see Oscar again. He had two cards left. One for Mr. Hide? Joy would appreciate the other, he thought. He tore the cards in half and walked out into the street. If ever he did see home again he would not resume with

Joy; if she heard no word from him now, the non-resumption would be simpler.

He found the post office and sent the two cards to Aunt Rhoda and Oscar airmail. In a more elaborately stocked shop than the one where he had purchased ice-creams and stale doughnuts, he bought two bottles of milk, bread, butter, jam, a dozen apples, a four-shilling safety-razor, blades, brushless shaving cream and a carrier-bag in which to put them. Then he set out back to the cottage.

The return from Balinspittle was as uneventful as the inward journey. His legs ached before he started. A mile from the cottage he left the road and hiked over the fields, seeking water. He found none, neither a stream nor a pond, and he dared not risk inquiring at one of the two or three cottages which dotted the headland. He noticed a tiny cove at a point where the cliff face had long crumbled away and flattened into the sea. A path led down to the cove across the fields. If he could find no fresh water, he could have seawater.

The cottage was as he had left it. There had been no callers, or if there had they had disturbed nothing. The parcel was in the cupboard. Weary now, he collected two buckets and plodded back across the fields and down to the sandy cove. To fill the buckets with water and not with water and sand, he had to remove his shoes and socks and wade out into the sea. The water was icy. Foley performed an agonised jig, gasping and trying to pretend that the sea's sting was in fact refreshing.

As he hauled himself back to the cottage, much of the water slopped out of the buckets. There remained ample for washing and shaving, rituals he performed slowly, lovingly, after first boiling the water and removing from his face the sticking-plaster. The plaster had become grubby and curled at the edges.

He selected two beef steaks from one of the packages and fried them medium-rare. He drank one of the bottles of milk and placed the other in a half-full bucket of seawater. The day might have been considerably worse, he reflected. He was still undiscovered. To-morrow he would telephone Shannon Airport. Extra flights might have been put on. He would also telephone Mary. Somehow he had to have his passport. Maybe he could alter the name on it. He could try. A magnificent mess he would make of it.

The problem of how to escape from Ireland was as insoluble as ever. He shelved it and from the bookcase chose a dog-eared paperback book of crossword puzzles. Some of the puzzles had been completed, others begun and abandoned. He sat in an arm-chair, the book on his lap, his mind on Shannon Airport and his passport. He rose leaving the book on the chair and climbed up the stairs to bed. The time was eight-thirty but he was ready to sleep.

When he awoke the time was a few minutes past midnight. He lay rigid listening. There were footsteps on the gravel outside the cottage.

Chapter 22

They had taken their time, he thought. One whole day's grace before they had twisted from Mary the information they wanted. Now they had arrived in the night, like secret police, like the machine-men in the Kafka books who came in the small hours and took you away. He held his breath and listened.

Nothing. Stillness. Then a curlew crying from the sea. Again, nothing. Then once more, the footsteps outside, treading, crunching.

A dog? An errant cow? Mary herself? Mary would let

herself in, not wander round the outside of the cottage. Foley scrambled out of bed and felt for the corduroy trousers and the sweater. He pulled them on. He knew the footsteps were the police; flat clodding steps which would have awakened a drugged man. If they were not the police, if they were Parker, McCarthy, so much the worse. With the police there would be a chance to explain. With Parker and McCarthy and Big Nose, he was finished.

Through the bedroom window he saw a moonless, starless sky, and beneath the sky the black unsounding ocean. The crunching on the gravel had ceased. Slowly, Foley turned the handle of the door, opened the door, and stepped out on to the landing. He knew he must take the parcel from the cupboard, fast, before they entered, and hide it. He should have buried it outside or concealed it in the shed, under the turf, but he had wasted the day on fatuous hikes after razor-blades and water and postage stamps. Now it was too late. He thought of the chimney and for an instant the idea seemed sound; but if he was able to think of the chimney, the police would think of it that much sooner. Probably the police took classes in hiding-places. It was their job. They would know of a dozen hiding-places, all superior to the chimney.

A board squeaked under his bare feet. He glanced through the window on the landing and saw two pinpoints of light where a car was parked on the road. One car, unless there were others which had switched off their lights. He wondered whether the police would come for him in just one car. He groped for the top of the steps and with one hand on the wall to guide him started down. Parker and McCarthy and Big Nose would use one car. But so would the police. They had no need of more for the job of arresting a solitary fat man.

He reached the foot of the creaking steps. He stopped and listened. Someone else might even now be inside the cottage, also listening. They could not have failed to hear him descend the steps. The darkness was almost total. Dimly Foley recognised the paler oblong of the windows.

The gravel crunched outside. From the window to his right, the window through which he had originally entered the cottage, a faint scrabbling sound reached his ears. Outlined against the window was the shadow of a man. The shadow moved but remained at the window.

A single bead of sweat started to crawl down Foley's forehead. His eyes were fixed on the shadow. The shadow, he sensed, was returning his gaze. The drop of sweat, tickling like a fly, found an eyebrow and lodged there. Too late to find the cupboard and take the parcel to the chimney, to anywhere. Foley no longer cared about the parcel, only about himself. The shadow shifted again. The window-catch scraped faintly.

For several seconds Foley heard only his own breathing, then the window squeaked open and he felt a breeze on his face. It must be a sea breeze, he thought. At the same moment his nerve broke.

"Come on!" he shouted.

His voice banged like gunfire in the cottage.

"Come on! I'm here! Why are you waiting? Come and get me!"

"Willie, it's me," called an American voice from the window.

Silence. Foley sank slowly on to his haunches, trembling. He sat humped on the bottom step, his bare feet cold on the stone floor.

"Willie," called the voice. "It's okay. It's me, Oscar. It's okay."

They let Mary in at the door and she felt her way to one of the shelves in the kitchen area and took down an ornate oil-lamp with a brass shaft and a mauve, glass shade. When she had lighted the wick she walked to the other end of the room and set down the lamp on the table by the fireplace. She crouched to strike a match and light the fire. Oscar had disappeared.

"You frightened me, shouting," Mary said.

"I frightened myself. Why the window? Why didn't you tell me it was you?"

"We were looking for a way in. My uncle has the key."

The kindling wood crackled. She took turf from the basket and placed it on the fire.

"Why didn't you knock or shout out?" he insisted.

"We would have if we couldn't get in. We weren't even sure you were here. Don't be angry."

"I'm sorry. I don't get any of it. It's not true. What's Oscar doing here? What's happening?"

"He flew to England with his wife. Her father had a stroke. He arrived in Cork this evening and telephoned me, at least he telephoned the house. You must have told him about my father. He found us in the book."

Like Minton. Like he himself after he had fled from Castleferry. Sooner or later everyone phoned the Caseys.

"I forget his wife's name," Mary said.

"Ann."

"Ann, yes."

Oscar returned carrying a bottle of whisky.

"Nobody say a word—not one word," he ordered cheerfully.

"It's good to see you," Foley said.

"Good to see you, Willie. You're looking almost skinny, you must have lost twenty pounds. Not another word. Where are the glasses?"

"Rory broke the last glass," Mary said. "You'll have to use mugs."

Mary brought two mugs from the Welsh dresser. Oscar made her return and bring another for herself. He poured substantial measures of whisky for Foley and himself and a more sober quantity for Mary.

"Is there water?" he asked.

"Seawater," Foley said. "If you like——"

"Not a word," Oscar commanded.

"There's a pump but it's nearly a mile away," Mary said. "William, I'm sorry, I should have——"

"Quiet please," interrupted Oscar. "We'll try it as it is."

The fire blazed higher. Mary unfastened her blue raincoat. Under the coat Foley saw the nurse's uniform.

Oscar manœuvred the rocking-chair closer to the fire and ushered Mary into it. He sat in one of the arm-chairs, Foley in the other. The three sat in a semi-circle sipping whisky and looking into the fire. For several minutes no one spoke. Oscar, a sizzling extravert, believed passionately in the need for calm and self-examination at times of stress. He leaned over with the bottle and sweetened Foley's mug.

"Okay?" he asked.

"Okay. Thanks."

"Ann had a wire from her mother saying her father had suffered a stroke. We dumped the kids with my people and flew to London. Ann said I was to stay home and go fishing but I couldn't let her go off on her own. When we get to Broadstairs the old man is all right. Knocked about a bit, but all right."

Oscar talked almost gaily. He took Foley and Mary into his confidence equally, looking from one to the other as he spoke of his domestic life.

"Everyone who arrives with a wreath he makes sit on the bed and play cribbage for three hours. I remember the first time I met him he asked were my intentions honourable and when I said no he said fine, let's play cribbage. He taught me the lousy game on the spot and took five dollars off me."

"I'm glad he's all right. Ann must have worried."

"She's fine. Now we're over here and down about thirty years' salary on the air fares she says we might as well stay a few weeks. The kids are all right. I remind her that Willie is living it up on his feudal estates across the water and she says go on then, maybe he'll keep you out of trouble, give him my love. So I fly to Cork, get Mary on the phone, hire a car, if you can call it a car, and meet Mary in Bandon. And here we are."

He put a cigarette in his mouth and lit it.

The sight of the cigarette pack with the familiar colour and design brought alive to Foley as though for the first time the fact that Oscar had arrived. Oscar was in Ireland, in the cottage with him, speaking of Ann and the children, and any moment he would relay the latest campus gag, or pass on a message from Joy, or spill some lying gossip about the Dean having absconded with the football scholarship funds. Foley's friendly, secure world of the campus, his one abiding world, was for a moment so eerily, depressingly present that he felt dizzy. He gripped the arm of his chair. It's the whisky, he thought. The campus was in the cottage, but unattainable, probably never to be attained again. Oscar's presence altered nothing.

Unless Oscar could carry the parcel back. Foley dismissed the idea in the same second that it came to him. He saw that as a spy he had one advantage over Oscar and the majority of men; he had no wife or children. He preferred not to dwell on the prospect before Ann and the children if Oscar marched off with the parcel like a marine into a battle and someone with an eye on the same parcel broke his skull, or tucked a knife into him, or whatever it was they usually did.

Foley looked at Mary and felt the blood beating in his chest and behind his eyes. He had never seen her so composed, so gentle. She sat motionless in the rocking-chair with her hands cradled round the mug in her lap. She was leaning slightly forward, looking into the fire, her thoughts her own. The flames cast moving shadows upon her hands and throat and across the regulation coat and uniform. Lying for him, she had probably told her mother she was off visiting one of the wives. The wide mouth was now dark, now illumined, as the shadows jumped and flickered. Once she reached her hand up to the black hair and tucked back a lock which had fallen over her forehead. She turned her head and looked at Foley and gave him a half smile, brief but tender. Foley smiled back. For an instant they looked into each other's eyes. She turned her head again and gazed into the fire, no longer smiling.

"That was good, Ann saying you'd keep me out of trouble," Oscar said. "It seems you've found your own trouble."

"Mary's told you?"

"I did," Mary said.

"I still say you should go to the cops," Oscar said. "I'll go with you. I guarantee we'll straighten this thing out in ten minutes."

"It's not that simple. It's supposed to be a secret but I guess I can tell you. Mary worked it out for herself. Most everyone seems to know. I'm a spy."

Oscar looked at him, uncomprehending.

"A what?"

"Minton recruited me. Then he was killed. I'm working for the C.I.A."

He spoke apologetically. The futility of it all oppressed him. He reached for the bottle by Oscar's feet and poured whisky into his mug. Minton had warned him not to mention that he was an agent, not even to the police. Nuts to Minton. What good had spying done Minton? What good had Minton done as a spy?

"How long have you been a spy?" Oscar was still incredulous.

Foley turned to Mary. "The night I was on the phone at your parents' place and you arrived back from the babies. Two nights ago. We had salmon for supper."

"Salmon?" Oscar said.

"There's a parcel in the cupboard over there, by the

bookcase. I got it from Minton, kind of indirectly. I've got to get it back to the States."

"Says who?" Oscar demanded.

"Well, says the C.I.A."

"Okay. I'll take it back."

"Nothing doing, sorry."

"Why not?"

"Reasons. Just forget it, just please forget it."

"Okay, okay. But the offer stands. Is this parcel so important?"

"I don't know. I think so. They murdered Minton."

Oscar did not speak immediately. He stared into his mug.

"Who knows about this parcel?" he asked.

"Everybody, I guess. Just about everybody."

"You're having quite a vacation."

Foley said nothing.

"The cops have taken your passport."

Foley nodded absently. He had been resigned to that. The wonder was that they had not taken it earlier.

"I could do nothing," Mary said. "It was that Inspector. They took it last night after you'd got away from them, and all your luggage, and the car. They came back furious. The Inspector said you hadn't a hope and he'd have you in a cell before the night was out. He threatened to charge me. I suppose he could have done. He was back this morning, asking questions."

"You should have told him the truth," Foley said.

"Don't be silly."

"I don't know why you're doing all this."

Mary was silent. She turned away and gazed into the fire. The turf glowed red. Oscar lit a new cigarette from the butt of the old.

"You could come back to England with me. You don't need a passport for England."

"I'd thought of that. I don't see that I'd be better off. Don't I need my passport to get out of England."

"I don't know. Maybe. We could find out. You could get a boat to France."

"Or Japan, or Tahiti. It sounds complicated. What about Interpol?"

"Who?"

"Interpol."

"Who the hell's Interpol?"

"I don't know. I've heard about them."

"You seem determined to be back where you started."

"I can't work anything out any more. Every way I seem to come back to the beginning, back to where I'm stuck in Ireland. Always I'm back where I started."

Oscar tipped his shaggy head back and rested it on top of his arm-chair. He wore a black hand-knitted tie and a lightweight suit which Foley had seen many times before.

"Willie," Oscar murmured, "you're really some spy. You of all people. You should never have been let loose from Chicago. I can think of no one less effectively equipped for the job than you—and that's a compliment. The whole business is too screwy. I know it's happening but I don't believe it. I don't believe a word of it."

He paused. Tobacco smoke curled from his nostrils.

"Boy, you've really some memoirs to write," he said.

"Someone else will probably have to write them," Foley said, "along with an epitaph."

For a while no one spoke. Finally, Oscar said to Mary: "You might as well tell him about your phone call."

"No," Mary said.

"What phone call?" Foley asked.

"It was nothing," Mary said. "Some crank."

"It was no crank," Oscar told her sharply. "You said it smelled like a trap and you're right. Whoever it was, it was no crank. He knew something."

"Who did?" Foley demanded impatiently.

"Those pals of yours," Oscar replied. "Parker or whoever he is."

"He phoned this afternoon——" Mary began.

"Parker phoned?"

"I don't know it was Parker. He sounded Irish. He said he'd tried to get me before. In fact my mother took one of the calls but he wanted me; he wouldn't say anything to her and hung up. He told me he could get you to New York on a charter flight from Shannon to-morrow evening. He said I was to tell you he could get you through the Customs with anything you happened to bring along. He'd give the details only to you and if you were interested you were to be at Bunratty Castle to-morrow evening at seven forty-five and ask for Mr. Smith."

"For heaven's sake," Foley said. "Mr. Smith."

"Mr. Smith-Parker is my guess," Oscar said. "Double-barrelled right down to the shotgun he'll be carrying."

"Is Bunratty Castle that tourist place near Shannon?"

"It is," Mary said. "Before he rang off he said, 'Tell Dr. Foley it's Mr. J. Smith—J for Jezebel.'"

"J for Judas," Oscar said. "I'm with Mary. It stinks. They're figuring they might get the parcel if they can reach you through Mary. They want to tempt you into the open with an easy exit out of the country. I can picture the exit. Feet first with shamrocks on the lid. Willie, the best bet is England. There won't be the same heat. We can go to-morrow. Once we're in London—what is it?"

Foley's features were a grimace of concentration. He was tapping his chin with his finger, staring sightlessly at a spot on the carpet, oblivious of the company.

"Seven forty-five," he said softly, as though to himself alone. "Seven forty-five, Jezebel . . . JZB 745. It could be on the level. It could be the way out."

Chapter 23

An hour later Mary said, " I must go."

She stood up and buttoned her coat. The men rose.

" I'll not be long," Oscar said to Foley. " It's thirty or forty miles there and back. Wait up for me, will you?"

" I'll walk you to the car."

Foley was glad to breathe the fresh sea air. Occasionally the smoke from the turf fire had billowed into the room, making his eyes smart. Oscar led the way across the fields towards the two pinpoints of light. Foley and Mary walked a few paces behind. He wanted to hold her hand but was restrained by an unexpected shyness. He kept his hands in the pockets of the old corduroy trousers. A half-mile to the south the lighthouse beacon flashed off and on. The night was very still. The sea was dumb, invisible, but its nearness could be felt.

" I don't want to say good-bye but if this works out to-morrow I shan't see you again."

His voice was husky. She'll put it down to the whisky and maybe she'll be right, he thought. Mary made no reply.

" If it doesn't work out——."

He did not know how to end the sentence. If it did not work out he certainly would not see her again, or anyone ever again.

" It'll be all right," she said. " I'm sure it will."

She seemed to believe what she said, or she was trying hard to believe it. Her voice had no life.

" Will you write to me?" she asked.

"Of course, of course I'll write."

"Don't if you don't want to."

God! Girls had said exactly the same to him before, word for word, ever since high school, exactly the same. "Don't if you don't want to." Girls, women . . . The difference was that before, with others, he had seldom cared.

"I'll write, I promise, and you must write."

They were almost at the car. The keys tinkled in Oscar's hand. Foley felt desolate. Some other age, he thought, it should have been some other age, some other place.

"I'll write to your mother and father," he said. "Please tell them that, that I want to write to them. It's terrible I can't see them to thank them. They've been so wonderful."

"I'll tell them. What will you do about Castleferry?"

"It's yours, Mary, if you'd like it, you have it. A farewell present."

"You're silly."

They halted. The car was a black and shiny Fiat 600. Oscar wrestled with first one key in the lock, then the other. He realised that he had not locked the car and opened the door. He climbed in. They heard him start the engine. Foley took hold of Mary's wrist. They faced one another in the dark.

"Good-bye," Foley said.

She came forward and kissed him on the mouth. Then she hurried away and climbed into the Fiat beside Oscar. Foley heard the car door slam.

"See you," Oscar said through the window.

He switched on the headlights. The car moved forward.

"I'll be here," Foley said.

The Fiat performed a U-turn in the road and over the edge of the field and accelerated away. Foley watched the diminishing rear lights, then he was staring into blackness and they were gone. Behind him the light in the lighthouse switched on, and off . . . on . . . off . . .

He walked back to the cottage and sat in his arm-chair,

looking at the rocking-chair. He wound his watch. At three o'clock he heard a car approaching along the road and stop not far from the cottage. The engine died, minutes passed. Oscar came back into the cottage alone.

The next ten hours or so should settle it one way or another, Foley thought. He lay in his makeshift bed of blankets without sheets and looked through the window at a nondescript sky. The day had dawned, but from the standpoint of weather that was all that could be said. The sky was dead, colourless, like blank paper. He had slept late and awakened to a day without weather. Judging from the stillness, Oscar was yet to wake up. The only sound was of screaming seagulls.

Ten hours to go, maybe something over ten hours. Seven forty-five, Bunratty Castle, Jezebel. Ask for Mr. Jezebel Smith. Speculating on the identity of Mr. Smith, Foley rose and went downstairs wearing a blanket. He preferred to picture Mr. Smith as another American, a ministering C.I.A. angel awaiting him at the castle gates at seven forty-five precisely with fast car, air ticket and some magic diplomatic document, signed and counter-signed by presidents and police chiefs, before which Customs men and lesser police would fall back bowing and tugging their forelocks. He was conscious that Mr. Smith might turn out to be a wholly different kind of animal, a dragon animal. But if so, how were the set of letters and figures to be explained? JZB 745. Minton had supplied this code on a scrap of paper sent through the post. The voice on the telephone had repeated them to Mary. Minton had entrusted him with the Professor's chloriodine formula and was a goody; a dead goody, but presumably a goody. In this unreal world existed few certainties, but logically, if Minton was one of the angels, so was whoever was ready to meet him at Bunratty Castle. Foley knew that events might rip even the most elementary reasoning into rags but the anticipation which stirred in him as he unbolted the two sections of the door was no less real for being irrational. The next ten hours would settle it.

A floorboard creaked upstairs. Foley heard a muffled sneeze. He stood in the cottage doorway wrapped in his blanket and looked out at the day without weather. There was neither shape nor colour to the sky, no wind, no dew on the grass. Anything might happen. The anticipation was in his stomach, stirring, causing him to give a small shiver. Oscar was part of the anticipation, his arrival was a gift worth gold . . . Oscar the ex-marine. He was moral support already and he would be infantry, cavalry and air power in the event of a rough-house. Bodyguard, bouncer, pug. This was not Oscar's war; Foley knew he could not allow Oscar to accompany him into Bunratty Castle any more than he could permit him to take the parcel. He knew even better that Oscar's will was stronger than his own, that he would be there if he chose to be.

The anticipation evaporated. He would never see Mary again. To say he had lost her could not be correct; what had never been possessed could not be lost. But she was gone. There had been impossible unsought moments when he had felt he had discovered her more intimately than anyone he could remember. They had been fleeting moments of eyes meeting, hands touching, but they were the stuff of happiness, and the sole experience in the whole vacation fiasco which made the smallest sense. She was gone. He would not cry or mope or build a goddess out of her memory. He would not write her name again and again on pieces of paper. He was thirty-nine and a spy, in danger, and he had another life a world away in Chicago, if ever he should see Chicago again. But she was gone.

"Hail Caesar!" said Oscar, full of sleep.

He stood on the stairs in pyjamas and slippers. A cigarette burned between his fingers.

"Hi."

"You've gotten skinny."

"I'm not surprised."

"A week back you'd have been, 'Hail Nefo'."

He joined Foley at the door and sniffed the morning.

"Great spying weather," he said.

"Did you sleep?"

"I always sleep."

Oscar dragged at the cigarette and looked out across the empty fields. The only evident mark of the twentieth century was the parked Fiat.

"This place is creepy," Oscar said. "It's not even wide open spaces. It's like being marooned. I think it's that lighthouse does it. Lighthouses are the creepiest places."

"You're a romantic."

"I'm for getting out of here. Where do I plug in my razor?"

"Great gas."

"Who?"

"Gas. You're an ignorant Chicago slob. Gas is Irish for joke—gag, fun, having a wonderful time."

"Is that right?"

"I'm not sure. I think so. You'd better check before you use it."

"You check. I need a shave."

"You're not going to this Bunratty Castle, you know."

"Says who?"

"This is my affair."

"You've got it wrong, buddy. I'm going, you do whatever you want. It's on my itinerary. Friday: arrive Cork, evening at leisure. Saturday: meet the Bunrattys."

"You don't know what you're doing. Think of Ann."

"I think of her. She's okay. She's got the great gas in England."

"That's not right. It should be, 'She's having the great gas'."

"Okay. She's having the great gas."

"That's not it either. Maybe it's: She's gassing it up. No. She's got the gas——?"

"I'm getting cold."

"You can have my razor. There's not even a bathplug here. I've a new blade."

"I bought a razor. They've the wrong current in England."

"There's a drop of seawater in the bucket."

"A drop of seawater is exactly what I'd been looking forward to."

"Mary said a pump was up the road but I've not found it."

"I'll find it."

Oscar threw his cigarette out of the door. He went upstairs and came down again with a bathrobe over his pyjamas and the car keys in his hand. He picked up a bucket and went out to the car. Ten minutes later he was back with fresh water in the bucket.

"You're a blind mathematical goof," he said.

They boiled the water and washed and shaved. The tweed suit was crumpled like a paper bag but it had dried out and Foley put it on. He returned the agricultural clothes to the chest of drawers and rescued his tie from the front of the bicycle, where it had secured the parcel. He wheeled the bicycle outside and leaned it against the wall of the cottage. He could think of nothing else to do with it. He folded the cloth cap and placed it tidily in the basket. He considered putting some banknotes inside the cap but rejected the idea. There was no knowing who would find them; almost certainly not the butcher.

They ate lamb chops which were slightly high and drank a jug of coffee. They washed up, and Foley tidied the cottage. He took the parcel from the cupboard. He still had not seen a key to the cottage, so they bolted the door inside and left by the window with the broken pane, closing it behind them and securing the catch. If someone should come along and open it again there was nothing they could do, but unless a carnival struck camp on the fields or the army arrived for manœuvres, no one seemed likely to come along. The Old Head of Kinsale was as empty as when he had arrived. Oscar took the parcel from Foley and locked it with his suitcase in the boot of the Fiat. They sat in the car, Foley in the passenger-seat. He was content to be a passenger. The anticipation stirred again in his stomach. He wished he had a pipe to smoke. Oscar opened a map and spread it on his knees.

"Which way do we go?" he asked.

"If you go any way but north you're in the sea."

"Do you want to go through Bandon?"

"No."

Oscar examined the map.

"I think we have to," he said.

"All right, if we have to. If they're looking for anything it'll be the bicycle. We should be safe enough in this, this—what did you say it was?"

"Fiat six-hundred."

Foley nodded vaguely.

"Here it is," Oscar said, tracing a finger over the map. "Kinsale, Cork, Mallow—where did you say Bunratty was?"

"Shannon."

"Where's Shannon?"

"God! Above Limerick."

"I've got it. Fine . . . Mallow, Limerick, Bunratty. A hundred miles, maybe a hundred and ten."

He partially folded the map and thrust it between the side of his seat and the door. He switched on the engine and lit a cigarette.

"Can't we skip out Cork?" Foley asked.

"We could but we're not going to. We're not skipping out anywhere else. If we start avoiding every place on the map we'll finish up back here, wherever this is. You just sit quiet and leave everything to Oscar."

" Could I have a cigarette?"

" Sure." Oscar shook one from the pack and passed it to Foley. " Are you comfortable? Cushions?"

" Nuts."

" Great gas. Let's go."

They drove off. The sky had acquired a smoky tint.

" It's a soft day," Foley said.

" Any more of that Irish poetry and you walk."

" I've already walked this road. And cycled it."

" How about donkey?"

" It would only have been a matter of time."

When they reached Balinspittle the weather came to a decision. Drizzle drifted lightly down. A signpost pointed left to Bandon, right to Kinsale. Half-way to Kinsale they crossed a long concrete bridge over a broad estuary. The tide was out and the drizzle floated greyly on to the mud. In Kinsale harbour were anchored a score of small boats, their gaudy colours deadened by the rain. Maybe the rain was an omen, Foley thought. It had rained the day he arrived in Ireland, maybe the same rain would see him safely out again. His stomach contracted nervously. He shivered. He did not believe it would be as simple as that.

They passed Cork Airport and drove without incident through Cork and on to the twisting open road to Mallow. They stopped in Mallow for beer and sandwiches. Foley bought another new pipe, tobacco and matches. He felt fatalistic about his purchases. If the evening went well he soon would be smoking the pipe aboard a charter flight to home; if badly, he might as well enjoy what he could, while he could. He puffed at the pipe while Oscar, swearing, inched the car round a patrol of cows. The rain stopped, started again, and continued tediously to turn off then on again, never heavy, never anything but dreary. The countryside was a dismal grey-green. The birds had flown into hiding.

"It's a helluva country," Oscar said.

Foley could only agree, but he said nothing. He was sleepy with the monotony of the road and the hypnotic ticking of the windscreen wipers. Oscar sang the first lines of "Chicago." He forgot the words and filled in with whistling.

They sang together. "By the Light of the Silvery Moon," "I'm Forever Blowing Bubbles," and "Alexander's Ragtime Band." Oscar started to sing, "Mary's a Grand Old Name." He stopped.

"She's a good girl," he said. "Tell her to get a job in the States."

"It's too late," Foley said. "It wouldn't have made any difference."

They reached Limerick at five o'clock and drew up outside The Brazen Head in O'Connell Street. They walked downstairs to the cocktail bar to kill time before the last lap.

The last lap . . . the Last Post. They sighted Bunratty Castle over the tops of the trees. Foley sang "The Last Roundup" loudly.

"Shut up," Oscar growled.

Foley was calculatedly awash with Irish coffee which had gone to his head and was on the point of overturning his stomach. Oscar, after two glasses of stout and five bottles of beer, was in an uncertain temper. He drove savagely, impatient to have done with whatever lay ahead. He was wholly in the dark over what to expect but sober enough to realise that an intoxicated Foley doubled his own responsibility. He did not blame his friend. Maybe in Foley's position he would have done the same. The fact remained that the condition of Foley made his own job even more that of nursemaid.

Bunratty, a huge tower of stone, was on the roadside at their right. The four sheer walls were slitted with windows only inches wide. From embattled turrets flew the Irish Tricolour and the flag of Munster; the gold crowns of the three kings of Munster were specks against a blue background; the background to the flags was a slate sky. Even in rain the castle was magnificent, a tourist's treasure. The fifteenth-century mound of feudal, impregnable stone had been restored by Tourist Board hands which were loving and simultaneously open for the visitor's fee.

Oscar swung the Fiat across the road and into the forecourt. He parked behind a motor coach. From loudspeakers high in the castle walls swirled the keening of bagpipes.

"Are you okay?" Oscar asked.

He switched off the engine.

"Yes."

"Sure you can walk?"

"I can walk. Let's get it over."

Probably he's not turned up, whoever he is, Foley thought. Probably the whole thing was an elaborate hoax, or they had the date wrong.

Foley did not feel that the date was wrong, or the hour. The time was seven-forty. Something was going to happen. Now that the time had come he could not make out whether he was relieved or terrified. Mainly he was aware that he had drunk too much and not enough. The turmoil in his belly was Irish Coffee and fear.

They stepped out of the car into the rain and saw a sign saying "Entrance" which pointed round the side of the castle wall. They walked across the forecourt, heads bowed into the rain. The last car parked against the castle wall was the fawn saloon.

Foley recognised the car instantly but continued walking, saying nothing until he was close enough to the car to read the registration plate: JZB 745. He halted and touched Oscar's arm.

"This is Mr. Smith," he said.

Foley walked closer to the car, Oscar following. Big Nose was in the driving-seat, alone. He wound down his window and inclined his head into the opening, watching the Americans approach. They stopped at the window.

"I'm glad you got my message," Big Nose said. "You'd better introduce me to your friend. Come inside, both of you. You'll get soaked out there."

Chapter 24

Foley sat in the back and delved in his pockets for his pipe. Oscar sat beside Big Nose. Big Nose swivelled sideways in his seat and leaned his back against the door. He wore a raincoat. Tiny red veins criss-crossed the marrow nose.

"Introduce us," he repeated.

"Friend of mine," Foley mumbled from the back.

"How much does he know?"

"As much as I do."

"Was that advisable?"

"Who cares what's advisable?"

"I'd have thought you should."

Foley said nothing. He tried to light his pipe, striking match after match and dropping them on the floor by his feet. Oscar kept his eyes on Big Nose. He came directly to the point.

"Are you getting him out of Ireland?" Oscar asked.

Big Nose looked steadily at Oscar. He gave a small shrug. "There's a charter flight at eleven for New York," he said. "He'll be on it."

"I'm glad—for your sake."

"You're very protective."

"It's been a little one-sided up to now. How do we know we can trust you?"

"I worked with Minton," Big Nose said. "In fact I recruited him four years ago. It was his idea to pass the Professor's formula to your friend when Shamrock became wise to him. Getting it to me would have been too dangerous. He sent my registration number as a precaution. It's as well he did."

Foley discovered that there was no tobacco in his pipe. He said to Big Nose: "Am I really going to get away?"

"Do you have the parcel?"

"Yes."

"You'll be met at Kennedy Airport."

"Can anything go wrong?"

"I don't see why it should."

Foley began to feel a warm glow of relief, almost of triumph. "Before we say good-bye," he said, "are we allowed to know just who you are?"

"It would be better if you didn't."

"You're a double-agent."

"Am I? You see too many films."

"Like microfilms, for instance."

"Like the cloak-and-dagger stuff."

"That's good, that's pretty good, coming from you. What about all these stupid codes? JZB——"

"Why stupid? You're here."

"Hokum."

"Call it what you like."

"What about that first time on the road to Bandon? You were 'Mr. Casey' and you happened to have the key to Castleferry. Parker and McCarthy just happened to be at

Castleferry at the same time. That was some coincidence. They beat me up."

"That was too bad. It couldn't be helped. I'd no choice."

"I'm sorry you'd no choice. If anyone asked me, I'd have guessed it was your idea."

"It was. I knew they'd get nothing from you but they had to be allowed to try. Minton already had the microfilm which you brought over for them——"

"For Parker and McCarthy?"

"For Shamrock—that's the organisation in Ireland, Parker and McCarthy, Kurt, myself. There may be others I don't know about. No one knows quite how far the ripples spread in this sort of set-up. Kurt's the guiding light. He manages the Erin Hotel. He's half a million connections on the far side of the Berlin Wall. I'd not be surprised if he personally let Parker and McCarthy into your room that first night."

"I remember him. Minton pointed him out when we were in the bar."

"Well, you're welcome to him. He was on to Minton, though we didn't know it until it was almost too late."

"I'd have said it was too late for Minton."

"Minton knew the risks. I was there when it happened."

"You did nothing?"

"What would you suggest?"

Foley looked away in disgust. It was not for him to know what to suggest, not in this jungle.

"Kurt looks after this end and takes a professional interest in guests sent to the Erin by the Thomas Hide Travel Bureau. His interest is more particularly the plastic folders the guests bring with them. Everything goes sweetly. Then he has to get a Travel-Wide tourist who assaults and ravages his folder and for all we know tosses the vital part out of the airplane into the sea. Bad deal for Shamrock."

"Bad deal for Foley," Foley said.

"You may not know it but removing that microfilm was the best day's work you ever did. We've got the chloriodine."

"So has your Shamrock. They've got Professor Holstein."

"They've had Holstein all along. We could do nothing about that. When Holstein came to Ireland he was disillusioned with the States and ripe for an affair with communism. Shamrock was set up in the first place to work on him. Holstein wasn't kidnapped. He came like a lamb."

Foley was suddenly tired of it all. He had heard enough. He wanted to be in the air, on his charter flight, away from it all, like the overworked businessman in the travel posters. He put his pipe back in his pocket, wound down the window and threw the empty matchbox out into the rain. The floor was littered with used matches.

"We've three hours," Big Nose said. "I've two places for the banquet inside—it starts in a minute. I'd thought Foley and I would eat together, but you've brought your friend."

"What are you talking about?" Oscar demanded.

"Every evening there's a tourist banquet in Bunratty Castle. Medieval style. I've only the two tickets. You can have them if you like."

"What do you do—take the parcel?"

"Can't you understand anything?" Big Nose spoke angrily. "All I want is Foley to get the parcel back to the States—fast. Take it into the banquet if it makes you happier. Sit on it."

"We may do that."

Oscar and Foley exchanged glances. Big Nose held out the tickets. Foley accepted them.

"I'll be here," Big Nose said. "Right here. We leave at ten-thirty."

Foley and Oscar stepped out of the car. Before Foley shut his door, Big Nose called after him: "Your pal Hide was picked up at his office yesterday. You'll hear no more of him, except for what you read of the trial."

"Maybe I'll have to be at the trial."

"That's right, you will. They've also picked up Dempster and two others. Quite a coup."

"Why don't they pick up Kurt, and Parker and McCarthy? Do the Irish leave everything until next year?"

"They'll get them when it's time. This thing isn't over yet."

"It's over for me," Foley answered, slamming the door.

He had never been more wrong.

A youth dressed in silks and velvets greeted them at the foot of a flight of wooden steps which led up into the castle. He asked Foley if he would care to deposit the parcel. Foley said he would hold on to it himself. Polished remnants of cannon decorated the ground as though put out for collection by a scrap-dealer. Through the door at the top of the steps sounded a hubbub of talking and laughter.

They followed the youth up the steps and into the castle. The unseen din was loud and merry. Cooking smells sidled through a half-open door to their left. Opposite the door, on the other side of the narrow entrance hall, was an arched opening in the wall, and the first steps on an ancient spiral stairway. The youth led Foley and Oscar over the worn stone flags into the banqueting hall. A hundred tourists with square white napkins round their necks were seated at refectory tables. Some who were not sitting were crouching with cine-cameras, or kneeling on the benches and pointing their cameras at their wives, or standing back from the tables and raking the hall with cameras as though with machine-guns. The noise was like a Rotary celebration on guest night. Paper hats and streamers were absent, but on the walls were Spanish and Cromwellian helmets, breastplates and swords, faded tapestries. The tables were lit with fat candles a foot long and laid with platters and pottery drinking vessels. The light from the candles threw shadows over the armour and the expectant faces of the banqueters, almost all of them American. A fireplace as wide as half a house occupied one wall, and aimlessly padding up and down in front of the hearth was an Irish Wolfhound, a great grey whiskery beast, supremely feudal, ravenous as a marching army and tame as a canary.

"You'll be here," the youth said, ushering the late arrivals into the only obviously spare bench space.

The bench was at a table near the entrance through which they had arrived and in the direct line of a tempestuous draught. They sat down, Foley with the parcel on the floor between his knees, and tied their napkins under their chins. Next to Foley was a blonde red-lipped girl of high-school age.

"Hi there!" she greeted Foley. "Isn't this swinging?"

A serving maid in medieval costume leaned low between Foley and Oscar. "Did you have the mead, sir?" she asked.

"We just got here," Oscar said.

"This is the swingingest," babbled the high-school girl. Any moment she would ask Foley if he came here often.

"I'll bring you your mead," the serving wench said. "Everyone else had their mead in the reception hall. I'll get yours now."

"I don't know what mead is," Oscar said to Foley, "but maybe you'd better go steady on it."

"We came to the lunch banquet as well," high-school announced.

"What's this mead?" Oscar muttered.

Bowls of soup were set in front of them. Foley reached across the table and picked up a menu but the words were all foreign to him. He dipped his spoon into the hot murky liquid. The high-school girl drank her soup as though frightened that it might be snatched from her if she did not finish it quickly. At the far end of the hall a colleen in a red and black velvet costume started to pluck a harp, her ear bent close to the strings, but the banqueting roar was too persistent for anyone but the girl herself to know whether she was playing the instrument or tuning it. The serving maid arrived behind Foley and Oscar with two vases of amber liquid.

"Now, sir, your mead."

"Thanks."

"There'll be spiced claret round immediately."

"Good."

Foley found the sweet, slightly cloying taste of the mead to his liking. He swallowed a long, unrepentant draught. Oscar slid his own vase in front of Foley.

"It's all yours," Oscar said. "I'm a spiced claret man myself, I hope. If I'm not, don't worry, live it up, I'll carry you on to the plane."

Foley pressed his knees against the sides of the parcel. Costumed young men and maids were arriving from the kitchens with smoking trays of spare ribs. Foley was thirsty but not hungry. Aided by whatever intoxicants might be set before him, he was ready to enter into the banquet's high-powered tourist spirit. He looked curiously round the banqueting hall.

His bespectacled eyes blinked as they lighted on the faces of two diners whom he had never imagined as tourists. On the opposite side of the next table, facing him, watching him, hemmed in by uproarious husbands and wives, sat Parker and McCarthy.

They had napkins round their necks. Tweedledum and Tweedledee, Foley thought, with razors. He started to tremble, fighting to keep down the vomit which rose in his throat.

"That bastard Big Nose," he whispered.

He touched Oscar's arm.

"Parker and McCarthy," he said.

"What about them?"

"They're here."

"What?"

"Over there, at that table."

"Where? No—wait, have they seen you?"

"They're looking straight at me. They probably saw us come in. What do we do?"

"Which are they? Show me which they are."

"What shall I do—wave?"

"Shut up. Which are they?"

"You see that helmet—by the girl with the tray; under the helmet, over to the right, next to the woman with red hair."

"The man with the bald head."

"Right. McCarthy's on his right, looking at us. Do I ask them to join us?"

"Be quiet. Let me think."

"Big Nose knew about this."

"You're telling me. We've been taken for the biggest boobies of the year, the two of us, two prize, lousy boobies."

"I'm scared, Oscar."

"We're as many as they are."

"What about Big Nose? Look—they're going!"

"Quick! Get out first!"

Foley did not know whether Oscar intended that they should escape from Parker and McCarthy and run for it, or catch them and fight it out. He did not stop to ask. Oscar was already scrambling over the bench. Foley picked up his parcel and followed, accidentally hacking the knee of the high-school girl as he clambered away from the table.

A youth carrying a dish heaped with spare ribs side-stepped as Oscar darted for the door. He failed to side-step a second time and collided head-on with Foley. They fell together on to the ground amid a shower of hot, dripping spare ribs. The hubbub faded as heads turned towards the mêlée on the stone slabs of the banqueting hall. Oscar hurried back to Foley and pulled him on to his feet. When they reached the door, Parker and McCarthy had already left.

Oscar and Foley went out into the narrow entrance hall. Foley jerked the door shut behind him. Facing them at the other end of the hall, at the head of the stairs which led down from the castle, stood McCarthy. He was alone. He fell into a crouch, his eyes glittering. Oscar moved in front of Foley and took a step towards the tensed figure at the end of the hall. A second step. No one spoke. McCarthy watched like an animal, motionless. At his back the rain slanted down. Oscar aped a similar crouch as he advanced.

"Stay where you are!" barked Parker.

He appeared in the arched opening at the foot of the spiral stairway. In his hand he held a gun. Foley stood immobile, hugging the parcel. Oscar turned, and as he did so McCarthy sprang forward and hit him on the side of the face. Oscar sprawled over the floor at Foley's feet.

"Get up here—fast!" Parker commanded. He gestured with his head at the spiral stairway.

Foley obeyed, hurrying past Parker up the stairs. Four stairs up he stopped and looked back. McCarthy had grasped Oscar's arm and was dragging him into the opening, on to the steps. He kicked Oscar in the ribs. "Get up," he snarled.

"You—keep going," Parker commanded, turning the gun on Foley.

Oscar came unexpectedly to life and with his free hand reached out, gripped Parker's ankle, and twisted. Parker grunted and came down on top of him. McCarthy started punching Oscar on the head.

"Get out of it, man!" Oscar shouted up the steps.

When would someone appear from the kitchen, or the banqueting hall? Foley watched the three men fighting like dogs in an inextricable tangle on the steps. He heard

Oscar gasp and saw his body slacken and go limp. McCarthy, panting, looked up at Foley and started to mount the stairway. Foley turned and lumbered upwards.

After only half a dozen steps his heart was thumping. The stairs spiralled from left to right. They were steep and narrow with a rope handrail attached to the wall on the left. Foley wanted to pull himself up by the handrail but his arms hugged the parcel and he could climb only with his feet, falling on his elbows, crushing the parcel under his weight, scraping his shins and knees. Close behind, mounting closer, he heard McCarthy's clicking shoes.

He arrived on a landing and glanced through an open doorway into a vast high-roofed hall hung with Flemish tapestries and furnished at the far end with a table and throne of oak. No hiding-place presented itself. The clicking shoes were behind him. Foley lurched across the landing and renewed the haul up the spiral stairway. He climbed gasping, his mouth open like a purse. He tried carrying the parcel on his shoulder. The napkin over his chest bore a wide grey smudge from where he had slipped on the steps. He did not know how far the steps wound upwards but he knew they would last longer than his strength. Clutching fingers brushed the back of his leg. He jumped up the next three steps, and turned round. McCarthy's head and shoulders swung into view round the central column. Foley raised his foot to kick. McCarthy froze, his head level with the poised foot, hands lifted defensively. He watched the foot, his hands close to his head. Foley watched the hands. If he kicked, he might send McCarthy backward down the stairway; or McCarthy might grab the foot.

Foley's nerve failed. He jabbed with his foot and in the same movement withdrew it, turned and stumbled higher up the steps.

He found himself on a second landing. He knew he could

run no farther. His body was water. An arm encircled his neck from behind and he began to choke.

He was propelled choking across the landing and through a doorway into a room. A sign near the doorway announced that the room was the Earl's Bedchamber. In the bedchamber were Kurt, a thin, stooping man whom Foley had never seen, and Professor Holstein.

Chapter 25

Oscar came into the bedchamber a few moments later. A purple bruise reached from his temple to his cheek. Parker held the gun in his back.

Kurt walked up to Foley and took hold of the parcel. His blond hôtelier's hair was wavy, meticulously shampooed and set. Foley stepped back, hugging the crushed, torn parcel to his chest. The two men eyed each other over the top of the parcel, one embracing it like a lover, the other with his hands gripping its sides, trying to pull it free. Kurt suddenly released his hold, humiliated before the many onlooking eyes to be so deprived. He punched Foley in the face. Foley fell backwards on the floor, still holding the parcel. The hotel manager lifted his foot and trod carefully, deliberately on Foley's arm. Foley squirmed noiselessly on the floor like an insect plagued by a boy. Kurt trod harder. Finally Foley gave a small groan and released his grip on the parcel. As Kurt stooped to take it from him, Oscar moved forward.

"Don't try it!" Parker snapped.

He held the muzzle of his gun close to Oscar's ear. Oscar stood still.

"Fire that thing and you'll have the whole castle up here."

"Unlikely," Parker said. "The castle closes at seven-thirty except for the banquet. We're on our own. They make so much noise downstairs they can't even hear themselves."

"Go ahead then, fire."

"Don't make me."

"Stay out of it, Oscar," Foley breathed from the floor.

Foley sat up on the stone slabs and adjusted his glasses. A squad of gnomes with pickaxes were at work inside his skull, trying to hew their way out.

"Oscar, is it?" Parker queried. "I don't know who you are, Oscar, but you should have stayed at home. Get over against the wall, by your chum."

Oscar walked to the wall. Foley remained sitting, nursing his ruined face. Parker held the gun on them. On the wall above their heads hung a painting six feet square of Adam and Eve. Against the opposite wall was the earl's four-poster bed. Ireland was alive with four-posters, Foley thought. They never mentioned it in the brochures. This one was the prize. A rich red canopy adorned the top of the elaborately carved deal posts. The gross weight would be that of half a battleship. They slept well in those days. Beside this Bunratty bed, the one at Castleferry was a cradle.

"You've got your stinking parcel—now what?" Foley said.

He looked up at Kurt, standing over him with the parcel under his arm, and from Kurt to Parker, and the gun. Foley was more frightened than ever before. He neither knew nor wanted to know what kind of gun it was. It was silvery and small, similar in shape to guns he had seen in movies, crime movies and cops-and-robbers movies, not the westerns with their notched, long-barrelled Colts. Though he tried to convince himself that the gun was really a toy and the brooding silence of the bedchamber a part of a game, a party game of spies and guns which would end with a bottle of bourbon for the winner and a forfeit for the loser, he found himself shaking uncontrollably.

"Now you can shut your mouth," Kurt answered. "Now you can be killed, both of you."

Foley started to stand up but Kurt settled a foot in the centre of the table napkin and thrust him back on to the floor. He looked from Kurt back to the gun in Parker's hand. Would the gun hurt more than the punching? he wondered. Would it hurt more than the running and sweating and weeping and the whole physical bag of tricks he had suffered since coming to Ireland? He looked away from the gun and saw McCarthy, polo-sweatered, on guard in the doorway. By the four-poster stood the Professor and the stooping stranger, unspeaking, watchful. He caught the Professor's eye.

"I want to go now," Dr. Holstein croaked.

Everyone looked at him. He was nervous. His tobacco-stained fingers fidgeted with his tie.

"I didn't want all this," he said. "It's time to go. I'll miss the flight."

In German the stooping man told him: "We've plenty of time."

"Be silent," Kurt ordered. "Parker, give me the gun."

Parker did not move. He said: "The Professor's right, it's time to go."

"We're going. Give me the gun."

Still Parker did not move. Foley sensed an air of indecision among the members of Shamrock. The occasion must be the handing-over of the Professor to the stooping German, he reasoned. Somewhere an aircraft was due, or waiting, presumably at Shannon. The arrival of Minton's recruit and his shaggy friend was a brutal complication. They had not been expected, Foley realised. The parcel was a windfall, an unearned, unbelievable bonus, but Oscar and himself were a problem for which Shamrock had not prepared. Whatever game Big Nose had played, Shamrock had no more expected this encounter than had Oscar and himself.

Foley was not certain but he guessed that Parker would be reluctant to use the gun. Parker was squeamish, and Kurt clearly knew it. The eyes of the hotel manager were without expression. Foley watched in fascination, witness to a silent war of wills. Kurt was not squeamish. The blond beast from the Erin was as squeamish as McCarthy, standing in the doorway like a heavyweight listening for the bell. Foley held his breath. He could hear Oscar's breathing close above him. He knew he would die in Ireland if Kurt got the gun. Oscar would die too.

Foley broke the silence. "What's the man with the big nose up to?" he heard himself say. "We just left him."

Foley broke the silence but not the tension. The air became electric. Whatever he had said had gone home.

"I told you!" McCarthy shouted from the doorway.

"Silence!" Kurt hissed. "It's too late now. Parker— the gun!"

Parker hesitated only for a second. As he stepped obediently towards Kurt, holding out the gun, a distant voice shouted: "Foley! Dr. Foley!"

The men in the earl's bedchamber were rigid, listening.

The voice came from below, from the spiral stairway. "Dr. Foley!"

The voice was nearer, louder, echoing up the stairway.

Foley opened his mouth to shout back but Kurt was already barking: "Watch the door! Get the Professor over there—behind the bed!"

Suddenly, as though set in motion by a switch, everyone was moving.

Kurt dropped the parcel and reached out for the gun.

Before he could seize it, Oscar flung himself on Parker. The gun exploded. For an instant everyone was still again, shocked into ungainly and contorted postures. Then they were fighting. Oscar and Parker were rolling on the floor. In the doorway, McCarthy and Sergeant Burke had their hands at each other's throats. The room was filled with struggling men. Foley shrank back against the wall. The explosion from the little silvery gun had burst against his eardrums with a violence which so deafened him that the scene on which he gazed resembled the last convulsive reel of a silent film.

He saw the gun spin across the floor and under the bed. He climbed to his feet, dodged behind Kurt and made for the bed. Around him men punched and wrestled, and he glimpsed Inspector Sheridan, in a raincoat, grappling near the doorway with the stooping German. Someone banged hard into his side and he was on the floor again, on his knees. He found himself against a pair of legs. He stretched his arms round the legs and pulled. Professor Holstein arrived squawking on top of him, heavy as a chicken. Foley struck out and hit something soft. The Professor rolled aside. A uniformed guard stumbled over him. Foley lay full length on his belly, his hands protectively over his head. Someone screamed as though from a long way off. Sergeant Burke was sitting on the floor with his mouth open, leaning forward and swaying, holding his stomach. Oscar and the Inspector struggled to hold Kurt. McCarthy was on his knees by the four-poster bed, groping on the floor. An instant later the bully-boy was on his feet, his eyes gleaming, silver glinting in his fist. The gun exploded a second time.

Foley closed his eyes in horror, opened them, and saw Oscar's back. Oscar had one hand round the gun in McCarthy's fist. The other hand, flat and open as a board, sliced down through the air. Oscar's knee jack-knifed up into McCarthy's groin and simultaneously the hand sliced down again. McCarthy dropped to the ground, the colour gone from his face, his eyes round and empty as two crystal balls.

"Watch Parker!" Foley shouted.

He could not hear his own voice. His ears sang like high-tension wires. If anyone heard, they paid no attention. Parker was on his own, edging towards the door.

Foley clambered unsteadily to his feet. He reached the door at the same time as Parker and grabbed his arm. They fought together in the doorway and out on to the landing. Parker was not the Shamrock strong-man but he was fitter than Foley. A blow which fell on the side of Foley's head knocked off his glasses and sent him careering backwards towards the top of the stairway. But he blocked the stairway with his bulk. Parker had nowhere to go but back into the bedchamber, or up.

He went up. Foley stumbled blindly after, shouting and hearing nothing. They climbed up and up, Parker scrambling ahead, extending the gap, Foley fumbling for each step. He smelled clean air and rain, and recognised the castle battlements through an opening on his left; but Parker was continuing up the next stairway, and Foley followed.

One after the other, at the end of a score of steps, Parker and Foley emerged into an open turret at the top of Bunratty Castle. The turret was an untenanted area of about ten yards by six, walled by a restored battlement. Ten steps led from a corner into a final, topmost turret, a tiny watchtower, also enclosed by four crenellated walls. From this turret drooped the blue flag of Munster, sodden in the driving rain. The stretching landscape was lost in the downpour. Far below, cars on the Limerick-Shannon road were the size of pin-boxes. A wide mud-coloured tributary of the Shannon crept past the south side of the castle.

Parker turned and lifted his fists.

"Get out," he rasped. "Get out."

The words were distant, Parker six feet away. Foley took a step forward. Parker stepped back.

"They'll come for you," Foley said.

"Get out—leave me alone!"

The voice grated with panic and fear. Intently they watched each other. Both were frightened, waiting to see what the other would do. Without his glasses, Foley could see Parker only dimly. The rain drenched them. On Parker's bald head the raindrops bounced and splashed like soft, watery bullets.

"Please go away."

A pleading note entered Parker's voice. Foley took another step forward. Parker spun round, darted to the corner of the turret and started to climb the steps up to the last pinnacle of Bunratty Castle. Foley clambered after. The steps were of wood, recently constructed. They had been built against the battlement and the open side was without a handrail of any kind.

Foley could see almost nothing. He reached the top of the steps and sensed rather than saw Parker above him. He reached out at the shape in front and heard Parker shouting. Fists or feet, he could not tell which, began to bludgeon his head and shoulders. A hand found his ear and pain scorched the side of his head. He fought blindly forward and hit Parker on the head. Parker slipped on the wet stone but was up in an instant. With arms locked round each other's necks they swung skidding and panting across the watchtower, each searching for a supremacy which they did not know how to win. Foley felt the battlement against his back. Parker seemed to be trying to lift him. There sounded shouts and running footsteps in the turret. They had arrived in time.

Still he was being forced back. He could feel Parker's breath in his eyes. They would have to hurry. His hands clutched the air. He saw only a blur of grey rain. Was this how it was to die in Ireland?

The shouts were on top of him but he was falling now ... falling fast ... faster ... there was only silence, and falling....

Parker gave no further trouble. Sergeant Burke snapped handcuffs on to his wrists and Guard Croft led him down the spiral stairway, past the earl's bedchamber, past the gently roaring banqueting hall, and down the steps from the castle. In the guard van, Parker found Kurt and the stooping German, both handcuffed. Dr. Holstein was taken to a garda car; he was not handcuffed, but two silent guards sat on either side of him on the back seat. McCarthy was dead, his neck broken. Someone took his embroidered red counterpane from the four-poster bed and draped it over his body.

Among the banqueters was a doctor from Minneapolis who willingly relinquished his plate of unfamiliar syllabub to climb the stairway to the summit of Bunratty Castle. He diagnosed a broken leg and concussion and demanded a stretcher.

Foley lay in a heap at the foot of the wooden steps leading from the watchtower down to the turret. They carried him out of the rain and laid him on the stone floor inside the entrance to the turret. Inspector Sheridan took off his raincoat, folded it and placed it beneath Foley's head. Foley opened his eyes, then closed them.

" What's the rest of the damage?" Oscar asked.

" Only McCarthy," the Inspector said.

He looked steadily at the American, waiting for a reply. Oscar remained silent.

" Otherwise nothing," the Inspector said. " I heard someone say there was a bullet-hole in Adam and Eve but I'm not going to lose sleep over that."

A guard reached the top of the stairs holding the crushed parcel and handed it to the Inspector. Inspector Sheridan pulled off the string and tattered brown paper. He opened the two cardboard boxes. Both were filled with old newspapers and magazines: the *Kerryman, Evening Echo, Cork Examiner . . . Life.*

"This is what Willie's been lugging around?" Oscar asked.

"This is what Minton passed him. People like Minton don't hand important papers to people like Dr. Foley—though they could do a great deal worse. Minton posted the formula to himself at Shannon Airport."

Oscar touched his mouth. The lips were swollen from the encounter with McCarthy.

"Okay," he said. "Where is it?"

"At the moment it's at Shannon. It belongs to the Irish Government. The agent Dr. Foley calls Big Nose arrived a few minutes ago to pick it up and fly out. Airport Security have them both."

"How did you know Big Nose would be at the airport?"

"We didn't. We hadn't the least idea. If we expected anyone it was Dr. Foley. I alerted the airport immediately Miss Casey told us he was supposed to be catching a charter flight."

"So how did you know about Big Nose?"

"Every garda in the country has had his description since the day he directed your pal to Castleferry. I've not met him yet but I gather he's not too difficult to identify. He was sitting in the departure lounge with a briefcase and a parcel addressed to one Phil Minton."

"Was there ever a charter flight for Willie?"

"No. There was a charter flight for New York but it was at nine and it was for Big Nose. The only other flight out which we were interested in was for Stockholm at nine-thirty. The Professor was supposed to have been on that one."

Oscar shook out a cigarette and offered another to the Inspector. The Inspector accepted.

"Minton and Big Nose were together in this," the Inspector said, "though it's my guess that Big Nose was inclined to work wherever the money was best. They both in turn used Dr. Foley as a decoy when Shamrock put the heat on them. Minton never made it. He'd about three hours to slip from under Shamrock, get to the airport and pick up the parcel. He brought in Dr. Foley as a diversion. If Foley had opened the parcel it didn't matter—Minton had expected to be out of the country by that time."

"Big Nose?"

"Big Nose was to take over from Minton if anything went wrong. But these Shamrock people were beginning to suspect they'd a bad apple in their barrel and Big Nose was scared. He arranged to get out to-night with the formula. Dropping Dr. Foley into their laps was the same diversionary technique Minton had used."

"Nice guy."

The Inspector shrugged. "That's the way of it. He'll not spend so much as a day in gaol. There'll be words between Dublin and Washington and we'll be told to let him go. We've nothing to charge him with except possession of stolen property."

Oscar said: "I thought Ireland and America were on the same side. If this chloriodine jazz belongs here, what's Washington doing trying to grab it?"

"Don't ask me. That's politics. They'll iron out something. We'll probably get the prestige and you'll get the big contracts to manufacture the stuff."

If the C.I.A. hadn't stepped in, chloriodine would now be in East Berlin, or Moscow, or wherever, the Inspector added to himself. There was no point in saying as much to Foley's friend. There was no percentage in admitting that Irish security had been whimsical, that he himself had been left almost wholly in the dark about the importance of the Marine Biology Station at Caherdaniel.

Sergeant Burke appeared at the head of the stairway

followed by Mr. Casey and Mary. The Sergeant held a whispered conversation with Inspector Sheridan. The Inspector nodded and saluted the father and daughter.

"We're waiting for the ambulance," the Inspector said. "He'll be all right."

Mary knelt beside Foley. Mr. Casey hovered in the background, twisting his hat round and round between his fingers.

"She told you where we were," Oscar said.

"It's as well she did," the Inspector said. "She had to have a little encouragement. Not too much. She was nervous."

Oscar dropped his cigarette on the ground and crushed it with his heel. He looked down at his friend. Foley had opened his eyes again. He was gazing up at Mary and smiling.

"I know you," he said.

"Don't talk," Mary said.

"I've a seat on a charter flight home. Will you come?"

"You must stay and mend your leg."

"Can I mend it in——?"

He winced. There was much pain.

"Is it disinfectant or perfume?" he asked faintly.

"Please."

"Bandon," he said, and smiled again. "Can you mend it in Bandon?"

She took hold of his hand. "You mustn't talk," she said. "Close your eyes and rest."

"Plenty of babies in Chicago," Foley murmured. "Town's full of babies. Why won't you come to Chicago?"

"You haven't asked me."

She held his hand tightly. Her eyes were moist.

"Please come to Chicago," he said.